THE SOUTHERN TRIAL

PETER O'MAHONEY

D1707559

The Southern Trial: An Epic Legal Thriller
Joe Hennessy Legal Thrillers Book 4

Peter O'Mahoney

Copyright © 2023
Published by Roam Free Publishing.
peteromahoney.com

1st edition.

ALSO BY PETER O'MAHONEY

In the Joe Hennessy Legal Thriller series:

THE SOUTHERN LAWYER
THE SOUTHERN CRIMINAL
THE SOUTHERN KILLER

*****

In the Tex Hunter Legal Thriller series:

POWER AND JUSTICE
FAITH AND JUSTICE
CORRUPT JUSTICE
DEADLY JUSTICE
SAVING JUSTICE
NATURAL JUSTICE
FREEDOM AND JUSTICE
LOSING JUSTICE
FAILING JUSTICE
FINAL JUSTICE

THE
SOUTHERN
TRIAL

JOE HENNESSY
LEGAL THRILLER
BOOK 4

PETER O'MAHONEY

CHAPTER 1

The outline of the man was barely visible in the rain.

Joe Hennessy slowed his pickup, trying to see through the windshield as the downpour became heavier. His headlights shone on the man—tall and thin, dressed in a long black raincoat. Broad shoulders. Long legs. The man stood in front of a red sedan, its emergency lights flashing through the deluge. The hood of the car was open.

Hennessy pulled up next to the man and brought his window down. "Need some help?" he called out.

"Broken down," the man called back. "The old girl just ran out of power."

"Tough night to break down."

"You're telling me," the man shouted, looking back to the open hood. "It's a flat battery. You got some jumper cables?"

Hennessy nodded and rolled his car forward. He turned around on the empty road and pulled up to the shoulder, his headlights facing the broken-down vehicle. Hennessy knew these back roads well. They were quiet roads, near only vineyards and farms, and had little traffic.

As the southern rain continued to come down with a vengeance, it reminded Hennessy of his forever ten-year-old son, Luca. Luca had always loved the rain. From the day he could walk, he splashed in puddles, danced in storms, and played football in the mud. Whenever the rains arrived, Luca would grab his father's hand, begging to play outside. Often, Joe laughed and followed him out the doors. Sometimes, he said no. He wished he never said no. For the past twenty-one years, Luca's unsolved murder had left a giant hole in his heart, filling him with regrets, aching, and frustration.

Hennessy left the engine on and reached back to grab the umbrella from the rear seat of the pickup's cab. He creaked his door open and opened the umbrella, looking toward the man. As the rain intensified with a gust of wind, the darkness of the landscape felt oppressive.

"You got help coming?" Hennessy called out.

"Nah, I should be able to fix it." The man turned to face the engine. "It's the battery. It died on me. All I need is some jumper cables."

"And the battery stopped while you were driving?"

The man hesitated. "I pulled over to relieve myself. When I got back in the truck, she wouldn't start. All I need is some jumper cables, and I can fix it."

"Where are you coming from?" Hennessy called out. "Not much back up that way except vineyards and farms."

"Yeah, I've been working on the farms."

"Which one?"

The man didn't answer, and his back remained to Hennessy.

"Which one?" Hennessy asked again.

"Eh?" the man called, turning around and shielding his face from the rain. "Sorry, my hearing is going these days."

"Which farm were you working on?" Hennessy pressed.

"Don't know the name of it. Just doing a cash job for a friend. Fixin' fences."

Hennessy stared at the man. He stood the same height as Hennessy at six-foot-five. He looked in his forties, younger than Hennessy by around fifteen years. When the man moved in front of the lights, Hennessy could see the man's face was scarred and weathered.

Joe Hennessy knew he was a marked man. Over the past five weeks, the criminal defense attorney had become cautious of every shadow, twitching at every unrecognizable noise. He'd become the target of one of South Carolina's most powerful men, and he was starting to feel the pressure. But no matter how dangerous it became, no matter how much pressure they applied to him, Joe Hennessy would not stop.

"Look," the man continued. "If you've got jumper cables, that'd be a massive help."

Hennessy paused, his instincts running on high alert. He stared at the man, searching for any hint of trouble, before he turned back to his pickup. The moment he turned to retrieve the cables, a fist slammed into the back of his head.

He fell forward onto the hood of his truck, the umbrella dropping beside him.

The fist cracked into the side of his jaw, a

crunching sound echoing through his skull.

He fell to the ground. Before he reacted, the man landed a kick, his foot connecting with Hennessy's stomach.

Hennessy felt the air forced out of him. He tried to roll and stand. He wanted to fight back. He wanted to spring to his feet and land a left hook on the man's chin, but he never had the chance. The man landed another boot into Hennessy's stomach, sucking any remaining air from his lungs.

"Leave the past alone, old man," his voice hissed from a few inches above Hennessy's face.

Another boot came from the shadows and slammed into his stomach.

As Hennessy fought for air while lying on the road, the man dropped the hood of his sedan and climbed into the seat. The car started on the first attempt. Hennessy watched as the taillights sped off into the night.

Someone had gone to a lot of trouble to send him a message, but it wouldn't work.

Joe Hennessy needed justice, and nothing was going to stop him.

CHAPTER 2

Joe Hennessy looked out to the hazy horizon.

Late in the morning, the air was heavy, covering Charleston in a sultry summer bath. The weather report had it right—it was hot all over South Carolina. It was sizzling in every part of the state, from the salt marshes to the enchanting fields, from the wooded valleys to the spectacular beaches. From Charleston to Greenville, from Hilton Head to Myrtle Beach, summer was drenching the state in humidity, forcing residents to take refuge in any air-conditioned space they could find. Another big storm season was predicted, and the predictions seemed to worsen each year.

"There was nothing in the attack on me," Joe said as he walked beside his wife of three decades. He wiped the sweat from his brow with his index finger. He could almost taste the river as the smells of the Charleston pluff mud filled the air. "It was a case of mistaken identity."

"Mistaken identity?" Wendy's tone showed concern. "Some guy jumps you on a back road near our vineyard, and he doesn't take your wallet or steal your car, and you think it's a case of mistaken identity?"

'Leave the past alone, old man,' the voice echoed in Joe's thoughts. He still bore the bruise of the boot from five days earlier, and his ribs still pinged when he twisted to his right, but he couldn't show that pain to his wife. Joe Hennessy had learned to be a stoic man. He had to be. Unresolved grief had consumed his world for far too long.

He tried to hide the grief, tried to push it down behind a thick wall of fortitude, but it was always there, always present. After twenty-one years, he knew the time had come to confront the heartache, he knew the time had arrived to face the pain, but it didn't make the journey any easier.

"It was a case of mistaken identity," Joe repeated, hoping his warm smile eased her fears. "He was a rough guy looking to blow off some steam. The sedan was stolen, and I couldn't ID him, so the cops had nothing to go on. There's nothing more to it."

Wendy didn't respond. Her concern was building for her husband. She knew how much their son's unsolved murder meant to him, as it did her, but she hated how it pushed him closer to danger.

Like many South Carolinians, Wendy Hennessy could trace her family history back hundreds of years in the state. Her forefathers arrived in the 1700s, proudly building a life in the colony. She had family spread all over the Low Country. After their son's death, she left Charleston and moved Upstate to buy a vineyard with her husband. At first, she missed the Low Country lifestyle, but she quickly settled into life on the vineyard, raising two daughters amongst the vines.

Affected by drought and then storms, several poor seasons on the vineyard pushed them to near bankruptcy. Joe returned to his first profession, criminal law, to make enough money to pay the ever-present bank loans. Wendy stayed at the vineyard while her husband worked in Charleston, but she still enjoyed returning to the Holy City to see old friends, drink coffee, and shop in the stores along King Street.

"How are your cases going?" Wendy changed the subject as a breeze blew off the nearby river.

"They're ok. Our books are good, but we could do with more work," he said. "And I can't say I'm overly enthused about taking Mrs. Hemingford's drunken disorderly case to court. She's the type of person who doesn't suffer from insanity." Joe's dimples showed as he smiled. "She actually seems to enjoy every minute of it."

"I'm sure she's not that bad," Wendy laughed. "But you know, yesterday I burned 1500 calories."

"Really? How?"

"By having a nap," she laughed. "I tell you, that's the last time I leave the cookies in the oven while I sleep."

Joe laughed with her before a long pause hung over them. They walked, trying to avoid the conversation, trying to suppress their emotions behind forced smiles. They both knew where the conversation was headed, and they both knew there was no avoiding it.

Joe looked out to the river lapping against the edge of the Battery, a seawall fortifying the southern tip of the Charleston peninsula. First built in the 1730s and rebuilt in the 1820s, the iconic location was bordered by stately antebellum mansions, lined by tall palmetto trees, and offered majestic views of the Sullivan's Island lighthouse. There was no better place to be on a blue-sky day, with the river simmering in the bright sunshine.

The couple walked hand in hand as a group of joggers passed them, followed by a person on an electric scooter. Wendy looked over her shoulder, and when she saw nobody around them, she drew a long breath.

"And Richard Longhouse?" her voice broke a little as she said the name.

Joe stopped and turned away from her. He put his hands on the railing, gazing at the water as two boats passed. Another light breeze blew through, easing the humidity, but it didn't calm his anger. He gripped the railing tightly, trying to hold his rage inside.

"Joe?" Wendy rubbed her hand on her husband's back.

"I don't have many answers yet," he whispered, avoiding eye contact.

"But you have some ideas?" There was hope in her voice, a type of hope that he didn't want to break.

He nodded but didn't respond.

Five weeks earlier, convicted felon John Cleveland

confessed to his involvement in the kidnapping of ten-year-old Luca Hennessy. Cleveland admitted he drove the van that was used in the abduction. He admitted that Justin Fields, his criminal colleague, beat Luca to death after the child fought back in the van. It wasn't supposed to happen like that, Cleveland had stated. They were supposed to keep the boy for a night and release him the next morning. It was a threat, a warning to Hennessy to stay out of other people's business.

Most importantly, John Cleveland admitted he was employed by Richard Longhouse, a former prosecutor and colleague of Joe Hennessy at the time, to perform the task. Five days after his confession, John Cleveland was dead, stabbed in a prison riot.

"Don't you dare hold back on me." Wendy's voice shook. "You need to tell me everything that's happening with Richard."

Joe sighed and hung his head. "Our son was kidnapped twenty-one years ago to put pressure on me. I knew Richard Longhouse was taking bribes to avoid prosecuting certain cases. I did the right thing and filed a complaint. A week later, Luca was kidnapped. Richard Longhouse paid those men to kidnap Luca. That's what John Cleveland claimed before he died. We have his written statement asserting the facts—Richard Longhouse paid him to kidnap Luca." Joe's grip on the railing tightened further, his knuckles turning white, and his jaw clenched tight. "And the police won't even look at it. They won't open an investigation into a sitting South Carolina Senator."

"I know you're angry they won't take action over the statement," Wendy rubbed his arm. "But all we have is a written statement from a convicted felon who's now deceased. And he made the statement twenty-one years after the event. That's not much to go on, and it's not enough to reopen a twenty-one-year-old cold case."

"I want to shoot him, Wendy." Joe turned to face his wife. "I want to put a bullet in Richard's skull. Right between the eyes. I've thought about it so many times. It's all I can think about when I close my eyes at night."

"No, Joe. We've been through this—you can't do that." Wendy softened her voice. "I can't lose you to prison, nor can our daughters. They need you around. I need you around. If you shoot him, you let us down.

18

There's no justice in that."

"I haven't slept in weeks," Joe whispered. "I can't sleep knowing he's still out there walking free after what he paid people to do. I've even sat in the same room as that man, and he talked to me like he was my friend."

"Even if you can prove that Richard Longhouse was involved, you must find forgiveness in your heart."

Joe turned back to the water and gripped the railing even tighter. He couldn't forgive Richard Longhouse. Not now, and not ever. He couldn't comprehend ever letting his anger go.

Wendy rested her hand on top of his. Knowing her husband was a man of action, she pushed his anger in the right direction. "What are the next steps?"

"I'm going over Luca's case with a fine-tooth comb. I'm talking to every witness, and I'm following every lead. Now that I know Richard Longhouse was involved, I have a direction to follow. I'm going to break it open, Wendy. I'm going to prove he did it."

"And then what?"

"If I can find one more piece of evidence, we'll file

a civil claim for wrongful death against him. We'll never win it, but it will destroy his reputation and any chance he has at running for the governor's job." Joe's grip eased. "And the pressure might force him into a mistake."

"He won't go down easily. He'll fight this all the way."

Joe drew a deep breath and looked at her. He offered a slight smile, pulled her in tight, and kissed the top of her head. He felt Wendy's arms tighten around his waist.

"I know," Joe said. "But I need to do this."

CHAPTER 3

Richard Longhouse knew politics better than most.

The Longhouse family was a political powerhouse in South Carolina, stretching back five generations. From a long line of lawyers grew a long line of dirty politicians. The Longhouse name was respected, admired, and feared. They could talk the talk, charm when required, and schmooze their way into the wallets of many. With a taste for power and a distinct lack of morals, the Longhouse family was perfect for the minefield of Southern politics.

Throughout his political career, Richard Longhouse had attended many functions at the Memminger Auditorium, also known as Festival Hall, nestled in the Harleston Village neighborhood of Downtown Charleston. It was a striking venue. Built in the 1930s and renovated in 2008, the building sat dominantly over the adjacent school and nearby streets. The neoclassical-inspired building had stately columns at the front, a grand entrance that impressed even the most hardened of critics, and a white exterior that contrasted against the blue skies of Charleston. Inside, the high ceilings made the space feel open and spacious, but the red décor was welcoming and calm.

In his fifties, Richard Longhouse's olive skin was tanned by many years in the sun. He was tall, slim, and well-groomed. His thick mustache was recognizable. He spoke eloquently, like he'd spent his life surrounded by money, and his accent had a deep Southern tone.

Longhouse knew political fundraising was seldom pretty, but he also knew he couldn't make it happen with his name alone. If he wanted the governor's job, if he wanted to upstage all his relatives and go further than they had, he needed allies, and he needed funds.

The 'Protecting Women from Poverty Foundation' ran a large annual black-tie fundraiser to raise money for women's shelters across the state. The purpose of the Foundation was secondary to most of the people in attendance. It was a place to be seen, a place to connect, and a place to make backroom deals.

Anybody who was anybody in South Carolina's political circles tried to attend, and Longhouse knew he needed to be at his schmoozing best.

He mingled with the attendees, greeting strangers like they were old friends, telling everyone how happy he was to be at the fundraiser for such an important cause. He was a salesman, a wheeler and dealer, and he was selling his ability to be governor.

His wife, Elise, was by his side, but they weren't talking, which wasn't unusual. She had put up with his many affairs, but the last one had made her more distant. Longhouse didn't mind. He had little respect left for the money-hungry woman, anyway. They stayed together for power and politics and knew they couldn't make it without each other.

His primary target for the event was landowner Thomas Clinton, who ran one of the state's largest cattle farming businesses. The Clinton family was a South Carolina family, just like the Longhouse's, and the two families had history dating back decades.

The MC announced a thirty-minute break in formalities when the opening speeches concluded. It was hunting time. Longhouse watched as Thomas Clinton excused himself from his table and made his way to the bar. Longhouse lurked a safe distance away while Clinton talked to another patron, and when their conversation ended, he pounced.

"Thomas Clinton, it's so good to see you." Longhouse held out his hand as he approached. "It's been a while."

"Richard Longhouse," Clinton shook the hand solidly. "I was wondering when you would hunt me down."

While some people were born into money, some gained it fraudulently, and some built their wealth by taking advantage of the vulnerable, Thomas Clinton had done all three. In his sixties, he'd spent a lifetime ripping people off. He thought any place, outcome, or person could be bought. His gray hair was wispy, his skin spotty, and his straight teeth were glowing white.

"Fundraising for poor women, I see," Longhouse smirked, patted him on the shoulder, and pointed to a quieter area, away from prying ears. "I always knew you were a good guy."

Clinton chuckled as he picked up his whiskey. He followed Longhouse to the quiet corner at the far end of the service area and then looked over his shoulder, checking no one was in hearing range. He leaned in close and lowered his voice. "I tell you, Richard, I do whatever I can to fight poverty. That's me. Just last week, I punched a homeless woman in the face."

Longhouse laughed more than the disgusting joke deserved. When he was finished laughing, he lowered his voice to deliver a joke of his own. "Yesterday, I asked a poor woman if I could take her home. She smiled and said yes. You should've seen her expression change when I walked away with her cardboard box."

Clinton laughed loudly and slapped his hand on the bar in joy.

"That's great. My sons will love that one," Clinton said with a wide smile. He sipped his whiskey, leaning one elbow on the bar, and then pointed his finger in the air. "But I tell you, it's the new money that gets me. These young entrepreneurs who strike it big. They have no class. These up-and-comers haven't grown up with money and have no idea how to behave when they get it."

"That's why we need true South Carolina families like ours to manage their wealth for them. Our families have had centuries of experience managing money." Longhouse leaned closer to Clinton. "It's up to men like us to maintain our state's great values."

"Agreed." Clinton eyed him. "I've heard about your run for governor. I've heard that your funds have almost reached two-point-five million. That's a good war chest, my friend."

"Every dollar helps, and I'm still fundraising for the campaign." Longhouse turned on his best smile. "I need the support of the state's most powerful and intelligent people. I need the backing of people who understand the values of our great state."

Clinton raised his chin slightly. "And if I throw my money behind you?"

"Your farms are the backbone of our local economy. Farming is at the core of our identity. It's at the core of our country's values." Longhouse gripped his fist in consolidation with Clinton. "We need to look after that backbone and protect those that have built this great country into what it is."

Clinton nodded. "And, of course, agricultural tax cuts would greatly benefit the industry, especially for large-scale operations. You know, another two percent in cuts could ensure our industry would thrive in this state."

"Yes, they would, my friend." Longhouse reached

out and patted Clinton on the shoulder. "And for the benefit of this great state, I can make that happen."

"I'll talk to the people I know to make sure they support you as well." Clinton looked around and then leaned closer. "If I look after you, you need to look after me."

"Of course."

"And before I attach my money to your bandwagon, I need to know if you have any skeletons hiding in the back of your closet. You'd be amazed at what comes out of the woodwork when people try to climb all the way to the top."

Longhouse's insides chilled at the words. "I don't have any problems." He forced a smile. "And if one arises, I'll deal with it."

CHAPTER 4

Hennessy cruised down Hope Plantation Lane in Jacksonboro, Colleton County, South Carolina.

Spanish moss framed the drive down the narrow lane, evoking memories of his past in the Low Country. Hennessy loved the Spanish moss, the gray-bearded plant swaying in the breeze, dancing to its own tune. The Spanish moss reminded him of the summers he watched Luca grow. He smiled as he remembered Luca eating cubes of ice with his friends, playing in the shade, hiding in basements, trying to cool down. He remembered Luca running under the garden hose and launching himself into the nearby rivers. He remembered driving Luca and his friends to the beach, which always felt cooler with the breeze from the Atlantic Ocean.

Some passages through grief are awful, heartbreaking affairs, others are relatively short and somewhat joyful, but for Joe Hennessy, the journey had been long, confusing, and seemingly, never-ending. For years after Luca's death, he couldn't contain his anger. He punched walls, kicked doors, and snapped at strangers. Whenever he closed his eyes, he saw his failure to protect his family. When the anger eventually subsided, his mind became lost in a sea of grief. He would break out in sweats for no reason, lose his breath at random times, and his heart would flood with sorrow every time he thought of his son. As he aged, as the grief became softer, it morphed into a knot in his stomach, always present, always there, always threatening to overwhelm him.

He'd read the details of Luca's case a thousand times. He knew the words of the police report off by heart. He knew every detail of the photos. Every color. Every drop of blood. During the early years, when the pain was so crushing, he couldn't read past the first page without tears, but as time passed, as the grief was hidden behind a thick wall of toughness, reviewing the files became easier.

There were things about the case that never made sense. There were names in the files that never gave a statement, there was a lack of DNA analysis even though there was blood on Luca's clothes, and there was a lack of witnesses, even though Luca was kidnapped at 5.30pm as he walked home after baseball practice.

Hennessy had spent years searching for answers, but he trusted the case files. He trusted the investigation. He trusted the names that signed the reports. Looking at the case in a new light, he saw gaps he'd never seen before.

As he pulled up to his destination, he wiped his eyes with the back of his shirt sleeve, clearing any remaining tears.

The small weatherboard home was recently repainted. Raised garden beds lined one side of the front yard, showing off a decent crop of celery stalks and carrot tops. On the other side of the yard, there was a long chicken coup. The trees around the house were large, providing a decent amount of shade, the grass was overgrown but very green, and yellow flowers were blooming below the porch.

As Hennessy climbed out of the truck, a voice spoke from inside the property's fence line.

"Oh my. Joseph Hennessy? Is that you?" There was no denying the owner of the voice, the thick Southern accent turning each word into a melody. "If

I didn't see it with my own eyes."

Hannah Channing was always a free spirit, a woman full of love and care. Her figure was full, her smile was broad, and her demeanor was entertaining. She radiated joy and tenderness. As she came closer, Hennessy could see that her gloves were dirty, as were her knees, and her wide-brim red hat had a line of sweat near the base.

"Hannah Channing. How could a person ever forget that fabulous smile?" he greeted her. "You haven't aged a day."

"I sure feel every one of my fifty-five years when I have to stand up after a morning in the garden." The pair embraced in a hug before she pulled back and stared up at him. "Can't say you've changed much, either. Still as handsome as ever with those cheeky dimples."

"I've aged plenty." Hennessy smiled and looked toward her house. "What a fantastic place."

"It might be small, but it's my dream," she said. "A single empty-nester doesn't need much to survive in this world. After my divorce five years ago, I downsized. Both kids have grown up, so I didn't need a big house. All I needed was somewhere cozy, with enough space for a garden and a workshop. I grow a lot of my own food and sell organic soaps at the Port Royal Farmers Market on Saturdays. That's all I need." She pointed to a setting on the porch. "Come in, Joe. Have a seat."

"Thank you, Hannah." Hennessy followed her up a couple of steps onto the front porch and sat on one of the two wicker armchairs.

"Let me grab a pitcher of sweet tea. I made some fresh before coming out to dig around in the yard. I like to plan ahead for these hot stints." She looked up at the blue sky. "And it's going to be a scorcher later today."

Not waiting for a reply, she disappeared through the front door. She reappeared a minute later, carrying a small tray with a pitcher of sweet tea and two glasses. As she set it down on the wicker table, the large ice cubes in the pitcher clinked. She poured two glasses, handed one to Joe, and then sat on the chair nearest the door. "My grandmother used this pitcher for her sweet tea, and then my mother, before she passed it onto me. I didn't have any daughters, so I've got to wait until a granddaughter comes along before I can pass it on."

"Now that's fine sweet tea," Hennessy smiled after he took a refreshing sip. He set the glass on the table between them and then wiped his brow with the back of his hand. "The garden looks amazing. And what's that smell? Azaleas?"

"Very good, Joe." She sipped her sweet tea. "You have an excellent nose. I bought some re-blooming Azaleas last year, and I say, they've certainly done that. This is the third time this year they've bloomed."

"It looks like you've built a pleasant life out here in the Low Country."

"Low Country living is real living, Joe. This is what life is all about—a slow pace, a great community, and people that wave hello to each other as they pass. We're surrounded by beautiful gardens, beautiful smells, and so much nature. All my family is within a fifteen-minute drive from here, and I work just enough to afford the things I want. I'm living the dream. Nothing in the world could take me away from here." She beamed. "And how's the beautiful Wendy?"

"She's well. Still as gorgeous as ever." Hennessy smiled. "And how's Shane?"

"He's doing great. He's in his thirties now.

Working in construction, managing the renovations of a few old properties. He lives about five minutes away on a nice piece of land. He got married a few months ago. She's a nice girl, and it was a beautiful wedding. They're planning on having kids, so I'll be a grandmother soon. And after having two boys, I'm crossing my fingers for a granddaughter." She paused and then grimaced. "I'm sorry if that's hard to hear."

"No, no, that's ok." Hennessy waved her apology away. "Luca would've loved that his best friend has built a great life. Even when they were little, they talked about living next door to each other as adults."

"You know, the day Shane turned eighteen, he walked into a tattoo parlor and got a tattoo that said, 'Luca Forever.'"

"Did he?" Hennessy raised his eyes in surprise.

"He did. Top of his left shoulder."

Joe looked down. He blinked back the tears. Luca's memory was living on in other people's hearts. "I know we've barely spoken in twenty years, but it was hard for us to stay around Charleston. I'm sorry if we seemed distant back then."

"You don't have to apologize. I can't imagine the pain you were going through. Everyone understood why you left, and nobody held it against you. We all would've done the same. The last time I spoke to you and Wendy, you'd just bought a vineyard and were planning to leave Charleston. Are you still there?"

"We are. The vineyard is past Greenville. We've been up there for twenty years now. We had two daughters, and they're turning into wonderful young women. Ellie is twenty and studying in New York, and Casey is seventeen and about to finish high school. Life is good up there."

She eyed him, leaving a pause hanging over them for a moment. "But you didn't just drop by to catch up, did you? There's something on your mind."

"You're right." Hennessy took another sip of the sweet tea and nodded his approval again. "I know it's been a long time, Hannah, but I was hoping you'd delve back into your memories and see if you can remember anything about Luca's death."

"It's a long time ago."

"More than twenty-one years, almost twenty-two." Hennessy avoided eye contact, trying to hold his emotions inside. "I've been reviewing the case, and your name was in one of the files, but nothing was attached. No witness statement or testimony. I always assumed you were one of the people that talked after the baseball game, and the missing statement was linked to the other parent's statements. But lately, I've been wondering if you knew anything else."

"I gave a statement about the man in the week after he died."

"About the man?" Hennessy squinted and turned to look at her. "There was never a statement on file about a man at the scene."

"That's strange because I clearly remember going into the police station and talking to a detective about what I saw that day. I even identified one of the men I saw."

"You identified one of them?" Hennessy sat up straighter. "What else did you say in your statement?"

"I'm sorry, Joe, but it's not fresh in my memory." She looked at him with concern. "But I'll tell you what I can remember."

"Please."

"Ok, but my memory isn't as clear as it was then." She saw the pain in his eyes and offered a half-smile. "I identified the man near the park. The detective showed me the man's photo, and I confirmed it was the same man I'd seen near the park earlier that afternoon. He was lurking around during baseball practice. I saw him go to a white van and talk to the driver."

Hennessy stood, unable to control the emotions growing inside him. He stood next to the railing on the porch, staring out to the yard beyond it for a few moments before he turned back to her. "Go on."

"As I waited for baseball practice to end, I watched him. He was looking at the kids. All these children were around after practice, and the man looked out of place. I was suspicious, so I took a piece of paper out of my bag and wrote the plate number of the van down. Then I think I also wrote something like 'White male, brown hair, six-foot,' for the first guy, and 'black male, young, skinny,' for the driver. I went off and collected Shane, and I remember Luca said he would walk home after practice." She drew a long breath. "I felt so guilty for years. I still do. If I'd done something or said something, then—"

"No," Hennessy cut her off. "You can't think like that. It wasn't your fault. Nobody is blaming you. You can't blame yourself for that."

"Thanks, Joe," she said quietly.

"Who did you talk to when you went to the police?"

"What was his name?" She snapped her fingers when it came to her. "Farina. Detective David Farina."

It was a name Hennessy knew well. He turned and stared at the deep blue sky for a while, trying to calm his breath before he turned back to her. "What did Farina say when you identified the man? Did he give you any names for the people you saw?"

"I'm sorry, but I don't remember," she said. "It's a long time ago."

"Do you remember if he said the name of John Cleveland or Justin Fields?"

"Those names ring a bell, but I couldn't be certain."

Hennessy clenched his fist and tapped it on the railing. "Those names aren't in the police files, nor is your statement that you identified the man near the park."

"Why not?"

Hennessy didn't answer.

He couldn't. His anger was too much. He stood at the edge of the porch, staring out to the hazy horizon, knowing one thing—no matter how painful, no matter how confronting, it was time to dig deeper into the past.

CHAPTER 5

As Hennessy climbed out of the truck, the oppressive humidity was almost unbearable.

The late July air was thick and heavy, almost like walking through a wet blanket. The weather report stated that it would only get hotter, and there was no end in sight.

"She's a toasty one today, mate," a strong Australian accent called out from behind him, and Hennessy turned to see Barry Lockett crossing the street. "Going to be a hot few weeks, I hear. Big storm season coming as well."

Private Investigator Barry Lockett was large enough to intimidate most people. His muscular frame was towering, his tattoos were threatening, and his scarred knuckles showed a lifetime of aggression. Dressed in a black t-shirt and jeans, he presented a menacing presence. But despite his hard exterior, Lockett's smile was cheeky, and his relaxed Australian accent was disarming.

"Let's get out of this heat," Hennessy said as the two tall men shook hands. "I'm going to need some good news, Barry."

Hennessy led them into the Harken Café, nestled into the French Quarter of Charleston. Inside, the café was cooled by two air conditioners working overtime. The place had a homey feel, with exposed brick and earthy tones highlighting a Parisian influence. Abstract art by local artists hung on the walls, and the smell of freshly roasted coffee filled the air. The café was a comforting escape from the heat, but more important than that, it served some of the best coffee in the state.

"Long week, huh?" Lockett asked as they sat down.

"Long decade," Hennessy replied.

The waitress arrived and took their coffee orders. Hennessy ordered a latte with one sugar, and Lockett ordered his coffee black and double strength.

"What do you have for me?" Hennessy loosened his tie, unbuttoned his collar, and rolled up the sleeves of his white shirt. "Tell me you've found something good."

"Two names and two possible leads." Lockett opened the screen on his cell and read over his notes. "Detective David Farina was the lead detective in Luca's investigation, and the rumors of his corruption have littered almost every part of the state. He was suspended from the force twice in Charleston in the five years after Luca's death. Both times he was accused of corruption and bribery, although nothing stuck. He was rumored to be taking money from drug dealers to look the other way, but nobody could prove anything. He was also rumored to have taken bribes from officials to make evidence disappear."

"The more I dig into this, the more his name keeps coming up."

"And this is the kicker—one investigation was based on accusations that Farina was taking money from Richard Longhouse to get rid of evidence in relation to the death of a local businessman, Carlos Hondas. Around two years after Luca's death, Mr. Hondas died under suspicious circumstances. No charges were ever laid, and guess what happened to the investigation?"

"The cause of death remained unsolved."

"That's right. At the time, Richard Longhouse was

still a prosecutor in the Circuit Solicitor's Office, long before he became a Senator. Mr. Hondas was a restaurant owner who complained to the media that Longhouse was refusing to prosecute the owner of the Pharmacy next door. The Pharmacy owner was rumored to be dealing drugs out the back of the store, causing Mr. Hondas many problems. The Hondas family were originally from Panama, and when I contacted them, they refused to talk. They moved back to Panama after Mr. Hondas' death and moved on with their lives. The investigation into the man's death went cold, and Farina was later accused of covering things up."

"Where's Farina now?"

"Eventually, after lots of accusations, Farina transferred to the Beaufort Police Department, and he's still there today. Life seems to be quieter there."

"I'm going to need to talk to Farina."

"He can wait," Lockett said. "You'll want to talk to this guy first."

Both men paused as the waitress placed their coffees down. Hennessy thanked the waitress and then sipped his latte. He closed his eyes and smiled gently. Coffee had that effect on him.

"Go on," Hennessy nodded when he was ready.

"You asked me to investigate Justin Fields and find out everything about him. Over the past few weeks, I've done a lot of digging, calling up contacts, and trawling through files. Everyone said the same thing—Justin Fields had a lot of mental health issues, and he self-medicated with drugs and alcohol. He was a loose cannon, and he was known to snap."

"According to the statement from John Cleveland, Justin Fields was the one who beat Luca to death in the kidnapping gone wrong. Luca fought back after being kidnapped, and Justin Fields hit Luca hard in the side of the head, which caused a brain hemorrhage." Hennessy drew a deep breath, trying to calm his anger. "We know that Justin Fields has been dead for five years, so what's the lead?"

"Justin Fields had a brother, and the pair were very close."

Hennessy leaned forward. "How close?"

"I went back through a lot of old records, and it's hard to find one charged for a crime without the other."

"You think his brother knows something about Justin's involvement with Luca?"

"I don't know whether he was involved with it, but I can bet that he would've known about it."

"And the brother is still alive?"

"Nate Fields." Lockett sipped his black coffee. The small cup looked tiny in his massive hands. "I tracked him down to a small town in Florida. From the photos, his house looks like it's barely standing. I imagine money would easily influence any information he has." Lockett swiped a few turns on his cell and opened a file photo of Nate Fields. He placed it on the table for Hennessy to look at. "Both the Field brothers, and their extended family, were in and out of prison most of their lives. Mother, father, uncles, cousins—their whole family has a history of criminal behavior. This family is so bad that the family dog probably has a criminal record."

"And Nate Fields' rap sheet?"

"His charges are mostly theft, while Justin Fields' records were almost all violence. Comparing the case files, it looks like Nate was the so-called brains of their partnership, while Justin was the enforcer. Nate's currently unemployed, and if I were you, I'd get down there soon because I'm sure he'll be back in the slammer before long."

Hennessy stared at the photo of Nate Fields before he sighed and leaned back in his seat. He stared off into the distance, not looking at anything in particular. "How did they miss all this?"

"Who?"

"The police. How did they miss all these leads?"

"Who knows? Choice, orders, laziness; sometimes they have too much on their plate to begin with."

"How did I miss it? How didn't I see all this?" Hennessy shook his head, confused by his own failures. "Why didn't I do more back then? Why didn't I talk to the names in the files? I should've chased down Hannah, and I should've investigated Farina. I wasn't stupid. I knew the law. I knew how criminal investigations worked. Why did I put all my faith in the police?"

"You just lost your kid, and you were working as a prosecutor. You were right to feel they would've done everything to help you. You were right to have faith in them." Lockett leaned forward, both his elbows resting on the table. "I couldn't even begin to know what that must've felt like to lose Luca. You had a lot more on your plate to deal with than this investigation. Don't be so hard on yourself, Joe. The grief must've been overwhelming."

"And by the looks of it, it was also blinding," Hennessy whispered and then looked at the picture on Lockett's cell. "I need to talk to Nate Fields."

CHAPTER 6

The drive to the town of Casper, Florida, took five hours from Charleston.

Hennessy started the drive at 5am, cruising through the early morning, listening to his favorites from Billy Joel, Phil Collins, and Fleetwood Mac. He drummed his fingers on the steering wheel, belting out the odd chorus, letting the music fill his soul. He wasn't a singer, but in his truck, out on the open road, he sang his heart out.

After several roadside stops, Hennessy reached the outskirts of Casper at five minutes past eleven. He didn't hesitate to go to the address Lockett had handed him the previous afternoon. This wasn't a town he wanted to linger in. He passed two mobile home parks, one scrapyard, and a strip mall with only one active shop before he turned down 5th Street. His truck bounced over several potholes as he approached the address. After a recent heavy storm, the street was barely staying together.

Nate Fields' home wasn't in much better shape. The single-story weatherboard home had cracked paint, one cracked window, and weeds growing in the gutters. The chain-link fence was broken, there was a tireless car in the driveway, and the grass was overgrown in the yard. Several nearby tall trees shadowed the house, but some almost touched the power lines. None of the other houses in the street looked in better condition.

Hennessy parked his truck, ensured it was locked, and walked toward the front door.

The front porch floorboards were rotten, and Hennessy cautiously took the first step. Despite creaking, the floorboards held. He knocked on the front door with several sharp taps and almost expected it to fall over. A dog barked, followed by a gravelly voice telling the mutt to shut up.

The footsteps came closer to the door, and when it opened, the gaunt face of a short man stared back at him. While just fifty-two, Nate Fields looked closer to eighty-two, resulting from decades of substance abuse. Pale skin, sunken eyes, and colorless lips. He gazed at Hennessy through gas station glasses held together by tape.

"I didn't do nothin', ya hear?" the words came out with a lace of venom. "You guys in suits think you can just accuse anyone of anything, but I didn't do it."

Hennessy nodded. "Mr. Fields, my name is Joe Hennessy. I'm not here to accuse you of anything. I'm here to ask you a few questions about your brother, Justin."

"Justin? You want him—you're gonna need to go to Evergreen."

"Evergreen?"

"Evergreen Cemetery. It's where he's buried. About five years back, he got into a bar fight, and some coward punched him in the back of the head. He was dead within a day. Bleeding on the brain or somethin'. He had no chance."

"I'm sorry," Hennessy said and tried again. "I know Justin is deceased. I need to talk to you about his past."

"Whatever he did, I ain't taking the fall for it. I ain't saying nothing 'cause I know how this works. You're trying to frame me for something my brother did, aren't you?" He pointed his yellow-stained finger at Hennessy. "But I ain't talking, ya hear?"

Fields went to close the door, but Hennessy stuck his foot out. He held Fields' eye contact for a few moments before he continued. "All I need is five minutes of your time, and maybe a twenty will help you out."

"You want to pay me twenty bucks to talk?" Fields looked Hennessy up and down. "Yeah, alright, but you cough up the note first."

Hennessy reached into his pocket and took out a twenty. Fields snatched it like a hungry animal. "What do you want to know?"

"In Charleston, twenty years ago, your brother was paid to kidnap a young boy named Luca Hennessy. I know about the kidnapping, and I know a man named John Cleveland drove the white van. I know Justin lost it and punched Luca. Justin killed him with that punch."

Fields held his mouth open to say something but then paused and stared at the ground. "That's some big claims you're makin'."

"I know it's the truth."

Fields continued to stare at the ground before he bit his bottom lip. Hennessy took a fifty-dollar bill out of his pocket. Money always talked in places like this.

Fields eyed him suspiciously before lowering his eyes to the money. He lowered his voice. "If you double that, I'll tell you everything I know. But it was nothing to do with me, ya hear?"

Hennessy nodded, reached into his pocket, and took out another fifty-dollar bill. He'd barely held it up before the man went to snatch it. With quicker reflexes, Hennessy pulled it back. "Talk first, then you get these."

The expression on Fields' face changed to the look of a kid locked out of the candy jar, but he nodded. "Inside, though. I ain't talking within view of the neighbors. Everyone 'round here is suspicious of guys in suits."

Hennessy followed the man inside, gently shutting the door behind him. He wasn't surprised at the state of the house. It was dark inside, with the curtains drawn to keep the July sun out. The kitchen table looked like nothing more than a spare bench, topped with empty beer cans, pizza boxes, and a pile of old pornographic magazines.

Fields pointed to a wooden stool at the end of the bench, and Hennessy leaned on it. Fields leaned against the metal kitchen sink and folded his arms, keeping his distance.

"Justin wasn't the smartest kid, and he had this thing… schizophrenia. If we'd been rich, I'm sure someone could've helped him. Given him drugs, or whatever. But he couldn't control it. He'd snap and become someone else. It was like he was possessed sometimes. Evergreen is probably the most peace he's ever had."

"He's buried there?"

"Yeah. Justin is lying next to our mother." He chuckled slightly. "She mightn't have been the richest woman in the world, or the kindest, but she loved her boys. She bought the plots before her death, saying something about us needing to be by her side forever. She even wrote it in her will. She left us five hundred dollars each on the condition we're buried next to her."

Hennessy leaned forward on the stool, resting his hands on his knees, careful not to touch anything else in the room. "I need to know everything about the day Luca Hennessy was kidnapped."

"Alright, but no cops and no statements. I ain't admitting nothing. Anything I say here is hypothetical, alright? I'll tell you everything for a hundred, but that's it. I ain't talking to nobody else."

Hennessy nodded his agreement.

Fields walked to the bench and grabbed the butt of an already smoked cigarette. He lit it, took a long drag, and leaned against the kitchen sink again.

"I knew about the job Justin was asked to do, but I wasn't around at the time; wasn't even in the state. I was locked up in Texas after my girl turned on me. That's why he brought in that other guy for the job. Cleveland, his name was. You don't know how many times I looked at myself in the mirror wondering how different things would've been if I'd been in that van with my brother. Justin was a hothead back then, always shooting his mouth off and stuff, but I could control him, you know? I knew what his triggers were. I made it my business to keep him as safe as possible. There would've been no way he would have hurt that boy if I'd been there." He took another long drag before he looked at the end of the cigarette. "It broke him, you know?"

Hennessy didn't respond.

"That death tore him apart," Fields continued. "After that day, he couldn't do anything normal anymore. He was shattered. That was the beginning of the end for him. He told me all about it when I saw him next. He said he was sorry, but he just snapped and beat the kid when he fought back. There weren't enough drugs or alcohol in the state to keep his mind off that event, and I mean not even close. Nobody wants to hurt a kid. Even the worst guy on the planet doesn't want to hurt a kid. It's against our nature, ya know?"

"Do you know anything about the job he was asked to do?"

"Yeah. It was a long time ago, but I remember it clearly. Like I said, I was in lock-up, and when I came back, everything changed. Justin was a different man after that day."

"What do you know about it?" Hennessy pressed.

"Justin took the job from one of his contacts and was supposed to hold on to the kid overnight and then release him the next morning. It was easy money." Fields paused and then looked at Hennessy. "It was all some ploy to scare someone. A guy paid Justin a big lump of cash to keep the kid overnight. That's all it was supposed to be. Keep the kid overnight in the van and let him go in the morning. A warning shot, ya know? Nothing serious."

Hennessy stared at Fields, struggling to hold his emotions together.

"But things went wrong." Fields took a final drag on the cigarette and then flicked the butt into the sink. "I'm sorry that kid died. Justin was as well. I don't know about the other guy—Cleveland—but it wasn't supposed to go down like that."

"Why didn't Justin get caught? How did he avoid the police?"

Fields scoffed. "The police? They were the ones that told him to get out of the state."

"What do you mean?"

"A cop called Justin the next day after the body was found. The cop told him to get out of the state and never return. He told Justin to run and forget about South Carolina."

"Do you remember the cop's name?"

"Yeah, I do." Fields raised his eyebrows. He nodded to Hennessy's pocket. Hennessy held his glare for a moment and then reached back into his pocket. He threw the two fifty-dollar bills on the table.

Fields walked over and snatched them up. "The cop's name was Farina."

CHAPTER 7

From the moment Hennessy spotted the memorial park, he could see it was missing something most other cemeteries had in abundance. There were very few headstones, with nearly every grave marked by small rectangular nameplates set at ground level. Enormous elm trees lined the edges of the area, the rusty fence was only half-standing, and the sign at the entrance had mostly fallen off. There were two mausoleums near the rear, and both were falling apart at the edges.

Hennessy drove under the overhanging branches of the elms guarding the entrance and rolled down the right-hand lane. The road followed a square pattern around the cemetery, with various sections set out both inside and along the outside. He came to a dirt parking area at the back of the cemetery and pulled up five spaces down from the only other car. After switching the engine off, he climbed out and was hit by the loud of sounds of Florida's bugs buzzing overhead. The air was thick and filled with the smell of freshly cut grass, but only a small section had been mowed. The remaining grass was above ankle height, green and full of life.

Hennessy walked around the cemetery, looking over the grave markers, searching for one name. As he walked, the bugs seemed to get louder. After twenty-five minutes, his shirt was damp with sweat. He tried to cool himself down by walking in the shade, but it made little difference.

At the western side of the park, he came across the name of Francine Fields. Hennessy froze, keeping his eyes on her small grave marker. He found it almost impossible to shift his eyes across to where he knew the name of his son's killer was waiting for him. The fear which had churned around in his stomach gave way to a hit of adrenalin.

Hennessy took another couple of deep breaths, and when he was sure he could manage, he looked at the adjoining grave. The marker, a dirty strip of metal, had the details of the tenant printed on it, and the letters appeared to almost lift off as Hennessy ran his eyes across them.

Justin Harold Fields
Born May 5, 1975. Died May 5, 2018
Son of Francine and John. Brother of Nate.
May you now find peace in rest.

It took Hennessy five tries to read through the small passage of words. The anger which had been simmering since early that morning felt ready to explode.

He wanted to spit on the grave marker. He wanted to scream and kick it. He wanted to rip it from the ground and smash it into tiny pieces. He wanted to destroy it and everything around it. His teeth gritted together, his shoulders tightened, and his knuckles clenched. Justin Fields had killed his child, and the marker represented the only thing that recognized he'd ever existed.

Hennessy fought the anger. He paced back and forth in front of the grave, struggling against the urge to stomp on the metal strip, wiping Justin Fields from existence.

After five minutes, the anger passed, and his heart rate eased.

With his head bowed, he walked to a wooden seat at the end of the row of graves. Under a sprawling elm tree, the seat was weathered by time and storms, with only a few scraps of white paint left. Hennessy sat down on the edge of it, careful not to put too much pressure on the seat. It creaked under his weight, but it held.

He sat in the Florida heat, with the insects buzzing overhead, and a voice came to him, one he had listened to for over thirty years. It was Wendy, speaking softly to him from another time, her words a comfort he hadn't expected.

The forgiveness she spoke of was reassuring.

When the strength returned to his legs, Hennessy walked back to the grave, looking at the name of a murderer.

After two decades of pain, after two decades of anguish, there was one person left for justice.

"Richard Longhouse, I'm coming for you."

CHAPTER 8

"Barry, I need David Farina's address."

Hennessy called Lockett as he drove on the open highways of Georgia. He did his best to suppress his anger, but it wasn't working. His knuckles were white as he gripped the steering wheel. His jaw hurt from clenching too much. And he couldn't relax his shoulders, no matter how hard he tried. He'd spent the last two hours doing breathing exercises, which worked for a short time, but as soon as he stopped, the anger returned.

"I'll text it to you. He lives in Beaufort, working for the Beaufort PD," Lockett responded. "Are you driving back today? That's a long day on the road, Joe."

"Nothing I can't handle."

"What did the meeting with Nate Fields give you?"

"As soon as I flashed some cash, he told me everything he knew," Hennessy spoke loudly into the speaker phone of his cell as he sped past another line of slow-moving semi-trucks. "He said Detective Farina told Justin Fields to get out of the state the day after they found Luca's body."

There was a long pause before Lockett responded. "So, Farina knew about the kidnapping, and he knew who the prime suspect was."

"He knew Justin Fields was involved and covered it up."

"Why?"

"I don't know, but I need to talk to Farina."

"Need me to come along?"

"Not yet. I should do this one myself." Hennessy's cell pinged. He looked at it, checking the message from Lockett. "I've got the address. Thanks, Barry."

Hennessy arrived at David Farina's address a little after 5pm. It was a two-story brick house in a pleasant part of the small city of Beaufort. White picket fence, grass slightly overgrown, and the American Flag hanging over the front porch. Hennessy pulled up to the driveway and climbed out of the truck. Even late in the day, he was met with a wall of humidity. The heat hadn't eased.

He flapped his shirt and then walked to the front

porch. A woman opened the door before he'd even had to chance to knock.

"Who are you?" Her tone was blunt, as was her demeanor.

"Hello, Ma'am," Hennessy used a gentle tone. "May I speak with David Farina?"

"That dirty old prick isn't here." Her words were spoken with hatred. "He'd be at O'Toole's, if you need him. And if you see him there, tell him to come home and mow the lawn. He hasn't done it in weeks, the lazy sod."

She slammed the door shut without another word. Hennessy stood in shock on the porch for a few seconds and then nodded and walked back to his pickup. He googled the bar's name and found it was only a short drive away.

Five minutes later, Hennessy arrived at Tommy O'Toole's Pub and Eatery, located in a strip mall between a medical equipment supply store and a Thai restaurant. He didn't waste time entering the pub, pushing through the doors in a hurry.

Inside, it looked like most other Irish pubs in the country—a smattering of memorabilia, several neon signs along the walls, and enough green to scare a leprechaun. Two college-aged boys were playing pool, several older men in muscle tops were at the bar, hunched over their drinks, and the bartender was busy talking to a patron about the ballgame on the large screen. The smell was a pungent mix of male body odor, stale beer, and fried foods.

Hennessy spotted Farina at the far side of the room. In his early sixties, Farina looked like he'd spent most of his life in the sun. His skin was a deep olive tone, and his hair, along with his mustache, was gray. He was solid but not muscular, standing around five-foot-ten, with a sizable stomach hanging over his belt.

Hennessy walked across the sticky floor and sat on the bar stool beside him, staring at the detective. Hennessy sat with an open posture, his legs spread wide, one hand resting on the bar and the other on his hip.

Farina lifted his beer to his mouth, not even looking at Hennessy. The detective took a long sip of his pint, placed it back down, and rested his hand on his belt, next to his badge and the gun in his holster.

When Hennessy didn't move, Farina turned to him. "You're either brave or stupid. And I'll tell you now, if you're looking to pick a fight, you've chosen to spend a few nights in lock-up."

"I know what you did."

"What?" Farina scoffed.

"Twenty-one years ago, you covered up the murder of Luca Hennessy."

Farina froze for a second. He squinted as his brain tried to search for the name. "Luca Hennessy, uh?"

"Justice has been a long time missing, but it's coming."

"And who are you?"

"Joe Hennessy. Luca's father."

Farina sat back slightly, studying the man opposite. "Yeah, yeah, I remember you. You've aged, Joe. Gotten grayer."

"You led the investigation into my son's murder and covered it up."

"You were a prosecutor then, right? All righteous and good." Farina turned back to his beer and took another gulp. "Yeah, yeah, I remember the case. The kidnapping and the boy turned up dead the next day under a bridge. We never did find that killer, did we?"

"You told Justin Fields to leave the state." Hennessy's teeth clenched. "You knew he was involved in the kidnapping, and you covered it up."

"That's a wild accusation you're making. You need to be careful when you talk like that." Farina seemed unfazed as he patted his gun with his hand and reached back to his beer. "And if my memory serves me correctly, Justin Fields is long dead, which means any evidence you have would be hearsay."

"I've got evidence," Hennessy lied. "And I'm coming for you, and I'm coming for Richard Longhouse."

The name caused Farina to freeze. He placed his beer down and turned back to Hennessy. He held Hennessy's stare before he stood. "I'm five months away from a nice retirement. I haven't got time for games with these old cases."

Hennessy stood as well, towering over Farina. "You'll spend that retirement behind bars."

"And who's going to make that happen?"

"Me."

"You don't have enough sway to make a criminal case against anyone," Farina stepped back. "You've got nothing to charge me with."

"I'm not starting with a criminal case."

Farina squinted and then chuckled. "You want to

do that in the civil court? You'd have to be crazy to go after Richard Longhouse in a civil court. The man has money coming out of his ears."

"Justice is coming for you, and it's coming for Longhouse. I'll do that any way I can."

Farina scoffed and then placed his hand on his gun. He left it on the weapon as he stepped closer to Hennessy and lowered his voice. "You don't want to go down that road, pal. Richard Longhouse isn't someone you should mess with."

CHAPTER 9

Hennessy sat in his office the next morning, tapping his finger on the edge of the boardroom table. He didn't sleep. He hadn't been able to sleep for weeks. His shoulders were tight, his back was sore, and a constant headache numbed his head.

The questions about Justin Fields wouldn't leave his mind. Was he happy that Justin Fields was dead? Was he glad that Luca's death tore him apart? If Fields was still alive, would he kill him?

He didn't know the answers to the questions, but they kept running through his head, leading to so many different scenarios. During the night, he couldn't stop the thoughts, no matter how hard he tried. Work was the only thing that provided some reprieve.

On the second floor of a plain red brick building, the Joe Hennessy Law Office was two blocks from the heart of law and justice in Charleston. He'd rented the space for cheap when he first returned to the city after an old associate mentioned it'd been empty for years. The walls were soundproofed, the windows double-glazed, and the air was cool, thanks to the overhead air conditioner.

"Morning, boss," assistant Jacinta Templeton said as she pulled out one of the coffee cups from the tray she was carrying. She handed the coffee to Hennessy. "Extra strong, with two sugars."

"Thank you," Hennessy said. "I'll need a constant supply of this today."

Hennessy found he couldn't function without the skills of his assistant. The mid-thirties blonde woman was organized, kind, and hard-working. At first, Hennessy was reluctant to hire a young mother, especially when she asked for flexible hours during the job interview, but he found she was more valuable than he could ever imagine. She asked for some afternoons off to spend with her son, and Hennessy never found a reason to say no. Despite his initial reluctance, he was happy to run an office with a good work-life balance.

"What do we have today?" he asked as he sipped the coffee.

"You need to draft the files for the Spencer case, and we have Mrs. Smithson coming in later today to talk about her son, Stuart. That's the car theft case." Jacinta sat across from her boss and took the lid off her takeaway coffee. She blew on the coffee gently before looking at her boss. "But before we get into that, do you want to talk to me about yesterday?"

Hennessy sighed and leaned back in his seat. He tilted his head against the top of his chair and looked at the ceiling. He remained there for almost a minute before he composed himself enough to lean forward. "I spoke to both Nate Fields and Detective Farina."

"And?"

"And it was eye-opening."

"What does that mean?"

"Nate said Detective Farina told his brother to leave the state the day after they found Luca's body. That means that Farina knew Justin Fields was guilty, and he covered it up."

"Why?"

"Because he would've been paid to cover it up."

"By Richard Longhouse?"

Hennessy shook his head. "I'm not sure, but I assume so."

"Why don't you take this to the media? Let them run with it and destroy his reputation?"

"They won't touch it. Most of the media outlets in the state want the advertising dollars that Longhouse is about to spend on his election campaign. They won't see his advertising dollars if they run a negative story against him."

Jacinta tapped her pen on her notepad. "So, what happens now?"

"What should have happened many years ago. I'm going to the civil court to file a wrongful death claim under the South Carolina Code of Laws. With two pieces of supporting evidence, I'll claim that Richard Longhouse was directly responsible for Luca's death."

"Two pieces?"

"The signed statement from John Cleveland and the testimony of Nate Fields." Hennessy tapped his head gently on the back of his chair. "Nate Fields doesn't know it yet, but he'll testify for me. I'm not going to give him the choice to say no."

"Even with those two pieces of evidence, it's still hearsay. And Richard Longhouse isn't just going to give up. He's going to be angry, and men like Richard Longhouse are dangerous when they're angry."

"I'm counting on it."

"You want to pressure him to make a mistake?"

"That's the plan. I need him to make a mistake and give us something that can be used in a criminal case. If we make enough noise, the Circuit Solicitor's Office won't be able to ignore us. Unlike some states, South Carolina has no statute of limitations on criminal charges."

Jacinta squinted. "But there's a time limit on civil cases?"

"There is," Hennessy confirmed. "For a wrongful death claim, the statute of limitations is three years, but we have two options."

"And they are?"

"One—we can file for a waiver of the time limit under the discovery rule. We can claim that this information was unavailable until John Cleveland wrote the signed confession. That's not likely to get up in court."

"And two?"

"Is a lot more personal."

"How so?"

Hennessy tapped his head against the back of his chair several times before he responded. "The statute of limitations doesn't apply while a person is still a minor, so the tolling period doesn't begin until a child turns eighteen. My eldest daughter Ellie is twenty, and her statute of limitations to sue someone for the wrongful death of her brother only started the day she turned eighteen. The court will weigh the benefits of the tolling period against the prejudice toward the defendant, but it's almost guaranteed that will get it through using Ellie as the plaintiff for a wrongful death suit."

Jacinta's mouth hung open.

"It's our best chance of getting the case through the courts." Hennessy tried to explain further. "Ellie will need to be the plaintiff, and we'll need to lodge in the next two months before she turns twenty-one."

"No, Joe," Jacinta shook her head. "You can't ask your daughter to be the plaintiff. That's too dangerous. You can't put a twenty-year-old girl through that sort of pain. It'll scar her for life."

"I can protect her."

"From Longhouse and a whole line of corrupt police?" Jacinta said. "Are you sure, Joe?"

He looked away, unable to answer her directly.

"And what about the mental toll the case would

take on Ellie?" Jacinta continued. "Luca's death occurred before she was even born. A court case like this isn't a simple walk in the park. The emotional turmoil will be huge. No." Jacinta shook her head repeatedly. "No. You can't ask her to go through that. That sort of pain would destroy even the toughest of people."

"It's our best chance in court."

"It's also your best chance to destroy her mental health. You can't ask your daughter to do that, Joe. You're asking one of your daughters to fight your fight. This is your fight, not theirs. You can't put them in that sort of danger," Jacinta pleaded. "Joe? Please, tell me you're not going to do that."

He didn't respond because he wasn't sure of the answer.

CHAPTER 10

"There's no way a civil case gets past the first hearing," Richard Longhouse grunted. He paced the edge of the executive boardroom with his fists clenched. "The court will throw it out the moment it sits before a judge. There's no way Hennessy has the legal grounds to win this civil suit. It's eighteen years outside the statute of limitations!"

Longhouse turned back to the dark mahogany table and punched his fist down on it, causing his glass to jump. The long wooden table was the centerpiece of the spacious room. Two tall indoor plants sat off to the side of the entrance, a black and white picture of Charleston hung on the left wall, and natural light filtered in from the window facing the street. The room smelled musty, but not a spot of dust could be seen. Off Meeting Street, Longhouse's political office had four separate spaces, including the executive boardroom. He also had a reception area managed by two young blondes, a private office for backroom deals, and a small meeting room he used to meet the public.

Around the boardroom table sat Longhouse's A-team. Christian Brockman and Leonard Minton led Longhouse's legal team, both with decades of experience. Their legal nous was only matched by their ruthlessness. Al Berry, Longhouse's media advisor, sat to their right.

"And you're sure he's going to lodge the suit?" Brockman sat at the far end of the boardroom table. His Italian suit was perfectly fitted, his thick brown hair was brushed back, and his soft, moisturized skin looked like it had never done a hard day's work. "What makes you think he'll file it in civil court?"

"A detective friend, David Farina, had a visit from Joe Hennessy yesterday. He seemed certain that Hennessy would lodge a civil suit for the wrongful death of his son against me. And although the death was over twenty-one years ago, Farina was worried."

"Is he a problem?"

"Farina? No. He was anxious, and I had to calm him down, but he'd never rat me out. Farina and I have done a lot of things together, and we're close.

And he also knows the consequences of ratting me out. He's seen that firsthand."

"If Hennessy lodges a civil suit, we have thirty days to file an answer," Leonard Minton stated. The older of the two lawyers, Minton, had an air of superiority to his voice. Equally well-dressed as his fellow lawyer, Minton presented an image of class and sophistication. He was balding, and as he entered his mid-sixties, his skin was sagging and becoming leathery, but that never stopped him from flirting with young women in bars. "This suit has zero chance of getting past the first hearing. And to show how outrageous this is, we have the option to file a frivolous claim against it."

"That's not the problem," Longhouse said as he paced back and forth again. "Regardless of whether he gets it through the system or not, the issue is what happens outside of the courtroom. If the press gets wind of what this is about, the ramifications for the campaign could be disastrous. With this kind of cloud hanging over my head, I can't start my run for governor. Could you imagine what kind of circus this would turn into if the press got their hands on it? They'd have a field day."

"We'll prepare a motion to redact any identifying information under Rule 41.2. That'll black out your name from the public files. The second he lodges the claim, we'll be prepared," Brockman stated. "And although this state doesn't grant many of these, given the lack of evidence in the claim, the court should approve the redaction. That means your name can't be mentioned in any public forum."

"That's good. Start talking to the judges and tell them that we're going to lodge this and would appreciate it being approved," Longhouse said. "But keep it quiet. I don't want any rumors floating about."

"We know the right people to ensure this never hits the papers," Al Berry stated. He was a bald, heavy-set man dressed in a dark blue suit with a red tie. "You might have to make a small 'donation,' but it's nothing to worry about. If the court decides to redact your name, that's the end of it."

Public opinion mattered in politics. Like a tiny seed that grew into a gigantic elm, the wrong rumors could destroy decades of hard work.

"Even if it does make it to the media, the case is frivolous," Minton stated. "We know Hennessy has a signed statement from a deceased prisoner, but it's worthless. Maybe Detective Farina will turn and testify against you, or maybe Hennessy has another witness lined up, but the signed statement isn't enough to convince a jury of damages. Any judge in South Carolina will find the claim laughable and throw it out."

"So, we have two options moving forward," Brockman continued. "First option is to crush him financially. We can counter-sue Mr. Hennessy for malicious prosecution. It would be a tort action, and we can claim damages, including the costs of defending against a baseless lawsuit. In that suit, we can also make slander or libel defamation claims, perhaps even damages to reputation."

"That only brings this case into the media forum," Al Berry shook his head. "That's not an option."

"Or we can prepare the answer to the summons with a motion to redact the identifying information. We'll state that the claim is frivolous and a waste of the court's time," Brockman persisted. "Not only is there a lack of substantive evidence, but the suit can't be filed on a matter of law. We'll apply for an expedited hearing under Rule 40, because this doesn't have a leg to stand on. The claim will be over in weeks."

"Hennessy will most likely apply for an expedited hearing, which I think we should join," Minton agreed. "The quicker we get to court, the quicker this is over. If this drags on, it might affect your campaign."

Longhouse clenched his fist again. He was so close to winning the race for governor, so close to achieving more than his father ever had, but it was at risk of all slipping away.

"However, we have a bigger problem." Brockman drew a deep breath and leaned forward, concern spread over his face. "Hennessy can file a wrongful death suit under his daughter's name."

Longhouse stopped pacing and squinted. "What do you mean?"

"If Hennessy claims he's the plaintiff, the case will be thrown out before the judge reads the first page. There's simply no way that he can convince a judge to extend the timeframe. However, the statute of limitations doesn't apply to a child until they turn eighteen. From what I've read, his daughters are seventeen and twenty. Both can become the plaintiff for damages, claiming they never had the chance to meet their brother. The judge would have to weigh up a lot of things, but if he uses his daughter as the plaintiff, there's a chance the suit makes it past the first hearing."

Longhouse snatched a glass off the table and threw it at the wall. It shattered on impact. He grunted as he paced the far end of the room, punching the wall as he walked. After a minute of pacing, he sat back down and groaned.

"Don't worry about the daughters," Longhouse said. "I'll take care of them."

CHAPTER 11

In his effort to keep paying the bank loans for the vineyard, Hennessy worked himself to the bone.

He worked early, he worked late, and he worked weekends. He worked in the office, at home, in coffee shops, and in bars. He told himself that he was working hard for the family, that his driving factor was for Wendy and the girls, but the reality was that he couldn't risk losing Luca's Vineyard. Losing that place, losing that precious piece of land, meant he would have to lose Luca all over again. He couldn't do that. He wouldn't survive the pain a second time. He had to do everything in his power to stop the banks from taking the vineyard.

He had a low-grade DUI to defend, a drunken-disorderly charge to handle, and another restraining order to refile. He had to file claims with the magistrate, respond to requests for information from the Circuit Solicitor's Office, and reply to emails from other lawyers. He had to research precedents, search the law, and scroll through appeals decisions.

When he could find time, often at the expense of sleep, he drafted the civil suit for the wrongful death of Luca Hennessy. The complaint was ready, drafted and redrafted fifty times, waiting for him to have the courage to lodge it.

As another long day in the office drew to a close, as if right on cue, he saw his wife's face staring back at him from her profile photo as the cell vibrated in his hand.

"Did you feel me thinking about you?" he said as he answered the call.

She didn't acknowledge his comment, and her tone alone was enough to capture his attention. "Joe, I've just gotten off the phone with Ellie."

"What's wrong?"

"A man came up to her in the street and was threatening."

Joe felt his insides tighten. His fist clenched. His daughter was studying in New York, but he knew she might be in trouble someday. "What do you mean 'threatening'?"

"I mean threatening," she said, amplifying the

urgency in her tone. "A man followed her yesterday, and then the same man stopped her on the street today. He told her that your meddling is going to get her hurt. And she said the man had a Southern accent, Joe."

"My meddling?" Joe pulled the cell slightly away from his ear as if needing space to think. "Is she safe?"

"Our Ellie is clever. She ran into a department store and talked to the service staff. She caught a cab back to her dorm and hasn't left since. She knows what to do, but it scared her."

"My meddling." He closed his eyes in dismay, trying to make sense of the words.

"Joe," Wendy paused. "Is all this worth it?"

"We can't be threatened by Longhouse anymore, Wendy. It's time to fight. It's time to see it through."

Wendy didn't complain, and their conversation turned to Ellie and how they could protect her. They chatted for a while before Joe ended the call and pressed Ellie's number. She was calm and measured, but Joe could hear a slight shake in her voice. She reassured him that she could handle it, that she'd seen worse in the city, but Joe still worried. He told her not to take any unnecessary risks, to be vigilant and alert, and she agreed. He told her he loved her, and they ended the call.

As a father, he fought the urge to drop everything, forget about the case entirely, and fly to New York to ensure his child was safe. Logic told him it wasn't a clever move. He shouldn't run from threats and wasn't about to be bullied by a scumbag like Richard Longhouse. It was time to fight back.

That afternoon, he filed a civil suit for the wrongful death of Luca Hennessy.

CHAPTER 12

"I've received the papers for the Summons and Complaint."

Richard Longhouse sat behind the large and imposing mahogany desk in his private office, staring at the two lawyers on the other side. To ·one side of his desk sat a glass of whiskey, to the other, a closed laptop. A large bookshelf was to the right of the room, and a dark Chesterfield leather couch was to the left. The room smelled musty, like an old bookstore. Brown was the predominant color, creating a subdued calmness that contrasted the childish rage of Richard Longhouse.

Brockman spoke first. "With the daughter as the plaintiff?"

"No," Longhouse shook his head. "Hennessy is going to try himself as the plaintiff first."

Minton nodded. "That won't last a day in court. Did he apply for an expedited hearing?"

"He did."

"I suggest we lodge the motion to redact your identifying information, and then we join the request for an expedited hearing."

"Agreed." Longhouse was firm.

"Do you think he's testing the waters before he uses the daughter as the plaintiff in a second claim?" Brockman asked. "Probing us and seeing how we'll play it?"

Longhouse stared at Brockman. "I'll deal with Hennessy," he gritted his teeth as he spoke. "Your focus is on this case. Get to the court and lodge the motion to redact now. I don't want a word of this leaked anywhere. It's your job to quietly get rid of this ridiculous claim."

"Consider it done," Brockman stated and then stood. "We'll go to the courts right away."

The lawyers picked up their briefcases and left the room without another word.

After they exited, Longhouse went to his jacket hanging near the door and removed his cell from the inside pocket. He peered around the door to make sure no one else was about to enter the room and then reached back into his jacket and removed a second cell.

He thumbed the screen awake and scrolled through his contacts.

Once he found the name, he activated the call and waited for an answer. A voice greeted him a few seconds later.

"Are you available again?" he asked. "I have a problem you need to solve."

The man answered that he was available and then ended the call.

Within five minutes, Longhouse was out the door and driving his black Mercedes sedan to Folly Beach, half an hour from Downtown Charleston. Known for its laid-back beach lifestyle, the area was a mecca for surfers, fishermen, and wildlife spotters. Longhouse drove through the main town and parked at the west end of the beach. The sun had started to set, and all the families and beachgoers had left for the day. A group of rowdy teenagers were left on the beach, most likely underage drinking, but otherwise, the parking lot was empty.

The parking attendant told Longhouse he closed the gates to the parking lot at sunset, but after Longhouse slipped him a twenty, the attendant waved him through. Once he'd parked, Longhouse exited his vehicle and leaned against the hood of his car, feeling the breeze from the wild Atlantic Ocean on his face.

Five minutes later, as the day turned to dusk, another black sedan pulled up beside him.

A man stepped out of the car, walked to the front, and also leaned against the hood. Dressed in an expensive suit, Dirk Taylor looked out of place near the beach. He was a slim man with dark hair and a pronounced chin. He was always wearing a suit and sunglasses. Longhouse had never seen Dirk Taylor without sunglasses.

"There's a new parking attendant," Taylor stated as he crossed his arms.

"They all like money," Longhouse kept his eyes on the Atlantic Ocean. "A twenty did the job."

"Same," Taylor agreed and nodded to the other cars in the lot. "There are still two cars here."

"Teenagers," Longhouse pointed to the beach. "Underage drinking, no doubt."

"What criminals," Taylor stated, and both men laughed. "You have a problem?"

"I do." Longhouse looked around the area before he continued. "A lawyer is trying to sue me for something I did in the past."

"Something bad?"

"You're here, aren't you?"

Taylor nodded his acknowledgment. "Any loose ends?"

"One. A cop in Beaufort named David Farina. He helped me cover it up, but he's not a problem. He's kept his mouth shut for twenty-one years, and he isn't the remorseful type. Farina and I have worked closely for a long time, and he's good."

"I'll talk to him. Anything else?"

"I need this guy off my back. He's causing me a lot of headaches, and I don't have the time to deal with him."

"And you've tried Diaz?"

"I had Frank Diaz rough him up on the side of the road a few weeks ago, and then Diaz threatened his daughter in New York, but this stupid guy didn't get the message."

"Name?"

"Joe Hennessy."

"And he's a lawyer?"

Longhouse nodded his response.

"Where else is he vulnerable?"

"He owns a vineyard named in his dead son's honor," Longhouse stated. "And he's very protective of his son's legacy."

"That's the next option," Taylor stated as he looked at the water. "Are you ok if I use Diaz again?"

"Diaz is good at what he does, but I can't be connected to him anymore. It's getting too close to the elections, and I need my contact list to be clean. From today forward, I can't be seen with Diaz. That's why I need you to be the middleman."

Taylor nodded and looked at the teenagers as they packed up after their day on the beach. "There's an easier way, and it would eliminate the problem for good."

"I know," Longhouse said. "And we're very good at solving problems. We've done it many times in the past to great success."

"But you don't want that?"

"Killing a lawyer is a lot harder to cover up than a nobody. Joe Hennessy has too many contacts and too many connections for his death to be swept under the carpet." Longhouse grunted. "We couldn't buy our way out of that one."

CHAPTER 13

"Looks like those ripples you talked about causing may have already begun creating waves." Jacinta leaned against the door of Joe Hennessy's office. "I've just got off the phone with the assistant for the Chief of Police, Roger Myers. He wants to talk to you."

"Did you set up a time?"

"I did, and he's an hour away. You have nothing on this afternoon." Jacinta offered him a grin. "Prepare yourself, Counselor. I think things are about to get a lot more heated."

Hennessy smiled. The thought that the waves he had anticipated finally hitting distant shores was a relief.

He turned his attention back to the laptop and continued searching through legal precedents for any sense of hope. He'd searched decades of cases and had found nothing to strengthen his argument for an extension of time. He figured there always had to be a first, and he hoped his would be it. An email arrived, confirming Longhouse and his team had agreed to join the request for an expedited hearing. Hennessy expected as much, and he was prepared for it.

Hennessy called Lockett and asked him to travel to Casper, Florida, and convince Nate Fields to sign a witness statement. Lockett agreed and stated he'd enjoy the challenge.

Five minutes after midday, Charleston Police Chief Roger Myers arrived. He was a solid man of Gullah Geechee descent who was proud of his heritage, which showed in his posture. He held his shoulders back, his thick chest out, and his chin held high. His black hair had grayed at the sides, but he still had a decent head of hair for a man in his early sixties.

Myers slowly entered the room, thanked Jacinta for her time, and offered his hand to Hennessy. The two men shook solidly, firmly, acknowledging their respect for each other.

"How can I help you, Roger?" Hennessy opened his hand and gestured toward the chair on the other side of his desk.

"Rumors are floating around, Joe," Myers said as he sat down. He leaned back in the chair and kept his chin up. "And I don't like rumors, so I go straight to the source."

"And what are these rumors about?"

"Word has gotten to me that you're looking to make a wrongful death claim against someone, but at this point, the name is confidential." Myers looked over his shoulder at the door and then back to Hennessy. "I've been told the civil suit is against a sitting South Carolina Senator."

"Who told you that?"

"People talk."

"Corrupt cops talk a lot."

"Come on, Joe," Myers moved in his chair, shifting his weight from one side to the other. "All cops talk to each other, and you know the force isn't perfect. We do our best with the resources we have. Sometimes, bad resources are better than no resources."

Hennessy raised his eyebrows. "Farina's already in your ear about it?"

"Yes, a detective from the Beaufort Police Department came and spoke to me. He was concerned that you're trying to upset the apple cart five weeks from his retirement. And he doesn't want the good name of the Charleston Police Department dragged through the mud. I agree with him. These old claims have very little evidence to back them up."

"I know we've had our differences in the past, but protecting corrupt cops?" Hennessy saw the words sting the man. "That's new for you."

"Calling a man corrupt without proof is a dangerous risk you don't have to take," Myers said. "The rumor is that Senator Richard Longhouse is the target of your civil case. It would kill his election chances in a heartbeat if this got out. You really think that's the smartest move?"

"I do."

"So, it's true. You've lodged a civil claim against Richard Longhouse for the death of your child."

"I have."

Myers grunted and then stood. He walked to the far end of the room, placing his hands behind his back as he looked out the window. The view from the second-floor window was partially blocked by a large oak tree, which also sheltered the office from the burning rays of the sun. Myers studied the tree for a moment before he turned back to Hennessy.

"And what could you possibly hope to achieve?"

Myers asked. "Any civil suit for a wrongful death claim has a time limit of three years. You know this suit will get thrown out the second it's before a judge."

"I've applied for an extension."

"You won't get it."

Hennessy nodded.

"But you don't care, do you?" Myers squinted. "You're trying to kick down as many doors as possible until you find one with what you like inside."

"All I need is justice."

"Making false claims in court will only take you further away from that goal," Myers walked back and sat down. "I've heard about the signed statement from the prisoner, but it's not enough evidence. The letter is from a convicted felon who was spending life behind bars before his death. He could've written anything on that statement. There's no way to confirm what he said about Richard Longhouse is real. The letter is worthless in a court of law."

"This isn't just some case, Roger. This is my son's murder." Hennessy's brow furrowed as he spoke. "His case has sat unsolved for twenty-one years, all those files sitting in a cardboard box in your department, not touched by anyone, and I've finally found out what happened to him. I can't walk away from that."

Myers nodded slowly, the realization setting in. When he fully comprehended the reasoning, he stood. "Ok. I get it. I understand. I don't like it, Joe, but I'd do the same given the situation."

"I could do with your help, Roger," Hennessy said as he stood. "I could use some of your resources."

"I respect what you're doing, but I can't help you. You're playing with bigger fish than I could ever hope to take on. Several very influential people have attached themselves to Longhouse's campaign, and they won't take lightly to someone trying to stop him." He held his hand out, and the two men shook solidly again. "But I'll give you some advice—be careful what you dig up. There's a long line of rumors about Richard Longhouse, none proven, of course, but he won't like it when you get close to the truth. He'll fight all the way, and it'll get dirty."

"I expected nothing less." Hennessy remained standing as Myers offered him a nod and left the room.

After Myers had gone, Hennessy sat down and

leaned back in his chair. He reopened the file on the side of his desk and read over the first page.

He looked at his name as the plaintiff and knew it was the right decision. He couldn't risk losing his daughters. He wouldn't survive that pain a second time.

He sucked in a deep breath and refocused. He had a hearing to prepare for, and he was sure Longhouse would apply for a summary judgment the second the motion for extension of time was rejected. It was a long shot, but it was the best one he could take.

The fight had begun, but he wasn't sure how long it would last.

CHAPTER 14

The lead-in to the case hadn't gone well.

Hennessy talked to every legal professor who returned his call, and none of them could find a reason to strengthen his argument for an extension of time. One law professor even openly laughed at Hennessy's case.

For five hundred dollars, Lockett convinced Nate Fields to sign a witness statement about the information he knew. It left Hennessy with two statements, one from a deceased prisoner and another by a convicted felon, whose claims were merely hearsay.

Fifteen days after the lodgment, wearied and exhausted, Hennessy stepped into courtroom five of the Charleston Judicial Center. It was an hour before the hearing, and the courtroom was empty.

With no one in it, the room felt soulless, like a vast vacuum of space. There were five rows of brown chairs in the public gallery, matching the dark wood paneling on the walls. There was little natural light, and one lightbulb near the jury box was flickering. The judge's seat was raised and in the center of the room, a symbol of power and strength. Behind the judge's seat was the Great Seal of the State of South Carolina, with the American Flag on one side of the seal and the flag of South Carolina on the other. A musty smell hung in the air.

Twenty-five minutes later, Barry Lockett and Jacinta Templeton led Wendy Hennessy into the room. They sat in the first row behind Hennessy, barely saying a word to each other. Their nerves were clear. Both daughters had asked to attend the hearing, but Wendy and Joe decided it was better if they stayed away.

Hennessy struggled to hold it together. His morning had been a rollercoaster of rage, nerves, and sickness, and inside the courtroom, it was no better. He looked at the claim, staring at the first page of the wrongful death suit, and felt like crying. He looked at the name, 'Longhouse,' and felt like exploding into a fit of rage. This was the beginning, his chance at justice after twenty-one years of heartache.

This was his moment.

At 9.55am, Christian Brockman and Leonard Milton entered the room, carrying briefcases and laptops. They looked calm and confident, unfazed by the civil suit.

"Where's Richard?" Hennessy looked over his shoulder at the door when no one else entered.

"He doesn't have to be here for such a frivolous claim," Brockman quipped as he opened his laptop. "But I'm sure you'll see him soon."

Five minutes later, the clerk at the front of the room read the case number and then asked the room to rise for Judge Arthur Clarence. The judge walked in, followed by his assistant, and sat down. The seventy-year-old adjusted his thick glasses, rubbed his hands together, and opened the file on his desk. Hennessy was standing, but he felt like his knees were about to give way.

Once Judge Clarence settled, he looked out to the waiting lawyers.

"Welcome to the court today. We have several motions to get through in case number: 2023-AB-05-855. Hennessy vs Longhouse. We have a wrongful death claim under Section 15-51-10 of the South

Carolina Code of Laws. I would appreciate timeliness in your presentation today. Keep it brief and to the point, gentlemen." Judge Clarence moved a piece of paper. "We'll start with the motion to redact any identifying information in the claim. Counselor?"

"Your Honor," Brockman remained standing. "This is a frivolous claim aimed to destroy the reputation of a current Senator of South Carolina. Under the South Carolina Code of Laws, Section 30-2-330, supported by Rule 41.2, we apply for the defendant's name to be redacted until such time as the case is completed, or if ruled in favor of the defendant, the information remains confidential. We also wish to keep the details out of South Carolina's public records." Brockman opened a file on his desk. "I note that there are several recent precedents for this in our state. Earlier this year in Florence County, a judge chose to close the courtroom and keep the details off the public record until a jury was chosen. In a case in Berkely County, the judge ruled that the frivolous lawsuit would do damage to the reputation of the defendant and ordered the courtroom to be closed while the pretrial hearings took place. I have noted other precedents in the memorandums you have in front of you."

"Your Honor." Hennessy had remained standing. His voice was firm. "This is highly unusual for South Carolina, and this case is in the public interest. This involves a sitting Senator, and the public should be aware of his actions. Previous rulings in South Carolina have stated courtrooms can only be closed if there's a substantial probability that the defendant's right to a fair trial will be affected. That's not the case here. The public deserves to know about this case."

"This case is frivolous, ridiculous, and a complete waste of the court's time," Brockman snapped.

"Gentlemen," Judge Clarence warned them, eyeing them off before opening a file on his desk. "I have already considered the motion, along with the affidavits and memorandums you submitted earlier. Given the evidence and the situation, the motion to redact any identifying information for the defendant is granted under Section 30-2-330 of the South Carolina Code of Laws." Without hesitation, he opened another file. "Next, we have the motion for extension of time under the discovery rule."

"Thank you, Your Honor." Hennessy's voice was shaky. "We've lodged a motion for an extension of time, pursuant to South Carolina Code of Laws, article 5, section 15-3-530 and the discovery rule. The intent of the discovery rule clearly states that a person may apply for an extension given such circumstances as we have in this case. This is a legal requirement in the great state of South Carolina. We must—"

"Your Honor," Brockman interrupted and argued before Hennessy could continue, "this is not a case this court can even consider. First, the evidence is laughable. He has two statements, one of which is complete hearsay. The other statement is from a deceased prisoner, whom we cannot cross-examine. These claims are as laughable as they are hollow. But secondly, and most importantly in the eyes of the law, the South Carolina Code of Laws clearly states the timeframe for any civil claim of wrongful death is three years." Brockman opened a file on his desk as he talked. "And we have precedents for the rejection of the claim. In Stein v. Brown, the plaintiff argued that they were entitled to submit a claim for the wrongful death of her husband five years after he died in a motor vehicle accident. The argument was based on new evidence that came from the manufacturer of the vehicle, however, the court found there was no exception to the three-year time limit. The time limit expired, so the Act didn't apply."

"Your Honor—"

"And in Wiggins v. Edwards, the supreme court held an objective test applied to any extension of time and stated that adopting a subjective test would have gone against 'well-settled law.' The court established the 'important date under the discovery rule is the date that a plaintiff discovers the injury, not the date of the discovery of the identity of the alleged wrongdoer.'" Brockman looked across to Hennessy and repeated himself. "'Not the date of the discovery of the alleged wrongdoer.'"

"Your Honor, if I may finish my arguments without interruption." Hennessy glared at Brockman, paused, and then turned back to the judge. "The discovery rule clearly defines that the statute of limitations on bringing a claim does not begin to run until the date on which a claimant actually discovers the injury. In this case, it's an unsolved crime. The police report does not define the method of death as murder. The police report states the death 'remains unsolved.' It does not state the way the death occurred. It was only discovered that the death was murder when John Cleveland signed that statement. That's the moment when the cause of the injury is uncovered."

"Ridiculous! This is outside the discovery rule as the actual injury took place twenty-one years ago."

"The moment the tolling period began was the day it was discovered the event was murder!" Hennessy argued. "Not a day before!"

"Your Honor," Brockman turned to Judge Clarence, "the intent of the discovery rule is for it to be applied when the risk of stale claims is outweighed by the unfairness of precluding justified causes of action and when there is objective, verifiable evidence of the original wrongful act. And that's the key here—objective and verifiable evidence. This case does not have that."

"We have a signed statement from one of the people involved in this crime!" Hennessy stated. "We know this is fact because the statement has information that was never released to the public. That statement has details that were only available in crime scene photos. Short of being at the scene of the crime, there's no way anyone outside the police force could've known that information. The statement is verified by the crime scene photos."

"The man is deceased!" Brockman argued. "Your Honor, this hearing is about the law, not some wild storytelling by the plaintiff. Even if we ignore the facts, the presumption provided under this section of the law does not apply. The death of the person in the suit occurred twenty-one years ago. Because it's outside three years, the extension cannot be applied."

"We have new information that has—"

"This is about the law! Not some fanciful claims written on a piece of paper that's merely hearsay! Under the law, the application for a time extension cannot be applied! The defendant has no right to file this claim!"

"This is the death of a child caused by the actions of Richard Longhouse!"

"There's no evidence of that!"

"We have the sworn testimonies of those involved!"

"Who are convicted felons!" Brockman slapped his hand on the table. "The discovery rule does not apply!"

"Gentlemen!" Judge Clarence shouted and raised his hands to settle the courtroom. "Let's calm this down again." He glared at both men, and when he was sure they were settled, he continued. "Apart from the issues raised, and the details presented in the affidavits and memorandums, is there any other evidence that needs to be considered in my decision?"

"Nothing further from the defense, Your Honor," Brockman said. "We have lodged our complete arguments in the affidavit, and our main point is that the extension of time cannot be granted on such frivolous and flimsy evidence."

"Mr. Hennessy, anything further?"

"No, Your Honor," Hennessy said. "Our complete arguments are lodged in the affidavit. I wish to reiterate that we have new information that was not available to us during the three-year time period, which under the law, means that we have the right to file this suit. The actual crime was discovered only when John Cleveland signed that statement."

"This is an interesting issue, and you both have strong arguments. On the one hand, the police report does not state the death was murder, despite the very clear evidence that it was." He drew a deep breath. "Legally, I can't ignore the fact that this was clearly a murder and should've been recognized in the police report. The missing definition is an administration error, rather than an error of fact. Thus, the tolling period for the three years to bring this claim to court started twenty-one years ago. Having reviewed the submitted documents earlier and after hearing what has been said today, the motion for extension of time under the discovery rule is denied."

Brockman responded immediately. "Given the motion for extension of time is denied, the defense moves for a summary judgment on the case. The case has no legal standing and must be rejected with prejudice." Brockman handed a piece of paper to the bailiff, who passed it onto the judge. He then turned to Hennessy. "And as I'm sure you're aware, Mr. Hennessy, with prejudice prevents the subsequent refiling of this case. Once the claim is adjudicated on merits, you cannot bring the same claim to this court again."

Judge Clarence looked over the papers and then looked to Hennessy. He paused and shook his head slightly. "Given the motion for extension of time was denied, I have a decision on the summary judgment. When deciding on a summary judgment, I must consider whether any genuine issue of material fact has been presented. I have done that, and as such, upon consideration of the South Carolina Rules of Civil Procedure, applicable case law, briefs of parties, and oral arguments, the motion for a summary judgment is granted. This case is dismissed with prejudice. Thank you for your time."

Judge Clarence closed his files, stood, and left the room without another word. His assistants hurried after him.

Hennessy remained standing behind the desk, staring at the Great Seal of South Carolina, not moving an inch. Brockman said something to Hennessy as he walked past, but he didn't hear it. He stood there, staring forward, trying to comprehend the judgment.

After twenty-one years, after two decades of pain, his chance in court only lasted fifteen minutes.

It was over.

CHAPTER 15

"Nice try, old boy," Longhouse taunted as Hennessy approached. "But the law isn't on your side."

The foyer of the Charleston Judicial Center courthouse was sparsely filled. Two guards stood by the security scanner, one man was reading his cell phone in the far corner, and Richard Longhouse and his band of merry lawyers stood near the exit, laughing about their win in court. They gathered at the far end of the marbled foyer, in front of the statue of William Pitt, where the words 'Where the law ends, tyranny begins,' were etched into the marble behind him.

Longhouse stood tall, proud, and arrogance seeped off his tone. He'd won again, and he felt invincible. He chuckled as Hennessy approached, the sound echoing through the foyer, grating on every piece of Hennessy's soul.

Hennessy walked toward the exit with his head down, shadowed by Lockett, Jacinta, and Wendy.

He tried his best to ignore Longhouse, he tried his best to move past without flinching, but that laugh, that evil chortle, was too much. He stopped, turned, and stared. He felt Wendy touch his arm, but he ignored it.

Hennessy stepped forward, coming face to face with the man that caused his son's death. His towering figure loomed over his antagonist. Hennessy wanted to say something, anything, but it was taking all his energy not to explode in rage.

"Didn't you hear me, Joe? I said, 'nice try.'" Longhouse chuckled. "The civil suit was a splendid effort, but you didn't do enough. Why don't you just keep your family safe and drop all this nonsense? It's been twenty-one years, and you make a frivolous claim against me, trying to destroy me with some old grudge. Don't you think it's—"

"Don't speak to me about my family," Hennessy gritted his teeth, stepping even closer.

"And your daughters didn't want to take the risk of being the plaintiff?" Longhouse scoffed. "But I understand that. I guess the question you had to ask yourself was how were you going to protect your daughters when you couldn't protect your son?"

Hennessy's rage exploded. His right fist connected with the Senator's stomach before anybody knew what was happening.

Longhouse fell to the floor, doubled over in pain. The guards shouted as they rushed toward the men.

Lockett pulled Hennessy back, telling the guards to stand down. The guards stopped five feet away, but their hands remained on their holstered weapons.

Doubled over, one knee on the ground, Longhouse began to laugh. Brockman went to help him up, but Longhouse waved him away.

"My Grandmother could hit harder than that," Longhouse scoffed. "Luca would've been embarrassed by that punch."

Hennessy sprung forward again, but Lockett held him back. Lockett wrapped his arm around Hennessy's chest and pushed him toward the door. Hennessy struggled forward, but Lockett was too strong.

"Get him out the doors!" One guard shouted. "Don't make us deal with it."

Lockett pushed Hennessy toward the door,

followed by Jacinta telling Hennessy to calm down.

Longhouse rose to his feet and waved to Hennessy as he was shoved outside. He laughed and then coughed, holding his stomach as the doors closed.

Wendy stepped forward, moving between Brockman and Milton.

Longhouse stopped laughing when he looked at the stern-faced woman. A silence descended over the foyer.

"I have faith," Wendy began, her soft-spoken words delivering her statement with impact. "And my faith has taught me to forgive you and allow God to be the one to judge your soul." Without waiting for a response, Wendy turned and walked toward the door. Once she was at the door, she turned back to Longhouse. "And He will be the one to deliver justice to you."

CHAPTER 16

As Joe drove through the light rain, the memories of Luca were at the forefront of his mind.

In the first years after Luca's death, he tried to avoid the memories because the pain was too much to handle. But as time passed, as the memories began to fade, he held onto those cherished moments. He never wanted to forget his son. He never wanted those images to disappear into the past.

His mind drifted back to one of the Clemson Tigers' football games they attended. Luca was so excited, filled with such innocent joy. He bounced up and down on his seat, he screamed when everyone else screamed, and booed when the crowd did the same. He ate hotdogs and drank soda. He high-fived strangers. The smile never left his face. As they left the stadium, he talked non-stop, barely stopping for a breath. When they got in the truck to drive home, Luca fell asleep before they'd even left the parking lot.

Joe never wanted to forget those moments.

As he continued to drive, he could barely keep his hands on the steering wheel, his fingers shaking with raw emotion. Grieving the death of a child knew no time limit, and the anniversaries were still so challenging.

Twice a year, Joe and Wendy arrived at the cemetery. In over two decades, they hadn't missed either date. One, to celebrate his birthday, and two, for the somber anniversary of his death.

Wendy sat silently as she watched the landscape pass by. It was a road she'd traveled dozens of times, maybe even hundreds, with the scenery barely changing in all the years since their first trip. The anniversary of his death had never gotten easier, the same heaviness weighing them down.

Hennessy parked in the small parking lot, choosing a spot near the back where the most spaces remained. He switched the engine off, and the couple sat silently for a few minutes, staring at the front gates of the cemetery.

Wendy reached across and held Joe's hand, indicating she was ready. She didn't speak.

With a deep breath each, they stepped out into the

humid air. Hennessy closed his door and took a moment, his hand resting against the handle. He lowered his head and tried to calm his breathing. It didn't work. It never did. Not here.

He walked around the front of the truck and reached for Wendy's hand. She gripped it tightly, holding a bouquet of flowers in the other hand.

Together, they walked the well-trodden path to the grave of Luca Hennessy.

The scent of jasmine hung heavy in the air, greeting them with familiarity. A few people stood scattered around the grounds, most with their heads bowed as they gazed at the headstone of their loved ones. A couple looked up as the new arrivals passed by, but nobody spoke. This wasn't a place for socializing.

They reached Luca's row, and Joe could sense his wife's grief beginning to surface. She didn't resist it. Together, they walked the final few steps until they reached the gravestone.

The day marked twenty-two years since Luca's death.

Just as she always did, Wendy first walked beside the grave and wiped away the leaves gathered around the headstone. She wiped her sleeve along the front of the marble, cleaned off the dusty coating covering his name, and placed the bouquet of flowers under the inscription. Once done, she returned to stand beside her husband, paused for a few seconds, then knelt.

Wendy greeted Luca with a smile. She took a small toy car from her pocket and placed it beside the flowers. Luca loved toy cars. Often Wendy would walk into his room at the end of the weekend to find cars all over the floor. At the time, she was annoyed that he'd leave such a mess. Now, it was one of her fondest memories.

Joe sat next to his wife, and for two hours, the parents remained by Luca's grave, sharing their life with him.

Wendy talked about the weather, the vineyard, and the changes in Charleston. She talked about his sisters, Ellie and Casey, and how their lives were progressing. She smiled as she told him about Ellie, studying in New York, and laughed as she talked about Casey and the dramas of the final year of high school. The girls were almost all grown up. She couldn't hold back the tears when she told Luca that she would've loved to see him grown up. How she would've loved to have known the man he would've become. She told Luca that she still kissed his photo every morning, and his smiling face was still the centerpiece of their house.

Joe talked about the storms, the humidity, and the recent rains. He smiled when he told Luca that the muds were thick enough to play football in. He told Luca that whenever he saw thick layers of mud, he remembered the football tackles, the dashing moves, and the yells of joy.

Together, they remembered his life as a toddler, his days at school, and his days on the basketball court. They remembered the jokes he used to tell, and how happy he was when his parents laughed. They remembered his friends and the joy they shared in the swimming pool. They remembered his innocent laugh, so joyous and free.

After two and a half hours, they left as a light summer rain began to fall. They felt guilty leaving him behind. Despite the years, that feeling of guilt as they left was always there.

When they reached the truck, Joe stopped and leaned both hands on the hood.

"I have to kill him, Wendy," Joe whispered. "I have to shoot Richard Longhouse."

"No, Joe. We've been through this." She rubbed his arm. "I know how angry you are, but I can't lose you as well. Ellie still needs you. Casey needs you. I need you. You can't help us if you're behind bars."

"But Longhouse paid someone to kidnap our child."

"And the man who killed our son is dead. Justin Fields is dead."

"But Longhouse is the man responsible."

"I know, Joe. I know." She hugged him as the tears flowed.

"I failed him," he whispered. "I failed Luca in a way no father should ever fail his son."

"No, Joe," Wendy said. "You didn't fail him."

When he reached his arms around her and pulled her close, Joe felt the warmth of his wife reach into his soul.

Together, in the soft summer rain, they grieved.

CHAPTER 17

Over the coming week, Joe found himself caught in a rollercoaster of emotions.

When Friday night arrived, he was relieved to be leaving Charleston and driving the highway to the vineyard. He arrived a little after seven, and Wendy welcomed him home with a hug. Casey, full of seventeen-year-old attitude, gave him a high-five. He asked for a hug, and she reluctantly gave him one. He smiled when she asked to borrow the truck to see friends in Greenville. He agreed in return for a proper hug. She smiled and hugged him tightly.

"Don't be too late," he tossed her the keys. "And be back by ten."

On Saturday, Joe spent time in the vineyard. He worked in the field, trimming some of the older vines. Casey helped him for a few hours, but mostly he worked alone, enjoying the sun and clean air.

That night he took Wendy out, first to El Tejano, a

Mexican restaurant twenty-five minutes from their vineyard, and then to catch a late movie session. Hennessy had little interest in a rom-com, but he knew how much Wendy loved Julia Roberts, and while he didn't expect much, he found himself entertained. On Sunday, he followed Wendy and Casey around the local farmers' market. Wendy bought up big, and Joe felt like a packhorse as he struggled to carry the five bags of produce back to their truck. By the time the afternoon rolled around, Joe didn't want to make the return trip. He'd had fun, enjoying the weekend the way he knew he needed to.

"One day," he whispered as he packed his bag with a heavy heart.

As he rolled down the gravel driveway, Wendy and Casey waved goodbye. He waved out the window for as long as possible, up until the moment he crossed the last rise and lost sight of his home in the rearview mirror.

For the next few hours, Joe felt his heart grow heavier. He made it back to his apartment a few minutes shy of 10pm, and all he wanted was to drop onto his bed and sleep. But as usual, he found himself unable to sleep despite the weight of fatigue fighting his eyelids. Each time he closed his eyes, the thoughts of failure returned.

After struggling with sleep all night, he rolled out of bed at 4am and went to his truck. He jumped in and began driving with no clear destination in mind.

He drove for hours, traveling as far south as Hilton Head Island. With nothing but the voices in his head for company, he drove in silence, winding the window down for fresh air and road noise.

He parked his truck, took off his shoes, and walked onto the beach as the morning light began to grace the horizon over the Atlantic. He strolled, hands in pockets, gazing over the water as the light sparkled on the waves. He breathed in the salty sea air, felt the fresh breeze on his face, and his pain began to subside.

As the morning clouds were painted in a magnificent pink, he stopped and looked out to the ocean. It was gentle but ferocious. Calm but menacing. Soft but powerful. Under the sky's gentle embrace, he remembered it all. All the living and dying, all the laughter and the pain. He remembered the good times and the bad, the gentle and the loud. He remembered the love and the anger, the tenderness and the violence. He remembered the love of his family, and the hatred he had for his foe.

At the edge of the ocean, he could feel the heartbeat of something more, something bigger, and he felt in harmony with the earth. He could feel the ocean's power, and its unrelenting force. He could feel the sky's beauty, and its threatening storms. He breathed deeply and stood taller.

He was no longer beaten. He was no longer defeated. He didn't know how, and he didn't know when, but he wouldn't let Richard Longhouse walk away.

He wasn't finished fighting yet.

CHAPTER 18

In the weeks after the civil suit was thrown out, Hennessy returned to court for hearings on a drunken disorderly case, a minor theft incident, and a fraud charge. There were bail hearings on a breaking and entering charge, a DUI, and a robbery charge. He tried to focus on the cases, he tried to push his life forward, but he hadn't managed to settle his anger. His muscles were tight. His eyes were tired. His jaw hurt. He still couldn't sleep, breaking out in cold sweats in the middle of the night, the thoughts of failing his son always present.

He spent the sleepless hours of each night searching for anything connected to Richard Longhouse. He searched his name online, clicking on every link he could find. He searched hundreds and hundreds of websites. He searched for anything connected to the Longhouse family, but it turned up little. He clicked thousands of links, read thousands of files, and reviewed thousands of connections.

Early one morning, at 2.05am, while he searched the insurance databases for anything connected to Longhouse's address on Ashley River Road, he found a lead.

Fueled by adrenalin, he was in the office by 3am. At 8am, he made several phone calls, confirming the information was correct. At 9am, he called a potential new client. She was receptive, almost enthusiastic, but he was a long way from making a case.

Later that day, Jacinta leaned against his office door. "Joe, you've put a new client meeting on the calendar for this afternoon at 5pm. Maria Santos. You've listed it as a civil case, but we don't usually take civil cases."

"It's a wrongful death suit, and we've had some recent experience with that. Plus, we don't have much new work coming in at the moment. This could be a good case to take on. A wrongful death suit might carry us through to winter."

Jacinta nodded but wasn't convinced by his reasoning.

Hennessy arranged his files on his desk. First impressions counted. His desk had a monitor to the right, a pile of folders to the left. His ballpoint pen sat on top of a legal pad, and he had a closed legal reference book next to that. There were two chairs in front of his desk, a potted plant in the far corner. The window behind him cast a soft glow onto his desk, and the ducted air conditioner hummed gently above his head. The room smelled pine fresh, thanks to a new automatic scent dispenser near the door.

At 5pm, Jacinta welcomed the potential new client into the office.

Maria Santos was a short woman of Latino descent, early fifties with curled black hair and small earrings. She appeared timid but powerful, kind but ferocious. She had a look of determination in her eyes, and her muscular forearms showed she wasn't afraid of hard work. Her eyes were green, and her perfume smelled like jasmine.

"Hello, Mrs. Santos." Hennessy stood and offered his hand. She shook it lightly and then sat down. "I've asked you here to discuss a wrongful death claim, but I must be upfront and say that civil suits aren't my specialty. Criminal law is my specialty."

"Good," she said and placed her handbag on her lap. "Because this is a criminal matter. I've shouted at the police for the past five months, but no one will listen to me. I've talked to just about everyone. I've filed complaints, I've written letters, but it goes nowhere. I'm so frustrated, and I must admit, I was quite happy that you called." She took a moment and looked over at Jacinta, who was sitting next to her with a notepad ready. "My husband George was a good man. He was a gardener. All his life, he was a hard worker and loved his job." She reached into her bag and removed a small photo of George. She placed it on Hennessy's desk while she fought back her emotions. She drew a breath and continued. "He didn't deserve to die in that incident."

"Can you tell us how the incident happened?" Jacinta asked in a soft tone.

"Five months ago, George died in a chainsaw accident while working on a property, but I don't think it was an accident. I think it's a criminal case, but the police won't touch it. I know he would want me to do this. I know he'd want me to get justice for him."

"And where did the incident occur?" Jacinta asked.

"On the property of Senator Richard Longhouse."

Jacinta swung her head to look at her boss, her

expression changing to something of concern. "Joe?"

Hennessy drew a breath and leaned forward, resting his elbows on the table. "Mrs. Santos, I need to be upfront and state that I have a past with Richard Longhouse. Richard and I aren't friends. I was searching his name on the internet when I came across the Life Insurance claim for your husband, and given the situation, I wondered why you didn't lodge a wrongful death civil suit. That's why I called you."

"I've already tried to lodge a civil suit."

Hennessy squinted. "What do you mean?"

"I've tried many different law firms." She looked across to Jacinta. "No lawyer in Charleston was willing to take on the case without a $100,000 retainer, and even then, I doubted whether they would see the case through. Once you scratch the surface, you find Richard Longhouse has his fingers in everything. Nobody was going to take the case seriously. All these lawyers were just going to take my money and brush the case under the carpet. One law firm agreed to look at it, but then one of my sons discovered that the lawyer had donated to Richard Longhouse's political campaign." She moved in her seat, shaking her head. "My boys wanted to kill

Richard Longhouse. Take him down to the river and drown him. I told them they were not to touch Richard and that I would take care of him. You're my family's last hope, Mr. Hennessy."

"How many sons do you have?" Jacinta continued with her soft approach.

"Two. They're both grown men. Both are married and have children of their own. I couldn't let them do something stupid, not when they had their own families to protect."

Hennessy sat back in his seat. "Mrs. Santos, before we go any further, I need you to know that I suspect Richard Longhouse was involved in the murder of someone very close to me. If we proceed with this case, I need you to know that fact might cloud my vision at times. You need to think long and hard about whether I'm the right lawyer to take on this civil case."

"You are." Her words were firm, like she was telling him off for doubting his judgment. "I could tell the second I walked in here that you were the man to do this."

Hennessy smiled. Maria Santos was warm but ferocious. He liked that. "For the cost structure, I'm willing to take this case on a contingency fee. That means there will be no upfront costs to you, and in simple terms, it will be a no-win, no-fee basis. If the case is successful, we will take any fees out of the settlement. Jacinta will provide you with the details of the fees and potential settlements as you leave."

"I have some forms ready and waiting on my desk," Jacinta added.

"In South Carolina, while there's no legal limit on the amount of damages that can be claimed in a wrongful death suit, there are some limits. When assessing the damages, the court looks at lost wages, medical expenses, and compensation for pain and suffering. If gross negligence is proved, then there are also punitive damages, which are capped at $500,000. It's good to note that South Carolina does not apply a cap to economic damages, nor the damages for pain and suffering."

"I don't want to settle for any amount."

"Pardon?"

"I want it proven in court that Richard was responsible for my husband's death." She reached into her handbag and removed five photos, holding them tightly in her hands. "George was an independent contractor and worked for Richard as a gardener twice a week on his former plantation home. The grounds are huge. George would spend Monday and Friday there every week, working on all aspects of the gardens. On that day in January, when he was cutting branches with a chainsaw, he fell off an icy ladder, and the chainsaw's blade cut his throat. He bled to death, but it wasn't an accident." She placed the photos on the table. "This is why I know Richard Longhouse was responsible for his death."

Hennessy picked up the photos and studied them. "An affair?"

"George had taken photos of Richard kissing his neighbor, a young 25-year-old woman."

"And what was your husband planning to do with those photos?"

Maria looked down at her hands. "I'm not proud of it, and I told him not to, but George didn't want to listen. He said this was our chance to make a better life for ourselves. He hated working for Richard and thought this was how he could retire comfortably."

"George tried to blackmail him."

Maria nodded. "George told Richard he would expose the affair to his wife and the media. He said it would ruin Richard's chances of being elected as governor. George said the cheating man needed to be exposed for the untrustworthy soul he was. The public would never trust Longhouse if they saw those photos. George gave Richard two weeks to pay him $500,000 to destroy the photos, but he was dead a week later."

"Did the police investigate your husband's death?" Jacinta questioned.

"They ruled it as an accident. It was a five-page report, but there was barely any information in it. There was not even a mention of the photos that George took." She rustled through her bag and removed a folded piece of paper. She placed it on the table. "There. That's all the investigation the police did into George's death."

"Did you tell them about the photos and the blackmail attempt?"

"I did. They told me to throw the photos out, or I could face court action for defamation. From that moment forward, I knew I couldn't trust the police. They told me it was a tragic accident and I needed to move on with my life. When I asked them to check the chainsaw for signs of sabotage, they refused. The detective even laughed at the suggestion and told me not to make inflammatory accusations against a sitting Senator. They said that because George was an independent contractor, he was responsible for his own safety."

"That's where we'll make our case," Hennessy explained. "Despite being an independent contractor, looking at his employment pattern on the Longhouse property and the jobs he was required to do, it's clear that the responsibility for his safety rested with the property owner."

For the next fifty minutes, Hennessy took Maria Santos through the details of the civil trial process. He explained where they could build a case. He'd already reviewed the life insurance claim, he had already reviewed the police report, and he'd already prepared a focus for the trial. He explained that Richard Longhouse would try to settle out of court, and the stronger the case became, the higher the settlement was likely to be. Maria repeated that she didn't want a settlement, and that she wanted Longhouse to admit guilt. Hennessy informed her that it was unlikely to happen, and without a settlement, the case would go to trial. They had a strong chance at winning in court, he said, but it wasn't guaranteed.

"Mr. Hennessy, I would like you to take the case to court," Maria said. "Because I need justice for my George."

CHAPTER 19

At five minutes past 10am the next day, Hennessy sat in the boardroom of his office reading over a paper file, with Jacinta to his right, typing on her laptop. His energy levels were up. He slept for the first time in weeks. He had hope.

The Joe Hennessy Law Office boardroom was long and wide, with a dark wooden table in the middle and five office chairs around the outside. A tall window at the end of the room looked out to the street, next to it was a whiteboard filled with notes, and there was a large painting of a Folly Beach sunset on the far wall. Folders were piled up on the boardroom table, organized by Jacinta. There were photos of the scene in one pile, witness statements in another, and evidence documentation in another.

The door to the boardroom opened, and investigator Barry Lockett entered carrying a small folder under one arm and a tray of coffee cups in one hand. "Delivery," he sang as he handed the coffees out.

"Well," Jacinta said as she looked up from her computer screen. "Look what you brought. All these donuts are not good for my waistline, you know?"

Lockett held up a small bag he'd hidden under his other arm and shook it. "Nor mine."

Lockett placed the donuts in the middle of the table and slumped his large frame into an office chair, which struggled under his weight. "I figured we needed a sugar hit for this morning. So, tell me all about this big break."

"We've taken a case for a woman named Maria Santos. She wishes to lodge a civil suit for the wrongful death of her husband," Jacinta looked at Hennessy before she continued. "And the defendant in the civil suit is Richard Longhouse."

"Whoa." Lockett pursed his lips and whistled. "That is a big break. Did that just fall into your lap?"

"No," Hennessy reached forward and grabbed a glazed donut. "It took a lot of research to find this lead."

"Much of a case?"

"That's what we're trying to figure out." Hennessy

began. He opened a file on the table and read over the first lines. "According to the police report, George Santos was an independent contractor working on Richard Longhouse's property twice weekly. He died when he attempted to cut the limbs off a tree but slipped off a ladder, and the chainsaw also fell. Although the chainsaw had stopped running, it fell on top of him, and the sharp point of the chain stabbed him in the neck, cutting his carotid artery. He bled to death in minutes. The police filed this five-page report." He passed the copy of the report to Jacinta, who handed it to Lockett. "It's obvious that there was very little investigation into the death."

"Who found him?" Lockett asked as he scanned his eyes over the report.

"Longhouse, about fifteen minutes after the recorded time of death," Jacinta said. "He claimed he drove into the property, saw the body on the ground, and immediately called 911. He was at a café only minutes before, and the police report says the statement checks out."

"Homeowner's Insurance?"

"From the details in George's life insurance claim, we've reviewed Richard Longhouse's Homeowner's

Insurance policy. While it covers accidental death, it does not cover negligence for wrongful death, which we will be arguing for. I'm sure it'll come as a shock to him when he finds that out. Most people don't read the fine print, Senator's included."

"That's got to sting," Lockett said. "Workers' Compensation?"

"Not eligible," Hennessy replied. "Because George was an independent contractor, under South Carolina law, he wasn't covered by Workers' Compensation. However, he did have a life insurance claim. Maria has claimed that amount, and it's a payout of $250,000. Maria also has the right to file a civil lawsuit for third-party actions if she believes negligence caused the injury."

"Third-party actions?" Lockett questioned.

"Third-party actions are a civil claim for pain, mental anguish, and other damages. If proceeds are recovered from both the defendant and the life insurance policy, the insurance carrier may have a lien on the amount, but if she wins this civil suit, I expect the damages will be much higher than $250,00."

Lockett expressed his approval with raised eyebrows and a nod. "And why do you believe

Longhouse is guilty?"

"This is where it gets interesting," Jacinta said. She reached for a file in the middle of the table and removed the photos from it. She pushed the images along the table to Lockett. In it, two lovers could be seen in an embrace with their lips locked together. "This is Senator Richard Longhouse and his twenty-five-year-old neighbor, Kathryn Moore. George Santos took these photos a week before his death."

Lockett pursed his lips and whistled again. "Blackmail?"

"That's right," Hennessy responded. "But clearly, Longhouse didn't pay up. Having these two events only a week apart is too much of a coincidence. Either Longhouse was involved in the death, or he paid someone to do it. It would be possible to set it up—pin the man down and then hit him in the neck with the sharp point of the chainsaw. The carotid artery is quite exposed at the top of the neck and doesn't need a deep cut. They knock over the ladder and make it look like an accident. I have no doubt that Longhouse's criminal connections can do that."

"But that's a criminal case. You can't make a civil case based on ideas," Lockett studied the photos.

"We'll need more than that. Is there enough evidence to file a civil suit for negligence?"

"And that's where the life insurance report comes in." Hennessy pointed to a file on the table, and Jacinta reached for it. She opened it and placed it in front of Lockett. "The insurance firm did a lot more investigations than the police. Their report presents several things on which we can build a civil case."

Lockett looked over the file, running his index finger along the lines of information as he read.

"The ladder is essential to the claim," Hennessy continued. "Longhouse provided the ladder which George Santos slipped off, and the ladder was discovered to have ice on it. Longhouse was negligent in providing the ladder to the worker without checking for ice during the month of January, which is the coldest month of the year. According to the weather report on the day of George's death, they had an overnight low of 30, and the temperature didn't rise above 50 degrees for the day, one of the coldest days in the area for the past ten years. Police found ice on the ladder rungs when they arrived twenty-five minutes after the death however, it doesn't say that in their report. That fact is only mentioned after the life insurance firm talked to the police."

"It was determined that Santos slipped off the ladder, and that's when he fell onto the chainsaw. The chain hit him in the neck," Jacinta added. "Longhouse is negligent because a reasonable person would've known there was ice on the ladder because he stored it outside, next to the gardening shed. Longhouse even states in the life insurance report interview that he knew the ladder was stored outside overnight."

"And the case will be built around his negligence not to warn George of the danger." Hennessy opened another file and read the first page.

"But if he was an independent contractor, then the responsibility of safety rests with him," Lockett added. "I know that because I'm an independent contractor, and any OSHA regulations don't cover me."

"Let's get technical," Hennessy raised his finger. "Just because he's paid as an independent contractor doesn't mean he's an independent contractor. The Occupational Safety and Health Administration uses several ways to determine whether a person is an independent contractor. One, and most crucially, is the work process. If you hire a true independent contractor, you request a specific outcome. It's up to the contractor to apply their expertise and judgment to arrive at the end result. However, if you dictate someone's process, you control their safety. Therefore, OSHA regulations protects them. Secondly, if safety violations occur, OSHA will use the Economic Reality Test, which considers the crucial nature of workflow control. The less control the independent contractor has over their work, the more responsible the property owner is."

"And George Santos was employed on the Longhouse property twice weekly for the past five years," Jacinta stated. "That's not a true independent contractor. That's an employee being paid as an independent contractor. The responsibility for safety rests with the employer."

"That'll be hard to prove," Lockett added. "His lawyers will fight this every step of the way."

"That's why we're here."

Lockett nodded his approval again. "Longhouse is about to announce his run for governor next month. This will cast a shadow over the entire campaign."

"It's perfect," Hennessy agreed. "We're going to come at it from two angles. One—the civil case based on the negligence of providing a ladder with ice on it. And two—the coincidence of the blackmail, which could lead to criminal prosecution later."

Hennessy closed one file and then opened another. "Barry, I need you to look into the girl in the photo— Kathryn Moore. I need to know everything about her—where she works, where she spends her time, who her friends are. Build a profile of her but don't talk to her yet. I'll talk to her once we have a clear picture of who she is."

"We could always just release that photo to the public?" Lockett stated. "It would destroy Longhouse's campaign right from the start."

"Not yet," Hennessy replied. "We don't need him pre-empting our moves. We'll wait until the court case to release those photos. Our ultimate goal is to win the civil case for the Santos family and gather enough evidence for the Circuit Solicitor's Office to investigate a criminal prosecution. We need to be professional and make the right choices for the Santos family."

"Sounds like a plan." Lockett closed the two files in front of him. "And where's your focus going to be?"

"I need to build a profile of George Santos. I'll talk to some people who worked with him and knew the man."

Lockett reached for another donut. "Do we have any hope of winning the civil suit?"

"We need to win it." Hennessy pressed his index finger onto the table. "Because this is our best chance to take him down."

CHAPTER 20

Antonio Smith lived in Mount Pleasant, which, as the name suggested, was a pleasant area. Across the Cooper River from Downtown Charleston, the suburban town was rapidly growing, with the laid-back lifestyle, excellent public schools, and low crime rates attractive to families, retirees, and anybody in between. With an abundance of fresh seafood, just-picked produce, and great local breweries, the calm pace felt like a world away from the hustle of the tourist hotspots.

Hennessy followed the GPS on his cell until he pulled into a quiet street. Most of the homes in the street had a white picket fence, a basketball ring above the garage, and an American flag above their porch. Toward the end of the street was a large two-story brick home with established oak trees and a sprawling garden. A tall hedge was clipped to perfection, and the grass was so green that it looked

146

painted.

"That's a gardener's home," Hennessy said to himself as he pulled up in the driveway.

"Hello?" The second he stepped out of his truck, a man walked out from behind the hedge.

Antonio Smith was a large man with large hands. He looked like he'd worked outside every day of his life. In his fifties, he looked fit enough to still go ten rounds of boxing with any young buck. He wore a red flannel shirt, blue jeans, and dirty boots.

Hennessy removed his suit jacket, loosened his tie, and threw them back in the truck. He then turned and approached the man. "Mr. Antonio Smith, my name is Joe Hennessy. You spoke with my assistant, Jacinta Templeton, earlier today."

"Ah yes, that lovely young lady that called. She sure was sweet."

"That's her," Hennessy smiled and held his hand out. As they shook, they gave each other a nod.

"My wife has fixed some lemonade," Antonio said. "She made it fresh this morning. Would you care for some?"

"In this heat, no reasonable man could say no to that," Hennessy agreed.

Antonio led them through the front gate, up the steps, and onto his porch.

"Make yourself comfortable," he said, pointing to the wicker settee with a white cushion before disappearing inside. Hennessy sat down and admired the view in front of him. A fan started to whirl over his head, and the draught was a welcome relief from the heat.

Antonio returned a few moments later, carrying two glasses filled with ice and lemonade. He handed one to Hennessy and sat on the wicker armchair beside him.

"Thank you for the lemonade," Hennessy said as he sipped his drink. "This is a lovely place."

"Thanks, we've been here twenty-five years now. Raised our children here and seen a few neighbors come and go. It's been a dream," Antonio said. "But you can't go wrong in Mount Pleasant. Most places here are lovely."

"I'm sure." Hennessy sipped his drink as condensation built on the outside. "Sorry to get straight to the point, Mr. Smith, but I'm investigating the death of George Santos."

"No, of course, I understand you're busy. Here's

to George." Antonio raised his glass to the sky and then took a sip. "George was a great man. Always willing to support everyone and would give the shirt off his own back to help. A genuine, good human being. The world lost a good one the day he passed away."

"And you had worked with him in the past?"

"Many times. We did a lot of jobs together, and we got along great. I used to do the work for Richard Longhouse, but I quit five years ago. I couldn't stand the guy. Treated me and all his workers like dirt. George took over the job on the Longhouse property after I left."

"You said that Longhouse treated you like dirt?"

"Yeah. He thought he owned us. As an independent gardener, I usually go to a place, and they tell me what they want, and I make it happen. It might be mowing the lawn, cutting trees, or trimming hedges. But I choose how to do it. With Longhouse, it was completely different. He wanted me there at 8am, and leave at 4pm, not a second earlier." He groaned and shook his head. "There was one time when I finished cutting the branches at about three o'clock and was packing up to leave, but he came out of the home and said I had to stay until 4. Said if I wanted to get paid, then I had to help the housekeeper clean up inside. I laughed because I thought it was a joke. But he wasn't joking. I quit a week after that."

"That's interesting." Hennessy made a mental note of the working habits. "Can you tell me if George was safety conscious when you worked together?"

"I was really surprised to hear he'd died in the garden, considering he was so meticulous when it came to safety."

"And he always followed safety guidelines?"

"Always. The man was a walking billboard of OSHA, if you can believe that. For a man who spent most of his days working alone, it always surprised me to see how cautious he was. Yes, to answer your question, the man always wore his safety gear, right down to the safety goggles."

"So, were you surprised to hear he slipped off an icy ladder and was cut by his chainsaw?"

"More than surprised—I was stunned. I'd only seen him maybe five or so weeks before his death. We worked together on a large job at one of the plantation homes. We were hired to clear a lot of fallen trees after a storm had ripped through the area. George wore all the gear that day—gloves, face mask, arm guards, steel-cap boots. You name it, he had it."

For the next fifteen minutes, Hennessy asked questions about George, his work habits, and his past. It became clear George was respected, hardworking, and safety conscious. Antonio smiled as he retold stories of their time together. He talked about George like he was an older brother, always looking out for everyone. Antonio was a good witness, a charming man with a friendly smile, someone who could sway a jury with his calm and likable persona.

"If the case went to trial, would you testify about George's dedication to safety?" Hennessy asked.

"Without a doubt. I loved that man like a brother. If you call me to the stand, I'll tell the court everything I know about him."

"And would you testify about your time working at the Longhouse property?"

"Absolutely. I hated working for that guy."

"Thank you, Mr. Smith. That's what I needed to hear." Hennessy drank the rest of the icy lemonade, brushing the condensation off the side of the glass. "Your testimony will be an essential part of the case.

My assistant will be in touch, and we'll need you to draft a statement of the facts as you know them, but it's likely we'll head to trial in around five to eight weeks."

After a solid handshake, Hennessy left the property and began the drive back to Charleston.

When his cell rang, and he saw Barry Lockett's number, he knew his day was about to get a lot more interesting.

CHAPTER 21

"You really do work fast, don't you," Hennessy said as he walked into the Blind Tiger Pub, a charming alehouse in the French Quarter, Downtown Charleston.

"It's what you pay me for, mate," Lockett said. He was seated at a table in the far corner of the room, next to Jacinta. Lockett was halfway through his pint, while Jacinta had only begun her gin and tonic.

For more than two hundred years, the Blind Tiger had been an iconic part of the Charleston landscape. Featuring a brick-walled courtyard at the rear and dark décor inside, the bar radiated class and history, and at 5.05pm on a Wednesday, it was becoming filled with workers, finishing their day with a quiet drink.

Hennessy ordered a pint of the local Westbrook IPA at the bar and returned to the table. Lockett placed a file on the table between them as he sat down. It was hefty, filled with different printouts and pages of information. The name 'Kathryn Moore' was written on the front of the file.

"Before we get to this," Jacinta pointed at the file. "I need to talk with you about the evidence from the insurance company. According to the report, the insurance company tested ten items from the scene, including George's water bottle and the chainsaw. They were looking for anything that might void the life insurance claim, such as alcohol use at work. Mr. Santos had a 'no alcohol' working condition on his life insurance policy. The insurance company, Mutual Life, found two water bottles in his truck. One in the back seat, and then one in the drink holder of his pickup, and they tested for alcohol. They found nothing. They returned all the items to Maria five weeks after the death, and she's kept them all in storage since then. I was wondering if we should request to have them tested by a private firm?"

"That's a good idea," Hennessy agreed. "The chain of evidence will be a problem if we find anything, but we need them tested. Barry, what was the name of the firm you used last time?"

"Precision Applied Technical on Calhoun Street. I

have a contact there. Nicki Chang. She's terrific."

"I'll send off the request tomorrow," Jacinta replied.

"Great. Thank you." Hennessy pointed to the file on the table and then sipped his ale. "Anything interesting on Kathryn Moore?"

"Lots of interesting things, and some fascinating things as well." Lockett turned the folder around to face Hennessy. "All of Kathryn Moore's social media profiles are public, so I didn't have to dig too deep to learn everything about her. We have a list of her friends, her workplaces, her schools, her cousins, everything we need to know at this point."

"Go on."

"Kathryn Moore is twenty-five, went to school in Charleston Collegiate before starting a major in Communications at Clemson. Dropped out in the second year and returned to Charleston, where she's worked in various upmarket bars as a hostess. She still lives at the address on Ashley River Road, next door to Richard Longhouse, and has lived there most of her life. She—"

"Ew," Jacinta cut in. "That means Longhouse would've known her when she was just a child?"

"I'm afraid so," Lockett nodded. "Her mother, Brenda Moore, was quite the socialite during her youth. I did a bit of digging on her as well, and this is very interesting—she went to her prom night with Richard Longhouse."

"Whoa." Hennessy sat back at the revelation.

"Longhouse has dated the mother and daughter who live next door?" Jacinta's face scrunched at the thought. "What a dirty old sleaze."

"In her twenties, Brenda Moore was in just about every social column in the state and was very well-known in the right circles," Lockett continued. "If she was a youth today, I'd suggest she'd be quite the influencer. Now in her sixties, she lives with her daughter at the Ashley River Road address. She really enjoyed the wealthy lifestyle, but it was mostly smoke and mirrors. They were heavily in debt and barely keeping afloat. The house was left in the mother and daughter's name in the husband's will. After his death, they put the house on the market, but no buyers were interested in the two-point-five million range. She applied to subdivide the land, but her application was knocked back due to the historical values of the property."

"And the father?"

"The father was Steven Moore. Died of a heart attack two years ago. He owned a large Veterinarian Clinic in West Ashley and started a chain of pet food supply stores, which spread across the country. They have several horses on their property and had previously owned a few racehorses."

"Kathryn is trying to fill a void in her life with Longhouse?" Jacinta asked.

"Not quite," Lockett said and continued. "According to a recent bankruptcy filing, the chain of pet food supply stores has gone bust. Steven Moore borrowed heavily to expand the business, leaving the estate with many debts. Brenda is running the business and doesn't seem to know what she's doing. She had to sell the Veterinarian Clinic twelve months ago and is looking to keep the debtors out of their property. Since the death of Steven, the family is barely keeping afloat."

"So…" Jacinta leaned forward, tapping her finger on the file. "Given the financial situation, would it be fair to assume that Longhouse paid Kathryn to sleep with him?"

Lockett nodded. "It wouldn't surprise me if there

was a financial incentive for Kathryn to have this affair. With her family's current debts, it would make sense."

"This will be front page of every newspaper in the state when this gets out." Jacinta turned to Hennessy. "This is so scandalous."

"It is." Hennessy leaned back in his seat. "First, I need to talk to Kathryn Moore and find out what exactly was going on."

CHAPTER 22

Hennessy stepped into the Vintage Lounge on King Street at 7pm. He was instantly impressed.

The swanky wine bar was classy, elegant, and stylish, and the clientele matched the décor. With the ambiance of a French café, with mohair upholstery and antiques from Paris, the space had a barrel ceiling, gilded in an uneven pattern to create a soft glow across the space. The marble-topped bar extended the length of the room, appearing like it had been pulled from the set of a 1920s Hollywood film.

"You look like you're after someone in particular," a voice said from behind him, and when he turned, he faced Kathryn Moore.

She was much shorter than he imagined, but her distinctive eyes and multiple shades of highlights in her auburn hair confirmed it was her. She held herself well, with the confidence that comes with being young and beautiful. A gentle smell of sandalwood surrounded her, and her demeanor was friendly.

"Miss Moore, my name is Joe Hennessy," he offered her a friendly smile. "I'd like to talk with you."

"You're not a cop, are you?"

"No, a lawyer."

"A lawyer? Why would a lawyer be looking for me?" She squinted as she looked at him. "This isn't about those unpaid tickets, is it? I'm going to pay them soon."

"No," Hennessy said and looked around. "Can we chat somewhere privately?"

"I'd like to know what this is about first."

"It's about your relationship with Richard Longhouse."

"Richard? What relationship?" Her eyebrows sprung up, and her tone lost any friendliness. "We don't have a relationship."

Hennessy pulled out his cell, thumbed the screen a few times, then held up one of the photos Maria had sent. Kathryn took one look before she turned away and swallowed hard.

Silence hung between them as Hennessy waited for her to decide the next move. To try and help her along, he scrolled through more photos. The tactic worked.

"Not here," she whispered. She looked around to ensure no one was watching, then pointed to a door near the back of the room. "I'll take a break in five minutes, and we can talk out in the alley."

Hennessy nodded and walked to the door. Once in the alley, he leaned against the brick wall and waited. The smell of urine hung heavy in the air, mixed with the stink of trash from the dumpster nearby.

Kathryn Moore walked out a few minutes later, but instead of stopping, she gestured for Hennessy to follow. Not even the shielded back alley was private enough for this chat. She led him around a corner to an alcove between two buildings. Cigarette butts littered the ground, mixed with broken bottles and snack wrappers.

"Before you start," Kathryn said as she stopped and turned to face him. Her defensiveness had kicked into high gear from the beginning. "There's no relationship. Yes, that's me in the photos, but only because he was paying me."

"Longhouse paid you to do what?"

She rolled her eyes. "He paid me to keep him

company, but we ended any connections about five months ago. My mother came into some money and there was no need for me to see him ever again."

"Did your mother approve of your relationship?"

"She approved of the money," she scoffed and fished into her pocket. She pulled out a cigarette and a lighter. Holding the cigarette to her mouth, she lit it and then took a long drag. "She never said no to that."

"Did your mother even know about your relationship with him?"

"I never talked to her directly about it, but she must've known that's where the money was coming from," Kathryn shrugged. "She was angry with me whenever I returned from his place. She'd ignore me for days, but she never once complained about the money. I was bringing in thousands."

"What sort of company were you giving him?"

"Geez, man." Kathryn looked up and met his gaze. "The type his wife wasn't giving him, but it's all over now. Like I said, I haven't seen that old sleaze in more than five months." She took another long drag of her cigarette. "I can't stand the sight of him or even hearing his name. I've tried to wipe those months from my memory. You gotta do what you can to survive."

"You were sleeping with him for money?"

"Come on, man." Kathryn shook her head at him. "What is this? Some sort of interrogation?"

"I need to know about your relationship with Richard Longhouse. He's involved in some very suspect activity, and I'd hate for you to be implicated in it," Hennessy explained. "We're beginning an investigation into the death of a gardener on his property, and that gardener had photos of you and Richard kissing. I need to rule you out of that investigation."

She stared at Hennessy for a moment before taking another long drag on her cigarette. "Yeah, I remember that death. Guy slipped off a ladder and cut himself with a chainsaw. It was pretty bad."

"His name was George Santos."

She nodded. "I stopped seeing Richard just after that. As I said, my mother came into some money, and I didn't need it from him anymore, so I told him to shove it. I haven't seen him since."

"Why didn't you need the money anymore?"

"We were trying to keep our property but had all

these debts. Then my mother found some way to make money. She never told me how she got the money, and I didn't ask. She said she could pay off the debts for the house so we could stay there. We're not rich, but we have a nice home. Mom and I own it half and half. That's what my father left in his will. I've still got to work for my money, and right now, I'm missing out on some good tips."

Hennessy looked around the alcove. The space was tight, and he stood between Kathryn and the only exit.

"Were you aware that George Santos tried to blackmail Richard with these photos before his death?"

Kathryn's mouth hung open for a moment. "I don't know what you're suggesting, Mister, but I suggest you tread carefully."

"Why's that, Kathryn?"

She moved nervously, unable to stand still, rocking from one foot to the other.

"Because Richard Longhouse is a very, very dangerous man." She flicked her cigarette out to the corner and tried to walk past Hennessy. "You don't know who you're dealing with."

THE SOUTHERN TRIAL

Hennessy stepped to his right, blocking her path.

"Listen to me," Kathryn lowered her tone. "Richard has connections everywhere. Police, politics, and criminal organizations. If he hears you're looking into our relationship, he'll come after you with everything he has. That's no joke. I've seen what he can do."

She held his eye contact before he stepped aside. Kathryn Moore hurried back down the alley and through the back door of the restaurant.

One thing was clear, she was scared of Richard Longhouse.

CHAPTER 23

Hennessy strolled through the historic streets of Charleston, stopping to eat his lunch in Waterfront Park. He loved the scenic location. It was a serene, picturesque park, only a short walk from his office. Complete with stunning views, an iconic Pineapple Fountain, and many shady areas out of the hot sun, the park felt a world away from the pressures of the legal system. Lowcountry living was all about slowing down and relaxing, and the Waterfront Park was the perfect location to do just that.

After finishing his sandwich, he chatted with a group of lost tourists, pointing them in the right direction. They laughed about the heat and were jovial despite their sweaty shirts. Hennessy wandered past the colorful homes of Rainbow Row and turned onto Church Street, two blocks from his office. As he did, a patrol car raced past, lights blaring and squealing around the corner.

As Hennessy approached his office, he spotted the patrol car parked on the sidewalk next to the front door of his office building. He sighed. Cautiously, he stepped inside the front door of the building and could hear raised voices upstairs.

He walked up the stairs to find Jacinta at the front door to their office, standing in the way of two police officers, her arms across the entrance.

"Can I help you?" Hennessy asked as he approached.

"Joe," Jacinta said, standing in the doorway. "They're demanding to come in without a warrant."

"Do you work here, sir?" the first officer was a middle-aged man with a stern look.

"Yes." Hennessy was blunt.

"We're going to have to ask you to step out here, please," the lead cop said as he stepped closer to Jacinta.

"What's going on?" Hennessy stepped between them.

"We were chasing a suspected drug dealer, and he was seen entering the building just now. We believe he's in this building somewhere, so can we have permission to search your office?"

"I assure you, officer, there's no drug dealer here," Jacinta said from behind Hennessy. "I've sat near the front door all day, and nobody unexpected has entered the offices."

"I'm afraid I must insist. We need to search the office."

"The answer is no." Hennessy's voice was firm. "And if you insist, you'll breach my fourth amendment rights."

The second officer stepped forward. He was older, shorter, and carrying a lot of extra weight. He hooked his thumbs into his belt and sniffed. "Under the hot pursuit doctrine, we have the right to search the premises for the suspected felon after we witnessed a felony occurring."

Hennessy stood up straighter. "Really? You followed a suspected felon into this building?"

"We did." The second officer sniffed again. "We noticed a drug deal in action and pursued the suspect until we saw him enter this building. We have reason to believe he's hiding in these offices. Under the law, we can enter these premises and search for the felon."

The first officer backed him up. "Unless you want to be arrested for obstructing the search, I suggest you allow us to enter these offices."

Hennessy glared at the man for a moment and then turned to Jacinta. He nodded. She raised her eyebrows. He nodded again, slower this time. She turned her stare back to the officers, held it on them for a moment, and then moved to the side of the doorway. Hennessy stepped aside.

The two police officers pushed past them.

They were aggressive and frantic in their search of the premises.

They pulled open each cupboard door and yanked the items out. They pretended to check in the tight spaces. In their haste, they knocked over a potted plant, pushed over chairs, and pushed papers off Jacinta's desk.

They returned to the door after only a few moments of frantic activity.

"Aren't you going to clean it up?" Jacinta snapped.

"Sorry, Ma'am, we're in pursuit of a felon. We can't stop now," the older officer said as he stepped out the doors. "We have a job to do."

The officers checked the door on the other side of the floor, and after they confirmed it was locked, they jogged down the stairs. Hennessy stood at the top of the stairs, listening as the officers knocked on the doors to the businesses downstairs. The officers asked the business owners if they'd seen the felon, and when the person answered 'no,' they left the building without further searching.

"They didn't even search the offices downstairs, did they?" Jacinta said as she looked at the pile of papers on the ground.

"No," Hennessy responded as he walked in and picked up some of the papers. "But that's not surprising."

"So, they were here to pressure us?"

"I imagine Kathryn Moore called Richard Longhouse last night, and now he's flexing his muscles."

"How can they do that, though?" Jacinta picked up a box of files and placed it back in the cupboard. "What about our fourth amendment rights? Don't we have the right to decline a search?"

Hennessy bent down and picked up the potted plant. "The Fourth Amendment requires law enforcement to have a search warrant to enter a private premises, but 'hot pursuit,' or 'exigent circumstances' are the exceptions to the protections.

Suppose the officer witnesses a felony that has just occurred and has chased the suspect to a private residence. In that case, they can forcefully enter the residence to prevent the suspect's escape."

"So, in theory, they can just make something up and search wherever they want?"

"There's one example I remember where the officers witnessed a drug deal in progress and then pursued the suspect." He checked the plant was upright and stable and then brushed his hands together. "They witnessed the suspect enter a laundromat and chased him inside. Once inside, they found extensive drug operations in a back room. The defense lawyers questioned the validity of the search and demanded it be thrown out, but the court ruled that the officers were in hot pursuit of the suspect and, thus, well within their rights to enter the premises."

"Sounds like they can pretend they're in pursuit of a felon and barge into any property at any time." Jacinta kneeled to pick up more of the papers from the floor. "Should we lodge a complaint?"

"We will," Hennessy picked up one of the chairs. "But it won't go anywhere."

"Because there never was a suspected drug dealer, was there?"

"Of course not," Hennessy agreed. "But at least we know one thing."

"What's that?"

"Longhouse is feeling the pressure, which means we're on the right path," Hennessy said. "And it's time to dig a little deeper."

CHAPTER 24

"Brenda Moore?"

The woman reading the magazine looked up. She was well-dressed in white tennis clothes and gold earrings. She smelled like a bouquet of red roses. Her eyes were a beautiful blue, and her teeth were perfectly straight. Her hair had volume, tied up in a ponytail, and she looked fit and strong, like she could tear the clothes off a man twenty-five years younger.

The décor of the Carolina Yacht Club was the height of South Carolinian opulence. It had history, class, and refinement at every turn, yet it was completely open to the water and the outdoors surrounding it. Founded in 1883, the club was housed in an old cotton broker's office, renovated to ooze sophistication. In the dining rooms, tables were covered in fine white linen, decorated with vases of freshly cut flowers, ready for dinner reservations. Brenda Moore sat at one of the tables overlooking the

Cooper River.

"And who might you be, Mr. Handsome?" She put on her best smile.

"My name is Joe Hennessy," he offered his hand. "May I sit?"

"Of course." She shook Hennessy's hand gently and then brushed a strand of loose hair behind her ear. "And Mr. Joe Hennessy, what do I owe this pleasure?"

"I wanted to talk about your neighbor, Senator Richard Longhouse."

Her demeanor changed instantly. She sat back and looked around. "Are you a reporter?"

"No, I'm a lawyer. I'm investigating a death on his property five months ago."

She gasped and moved back further.

"Why does that shock you? What do you know about his death?"

She tried to brush off her shock with a slight wave of her hand. "I only know what I've heard around the place. Death always shocks me. Now, if you'll excuse me, I—"

"You seem like you're avoiding the subject." Hennessy held out his hand to stop her. "What do you know about Richard Longhouse?"

"I don't know Richard anymore. I haven't talked to him in months."

"You knew him well enough to go to prom with him."

She glared at Hennessy. "How did you know that?"

"I'm preparing a civil suit for the wrongful death of the gardener, and that court case will bring out a lot of information about Richard Longhouse. That means a lot of his past will be exposed in court, and that will be an open forum." Hennessy watched her reaction closely. "Including any relationship that Longhouse had with your daughter, Kathryn."

Her face went stiff. She swallowed hard. "There's no relationship between them."

"That must've hurt. Your daughter was dating the man that took you to prom."

"I hate that man." Her face twitched as she fought back the emotions that were threatening to come out.

Unable to contain her feelings, she stood and began to walk away.

She'd only taken five steps before she stopped. She faced away from Hennessy for a moment and then swiveled and came back to the table. She sat back down, a calmer presence on her face.

"You said you're a lawyer?" She smiled gently. "The same one that spoke with Kathryn yesterday?"

"I am."

"Then you can tell me something." She looked over her shoulder to check no one was listening. When she was sure they weren't, she leaned forward on the table and kept her voice low. "If someone signed a Non-Disclosure Agreement, when can that be broken?"

"There are a variety of circumstances where an NDA is not enforceable. It depends on what the NDA covers."

"It doesn't matter what it's for. When can an NDA be broken?"

Hennessy squinted. "Have you signed an NDA with Richard Longhouse?"

She waved her hand at him and then stood. "Forget I asked."

"What did you sign it for?" Hennessy stood as well.

This time, Brenda didn't turn back. She strode out the door without stopping.

Hennessy stood at the table for a moment, thoughts running through his head.

The conversation with Brenda Moore had left him with more questions than answers.

CHAPTER 25

As Hennessy parked his truck on the street and stepped out, he noticed the outline of a man on the front porch of his ground-floor apartment.

He groaned and then stepped out of the truck. Briefcase in one hand, keys in the other, Hennessy jogged through the light rain to his front porch.

Hennessy's rental was a small, two-bedroom apartment on a quiet, tree-lined street in the Harleston Village neighborhood. While the apartment only had a small kitchen and living space, it was blessed with a gorgeous view of the nearby park.

The man stepped forward as Hennessy jogged up the steps to his porch. "Mr. Hennessy, what a pleasure. Might I have a moment of your time?"

Hennessy recognized the man instantly. Al Berry was a well-known media advisor in political circles, having helped many politicians into their positions. His face was round, his skin was soft, and he was well-dressed and well-groomed. Al Berry was a man who made things happen by conducting conversations in dark corners. Hennessy wanted no part of it.

"How can I help you, Mr. Berry?"

The man stepped closer, keeping his tone low. "I'm not here on behalf of Richard Longhouse," he began. "I'm here on behalf of several other people who have, what you might call, an invested interest in the outcome of next year's gubernatorial elections."

Hennessy didn't respond as he put his key in the front door. Berry stepped forward when the key opened the lock, but Hennessy turned and stared at him.

"May I come in?" Berry asked.

"No." Hennessy's response was blunt. He kept his eyes on the man, towering over him.

"Well, that's not the Southern hospitality I'm used to," Berry's tone was as fake as his smile.

Hennessy didn't budge. "Say what you've got to say and get off my property."

"Now, now. We're all friends here."

Hennessy didn't respond.

"Ok. It's like that." Berry straightened himself out

and coughed. "The potential governor aside, many others have a keen and vested interest in Longhouse's campaign. With the current governor stepping aside next year, many people are backing Mr. Longhouse. And that means many people have spent a lot of money to see him get into office."

"Like who?"

"Some of the backers are private." Berry looked around the street. There was no one else walking in the rain. "But I should warn you that a lot of influential people connected to the Charleston Police Department have their wagons hitched to the senator's campaign."

"It seems like it's us versus the whole system."

"Yes, it is, which is why I've been asked to come here and ask you to reconsider lodging your claim of wrongful death for the unfortunate accident of George Santos. Wrongful death claims tend to rile up constituents, and we feel that it might be best to let things lie."

"Lie is such an appropriate word for you to use."

Berry groaned as a gust of wind brought through a sheet of rain. "Come on, Joe. Don't be like that. We've known each other for a very long time. There's no need for hostility."

"The civil suit is getting lodged on Monday, whether you like it or not," Hennessy said. "But tell me, what did Brenda Moore sign an NDA for?"

Al Berry stood back a little, shocked by the name. "I don't know what you're talking about."

"You do."

"I'm not here to talk about rumors." Al Berry composed himself and flattened the tie down the middle of his shirt. "Listen, many people are worried that their monetary donations will be worthless if this goes to court, which is why I've come to make an offer."

"An offer?"

"Yes, an offer for you, but I'd much rather discuss it inside."

"The answer is still no."

"That's not how we do things in the South." Berry indicated toward the door.

Hennessy shook his head.

"Fine," Berry grunted. "My question to you is simple—how much would it take for you to remove yourself from this wrongful death claim by Mrs. Santos? We know that Mrs. Santos moved this case around to different lawyers, but no one wanted to touch it. So, simple question, how much for you to remove yourself from the case?"

"That is a simple question," Hennessy said. "And the answer is just as simple—I won't do it."

Silence hung between the men, with Berry unsure of how to proceed. He wasn't used to rejection. "I'm not asking you to stop the civil suit, Joe. All I'm asking is that you step away from it. Leave it to another lawyer. That's all. How much for you to remove yourself?"

"This isn't about money—"

"Everything is about money," Berry barked. "Every man has his price. Think of your family, Joe, your wife, and your daughters. Think of how much their lives will change with some extra money. We can discuss keeping the banks out of the vineyard. Luca's vineyard. It's beautiful that you named it after your son, but it sure would be a shame if you lost it."

Hennessy's jaw clenched tight. "Get off my property."

Berry held his stare for a moment and then backed off. "Think about it. We can make an excellent offer. In the tens of thousands. It might even save your vineyard."

Hennessy didn't respond as the man returned to a black sedan parked nearby, brushed the rain from his jacket shoulder, and entered the back seat. Hennessy watched the car drive to the end of the street and turn without stopping.

It was clear the whole system was against him, but in his mind, one thing was now clear—nothing was going to stop his pursuit of justice.

CHAPTER 26

Richard Longhouse slammed his fist down on the table.

The glass of water next to him jumped, the sound echoing around the boardroom as the other men shifted uncomfortably in their seats.

"I don't care how you do it," Longhouse said, the words forced through clenched teeth. "This is a personal vendetta against me and my family name. Hennessy is out to get me for personal reasons and cannot be allowed to continue." He pointed to Al Berry. "You get that out to the press before he lodges the suit on Monday. Two wrongful death suits within a month? That's got to be our angle. This is a vindictive goose chase."

Al Berry shifted uncomfortably and looked at those seated next to him, his eyes flicking nervously from one to the next as if looking for help.

"That would be a great course of action, sir, but

unfortunately, we've already introduced a motion to redact identifying information on the first case," Brockman stated. "We can't say anything to the media in relation to the matter unless we remove the request for a redaction, which I don't suggest is a great course of action."

Minton, the other lawyer in the boardroom, nodded his confirmation. "And redaction aside, you'll win this case, regardless. Given the evidence in the matter and our influence over those involved, Hennessy doesn't have a chance of making this fall in his favor."

"And what do we know about the Santos family?" Berry asked.

"I'm sure we could find a few skeletons in the family closet and make it look like the Santos family is only after money," Minton replied. "No one is squeaky clean."

"Then we'll play it as a money-hungry widower trying to get more than her fair share of the pie," Berry said. "She's already received the life insurance payout, and now she's just getting greedy. He was an independent contractor responsible for his own safety, and he fell off a ladder and onto a sharp chainsaw. You shouldn't be held responsible for that. The public will see it the same way. They'll be on your side."

Longhouse didn't react, looking at the others seated around the table and, as if hooked up to a sequential trigger, each man nodded their confirmation in turn.

"And are you sure the Homeowner's Insurance doesn't cover negligence?"

"We reviewed the policy again, and unfortunately, the policy that you took out doesn't cover negligence for wrongful death. While the policy covers slip and falls, and accidental death, it doesn't cover negligence for wrongful death, which is what the suit will be based on."

"It was my stupid wife." Longhouse thumped his fist on the table again. "She handles the insurance and everything with the home. I sign the papers and pay her credit card bill, but I shouldn't have let her handle anything. Stupid, stupid woman."

Longhouse leaned forward in his seat and, for a brief moment, looked at the tabletop between his arms as if trying to find patterns in the timber. The others sat in silence as they watched him, unsure of what he would do next. In public, Longhouse was a charmer, complete with a quick wit and easy smile. Behind closed doors, he was ruthless. His anger had caused many assistants to quit, and he'd pushed many employees to the edge. No employee wanted to be caught in a room alone with him.

"How long can we delay the suit?" Longhouse asked.

"Years." Minton's response was quick. "We can delay it for more than five years with some decent motions. That won't be a problem."

"Except it is," Berry stated. "Something like this hanging over an election campaign? Your opposition will think this is pure gold. They'll say that a negligent lawsuit shows that you can't even manage your own yard, let alone the state budget."

"You're right." Longhouse looked around at each man. "One of the most important things during this run for governor is reputation, and with a case like this, mine could easily come off second best. A reputation in tatters means a lot more than winning or losing a civil case. A lot of people are depending on me right now, and I'm not about to let them down because some lawyer is out for vengeance."

More silence followed as the lawyers looked at their boss, each afraid to make eye contact. Longhouse leaned back in his chair, swiveled it away from them, and looked out toward the window, his mind trying to make sense of the situation.

"We have to put it through for an expedited trial under Rule 40, which I imagine the Santos family will agree with," Brockman said. "If we can't delay the trial, we need to get it out of the way before the election campaign begins. That's our best option."

"I agree."

"We do have one slight other problem," Berry squinted as he spoke. "Hennessy asked what Brenda Moore signed the NDA for."

Longhouse swiveled his chair back to face them. "How did he know she signed one?"

Berry shrugged and held his hands out.

"Argh." Longhouse let out a deep groan. "We need to stop this mess. It's becoming too hot."

"We could try to pressure the widow," Minton said. "Have her sign an NDA before it gets to the courts."

"We tried that," Brockman said. "She rejected the $50,000 offer when she first presented the case and then rejected the $100,000 offer two months ago. She kept shopping for a lawyer until one was brave enough to take it to court."

"Everyone has a price," Longhouse said. "What can we afford to offer her?"

Brockman drew a long breath. "Given the impact that a case like this might have on the run as governor, and given the timing of it, I suggest we throw everything at her."

"I agree," Longhouse stood. "And I'll present the offer to her myself."

CHAPTER 27

Losing wasn't an option for Richard Longhouse.

His father, Gerald Longhouse, had been a Senator, and Gerald often told Richard how disappointed he was in him. Gerald was distant, mostly drunk, and obsessed with his own greatness. Gerald hit him weekly when he was little, trying to teach Richard discipline through the back of a fist. The run for governor was Richard's chance to trump his father's legacy. It was his chance to show his father how much better he was. It had been ten years since Gerald passed, but the desire to be better still burned deep inside.

Longhouse drove to the home of Maria Santos in his black Mercedes sedan, followed by a black SUV carrying the lawyers and his media advisor. In the passenger seat of his sedan sat Dirk Taylor, his private investigator, and man with a myriad of criminal connections. The silence hung heavy between them.

Each man was aware of what was on the table. If this failed, Longhouse's run for governor would become much more complicated.

The two vehicles sped the fifteen miles to Maria's property. Longhouse pulled into the driveway first, and the black SUV parked on the grass. The white one-story weatherboard home was small but cute and was surrounded by a garden that was still perfectly maintained. Longhouse didn't take time to smell the roses, he never did, charging out of the sedan toward the front door.

Nobody said a word as he knocked, with the two lawyers standing behind him, carrying briefcases. Taylor brought up the rear, standing half on the porch and half on the top step.

When Maria opened the door, Longhouse took great pleasure seeing the fear in the woman's eyes. The sight of five men in suits standing on the porch was intimidating.

"Hello, Maria," Longhouse said as he held out his hand. "It's been a long time."

She didn't accept the handshake, but that didn't surprise Longhouse.

"What do you want?" Maria's voice shivered.

"May we come in?"

"Why?"

"We have business to discuss, and it would be better if we sat down for it. Please, Maria."

Maria glared at Longhouse and then stepped back from the door. Despite her fear, she remained committed to Southern hospitality.

"Thank you," Longhouse said, and as he held Maria's gaze, he waved the rest of his party inside ahead of him. Once they were through the door, he followed them into the small but comfortable living room.

Two couches sat facing each other, with a single recliner opposite a television. The two lawyers sat on one couch while Maria sat on the other. Longhouse sat on the edge of the armchair, leaning forward, while Taylor and Berry stood at the entrance of the room.

Longhouse didn't waste time getting to the point. "I understand you've suffered because of the loss of your husband, and for that, I'm truly sorry. George was a good man and a talented gardener who didn't deserve to go the way he did. His dedication to his work was second to none, and I was so grateful for the work he did on my property. He truly was a gift to this world."

Maria didn't fall for the charm offensive. "What do you want?"

Longhouse looked around the quaint room. "I can see that George didn't leave you with much, which leads me to believe you could use some extra funds."

He gestured to Brockman, who opened his briefcase and pulled out a check. Longhouse took it, set it down on the coffee table in front of Maria, and forced the warmest smile he could manage.

"What's this?" Maria asked, her eyes scanning the amount.

"It's a check for five-hundred thousand dollars."

Maria stared at the check. "In return for what?"

"This check is a gift to you to ensure you're comfortable in the way George would've wanted. This second piece of paper," Longhouse indicated to Brockman again. Brockman removed a piece of paper from his briefcase and placed it on the table, "is a nondisclosure agreement between you and me."

Maria looked up at him, her mouth hanging open as if caught off guard. Longhouse took it as a sign that he'd grabbed her attention.

"Half a million…" she began.

"Yes," Longhouse said as her voice trailed off. "Half a million dollars, and we never speak of this again. Imagine what you could do with that kind of money. Imagine how you could help your sons and their families." Again, he looked around the home. The small and chunky television looked like it'd been purchased in the nineties, and the rest of the room followed suit. Old, worn-out carpet, couches with faded fabric, curtains sagging in the middle. "This is like winning the lotto."

Once the shock subsided, any hint of emotion disappeared as Maria put on her poker face. "I need to speak with my lawyer first."

"You don't need to do that. Christian Brockman and Leonard Minton are both lawyers and are happy to answer any questions you may have. We can explain it all to you. And if you sign this today, we can all walk away from this."

"No," Maria shook her head. "I should talk to Mr. Hennessy first."

Longhouse's face snapped into a snarl.

"This isn't up for debate, Maria. You need to sign it," he tried again, forcing himself to keep his temper in check. "It's a once-only offer from me to you. Here and now. That's it. Five hundred thousand dollars for you to sign the agreement." As if needing to give her an extra nudge, Longhouse reached into his shirt pocket and pulled out a pen. He set it down on the sheet of paper, then slid both closer to her.

Maria didn't move.

"Sign it," Longhouse repeated.

"I can't sign it like this, not without talking to—"

"You don't need to speak to him," Longhouse growled. His voice rose and turned nasty as any hint of warmth faded away. Maria flinched but remained seated. Wanting to keep things peaceful, Longhouse calmed himself and repeated with a softer tone, "You don't need to speak with him. I have a team of lawyers right here who will answer any questions."

Maria's defenses were up. She shook her head. "No. I have to talk to Mr. Hennessy first."

"No, you don't!" Longhouse slammed his fist on the coffee table. "Just sign the piece of paper, Maria!"

Brockman went to interject, rising halfway up, but Milton pulled him down. Longhouse glanced briefly at the lawyer before turning his attention back to Maria.

"Sign the deal," he said, all friendliness gone, but Maria shook her head again.

"I won't. Do what you will to me, but I won't sign this or anything else you give me," Maria stood. "Now get out of my house."

Longhouse tried a softer tone again. "Maria, all I need is—"

"I said get out." Maria reached for her cell on the table next to her couch. She held her finger over the call button.

"Ok, fine," Longhouse said, eyeing the cell. "We'll double it. One million to sign. Right here, right now."

"I need to talk to Mr. Hennessy first."

Longhouse grunted and stood. He stepped toward Maria, but Maria held the phone up, showing the cell phone was about to call her son.

Longhouse raised his hands in surrender and took a step back.

"This is the biggest mistake of your life, Maria." He pointed at her. "Because if this makes it to court, I'm going to do everything I can to destroy you and your family."

CHAPTER 28

"Richard Longhouse came to my house."

Despite trying to sound calm and composed, Maria's voice wavered. Her words came through in short spurts as if the nerves throttled them down to just one per second. Hennessy heard the name 'Longhouse,' and his fists tightened.

Maria was rattled. Her eyes darted around the café, and she studied the entrance every time the door opened.

Ava's Diner sat just off King Street, a small eatery in a plain red brick building. They served Southern food, with an abundance of sweet tea, and a side of Southern hospitality. Hennessy and Maria sat in a booth near the back of the diner. As if on cue, a waitress came and introduced herself and, after filling up their water glasses, took their order of coffee and left again.

"Tell me what happened," Hennessy said.

"They just showed up at my house. Five men, all in suits. Longhouse, two lawyers, and two other men who weren't introduced. The fifth guy looked rough, despite his suit. He had a neck tattoo that was poking out under the collar. He didn't say anything but stared at me the entire time with his cold eyes." A shiver ran through Maria. "I shouldn't have let them in. I should've shut the door the second they arrived."

"It's ok." Hennessy used a soft tone, trying to calm her. "They were trying to intimidate you. Nothing more. It's a ploy used by people like Richard Longhouse. I'm very impressed that you told them to get out. That would've taken a lot of strength."

"I don't want to take the deal. Not for a million or fifty million." Her eyes shot to the door as it opened. Once she saw it was a young couple, she turned back to Hennessy. "This isn't about the money. This is about standing up for my husband. The police didn't want to touch it, but I know, I know, Richard Longhouse was involved. This is about justice."

The waitress came with their coffees. The woman set a mug down before each of them, reminded them to give her a shout if they needed anything else, then turned her attention to a couple at a booth further along. The diner began to fill behind them as the mid-afternoon crowd filtered in. There were office workers looking for a caffeine hit to make it through the day, young mothers with babies in strollers, and tourists wandering through, looking for a touch of Southern hospitality.

Hennessy leaned in closer to Maria. "Are you scared he'll come back?"

Maria looked away. "One of my boys is moving back home for a while to make sure nobody else comes around. He's a tough boy, and he'll do anything for me. I told him I didn't need the protection, but he insisted. He lives about fifteen minutes away, and his wife is amazing. She's the one that insisted he stay with me for a while. She set up speed dial on my cell, so if I see a suspicious car in the street, I have to call her right away."

"And do you have a weapon?"

"I have a small pocket pistol in the drawer beside my bed, but I don't use it."

"Understandable." Hennessy gave his nod of approval. "You don't have to take this deal, Maria, but as your lawyer, I need you to consider it. He offered—"

"No. I don't even want to think about it. The answer is no," the stoic woman blinked back a tear. "George's death is not for sale. Somebody needs to stand up to these bullies. How many people has this happened to before me? Do they think everyone is for sale? They can just throw their money around and avoid justice? No, Mr. Hennessy. I need to stand up to them. I don't care if it's us versus the whole system. I need to get justice."

"The closer we get to the civil trial, the more pressure will come at you. It's going to get dangerous. We're going to lodge the case tomorrow morning, and that will increase the pressure even further. They're going to play dirty."

"I understand." She sat up straighter. "It might look like I don't have much, but I have everything I need. I have family, friends, and a great community. I have a nice little home that I own and everything I could ever want to buy." A tear escaped down her cheek. "All I'm missing is my George. I've got this empty hole in my heart that he used to fill. No, my George's death is not for sale. Not for a million or a trillion. My George deserves justice."

"He does," Hennessy agreed, "and we'll make sure

we get it for him."

CHAPTER 29

The pressure was building for Joe Hennessy.

He'd received a phone call from Wendy that evening, and she said someone was lurking around the vineyard. She said one of the workers had chased the guy, but they didn't catch him. Her voice crackled a little when she talked about their daughter, Casey. She was seventeen and finding her independence. Hennessy assured her she was safe, but he wasn't convinced.

On Sunday afternoon, he received a call from Jacob Aster, an Occupational Safety and Health Administration specialist. Aster had reviewed the facts of George Santos' employment and workflow. He agreed that while Santos was paid as an independent contractor, he was legally an employee. The OSHA regulations protected Santos, and the employer was liable for the negligent behavior.

Aster's report was the last piece of the puzzle.

He would be their star witness if the case made it to court. His testimony was essential to winning the civil trial for wrongful death.

Aster confirmed he would finalize the report and agreed to testify.

Buoyed by information from Aster, Hennessy ordered Thai takeout for dinner, Red Duck Curry. The spicy dish was one of his all-time favorites. He washed it down with a beer while watching a ball game on television. It was a simple escape from the stress of challenging Longhouse.

He considered pressuring Detective Farina, compelling him to expose the truth about Longhouse, but he knew men like Farina didn't respond well to aggression. The more Hennessy investigated Longhouse, the more Farina would feel it.

With enough pressure, Farina might come forward with a deal.

As Hennessy watched the bottom of the fifth inning, he tried to rub the tension out of his shoulders. The tightness in his shoulders had been there for twenty-two years, a constant in his life. Over time, he'd lost some of his range of movement and often woke up with a thumping headache. He tried everything to ease the tension—massage therapists, acupuncturists, physiotherapists. None of it worked. Deep down, he knew the answer. He knew the only way he could find respite. Justice would be the only thing to give him relief.

Again, he didn't sleep. The humid night did little to ease his stress.

He woke Monday morning and popped two Advil before two cups of coffee. After an apple and a banana, he dressed in his best suit. He stared at himself in the mirror as he tightened his tie and gave himself a nod. The time had come. The next step had arrived.

It was time to go after Richard Longhouse.

Hennessy drove to the courthouse in silence and remained quiet until he turned onto Broad Street.

He groaned when he saw five police cars in front of the courthouse.

The patrol cars took up an entire side of the street. Five uniformed officers stood outside their vehicles, and when they spotted Hennessy's truck approaching, they moved to one side of the sidewalk. They watched closely as Hennessy parked in a space further down.

He picked up his briefcase and stepped out into the humid weather. He wiped his brow and looked up to the clear blue sky before he crossed the road toward the entrance of the Charleston Judicial Center.

The five officers waiting for him formed a blockade across the walkway, with every eyeball on him. They stared at him with contempt. Hennessy walked toward them, but nobody moved.

"Excuse me," Hennessy said as he approached. "I'm trying to get past."

After a moment of agonizing silence, one of the officers stepped aside slightly. Hennessy recognized him from his office a few days earlier.

"Watch your step, pal," the officer said. "There are dangerous footpaths around here."

Hennessy looked at the man and went to walk forward, but another officer stepped ahead of him. The officer lifted his chin when staring up at Hennessy. "It'd be a real shame if you fell over and hurt yourself."

Hennessy ignored him and walked forward. They knocked shoulders, but Hennessy didn't stop.

He continued toward the courthouse and felt relief as he went through security without a problem. He strode across the foyer toward the administration desks.

"Mr. Hennessy."

He knew that voice. He turned. Al Berry, dressed in a pressed suit, approached.

"Mr. Hennessy, I'm asking you to consider the ramifications of what you're about to do. Think about the people of this great state and how this will affect them," Berry stated. "This is bigger than just your case, and I want you to think about the people this case will hurt."

"The people of this city deserve to see the scales rebalance after this miscarriage of justice." Hennessy stood tall. "The time is now."

"That's not how this will be perceived, and you know it." Berry's voice rose, but after taking a quick look around, he lowered it. "The offer presented to Mrs. Santos is still on the table. Think about what's best for your client, and encourage her to take the deal, because the second you lodge that suit, the offer is gone."

"Mrs. Santos is not interested in a deal."

"But Joe," Berry changed his tone to a friendly one. "There's so much more riding on this than you could understand."

"I know exactly what's riding on this. And you can tell your powerful friends that money and intimidation doesn't work for people whose only goal is justice."

Berry's jaw hung open, and before he could launch a further attempt to change his mind, Hennessy continued into the building.

The case was about to begin.

CHAPTER 30

Frank Diaz sipped his drink.

He cast a lonely figure at the far end of the 555 Bar and Steakhouse. In North Charleston, the bar contrasted the classy establishments on the Peninsula. Neon lights hung on the walls, glowing purple and red, contrasting against the lack of lighting in the rest of the room. The carpet was stained, worn, and, in some places, sticky. The tables were dirty. One television had a crack in it. A hip-hop song played through old speakers, muffled and loud. The smells of beer and bourbon covered every inch of the bar.

Diaz tipped his Jack Daniels and Coke to the left, and the ice cubes clinked against the side of the glass. His parole officer said he wasn't allowed to drink, but he didn't care anymore. He'd had enough of adhering to their rules. Diaz had enjoyed crime like some people enjoyed amateur sports. He'd been charged with assaults, robberies, and carjackings. Arson, sexual assault, and theft. The last time he was arrested, he joked with the officers that he was going for the complete list. They didn't find it funny.

Daylight flooded into the bar as the entrance door swung open. Diaz looked up and squinted.

Dirk Taylor entered the bar first, followed by a second man. Taylor sat down next to Diaz without a word and looked around. Once he was sure nobody was watching, he nodded to the back corner. Diaz picked up his drink and followed Taylor to a booth at the far end of the room, near the emergency exit. Taylor nodded to the other man, who had waited at the bar. The man at the bar wore a black facemask, a black cap, a grey sweatshirt, and black pants.

The man with a facemask walked over and sat down, his back to the rest of the bar.

"I can't meet with you anymore," Richard Longhouse grunted as he lowered his facemask. "I have an election coming up, and I can't be seen with convicted felons. One photo with you and it could derail the entire campaign, which is worth millions of dollars. I can't risk years of hard work going down the drain."

"Now, come on," Diaz smiled. He was missing

two of his lower front teeth. "Nobody here has even heard of you."

"Next time, we do it through an intermediatory." Longhouse nodded to Taylor. "He'll talk to you."

"No," Diaz scowled. His face squeezed together as he clenched his jaw. He pointed his fist at Longhouse. "We do it however I say we do it."

The meeting was a power trip for Diaz, a way to exercise a sliver of authority over Longhouse. Longhouse didn't react to the statement, staring at Diaz with cold eyes.

"We have a job for you," Taylor interrupted and took the lead in the conversation. "We need you to put pressure on someone."

"We've done a lot of bad things, you and I." Diaz kept his eyes on the Senator as he took another sip from his Jack Daniels and Coke. "We've done things that nobody should ever know about."

Longhouse leaned in closer. "If you think you're going to rat me out, then you won't survive the walk to the car."

"I'm not going to do that." Diaz spat as he talked. "I'm no snitch."

"Report on the vineyard?" Taylor calmed the

discussion.

Diaz snarled at Longhouse and then turned to Taylor. "There are no cameras on the far side of the vineyard, and I can get in and out quickly." Diaz leaned back in his seat, raising his voice. "Is this the same vineyard owner I roughed up a few months ago?"

"Keep your voice down," Longhouse told him off. "It's the same vineyard owner, but we need to be careful. He's looking into us."

"Us? Why's he looking at me?"

"Because he's looking at me, and that means he's going to find you. He's not going to stop until he uncovers everything." Longhouse kept his voice low. "And that means he's going to find out everything you've done in the past, including the housekeeper."

Diaz didn't appear fazed. "You want me to kill him?"

"No," Longhouse shook his head. "It's too much heat. We'd never get away with it like we did the others. We could cover the others up easily, because nobody would investigate it, but a lawyer... no. They'd have to put all their resources into investigating that. We couldn't buy our innocence then."

Diaz nodded. "What do you want me to do, then?"

Longhouse leaned forward. "It's time we sent Joe Hennessy a message that things are about to get a lot worse for him."

CHAPTER 31

A long summer dusk had settled over the vineyard.

The sun had set behind the mountains, and the horizon had been drained of almost all its color. As Joe made the long walk back to the household, the sky was clear, the air was cool, and the stars were beginning to twinkle.

Under the fading light, the trellises of Merlot looked like a painting, flowing down the hill in even rows toward the valley. He stopped for a moment and gazed at the view. The grand show was eternal. Always changing, always impressive. No matter how often he'd seen it, the vast landscape could still take his breath away. He was so proud of what they'd built in Luca's memory.

Set on fifty-five acres, Luca's Vineyard featured a chateau and small café to the east of the property, along with a small store for wine sales and a wedding space. The Hennessy household sat on top of the crest of a hill to the west, overlooking the neighboring lands. The vineyard employed ten workers, all who felt like family.

Joe had left Charleston early on Friday morning to spend the day working among the vines, tending to their next harvest, filling his lungs with fresh country air. The harvest was looking promising. Healthy. Perhaps one of their best ever.

He walked back into the homestead at just after eight, greeted by the beautiful smells of a lamb roast. He gave Wendy a kiss, and she suggested they open one of their older Merlots. Joe agreed and went to the cellar.

Casey joined them for dinner, and they ate, joked, and laughed most of the night away. After dinner, they played cards, chatting while challenging each other. Casey talked about her upcoming final year of school, her friends, and her volleyball team. She still didn't know where she wanted to go to college, and Joe didn't pressure her. She had good grades, which gave her options. She talked about the boys and how one had already asked her to prom. Wendy told her she still had time to decide, and Casey agreed. Joe was quiet when the conversations of boys came around, but he knew he had to let go of his youngest one day. He just wasn't ready for it yet.

He slept well that night. Wendy always said the country air put him into a deep slumber, but he knew it was the sense of calm his family provided. He awoke Saturday morning refreshed and with his batteries recharged.

Birdsongs greeted him as he stepped out into the sunshine, and he marveled at the beautiful smells he breathed in.

After breakfast, he headed to the heart of the vineyard, the long rows of vines greeting him near the edge of the home. Pausing just inside the first row to take in the sight of the crop, Hennessy smiled at the thought of a new batch turning into wine. Together with the weddings, he hoped the dual income streams would eventually be enough to keep the banks happy and their accounts topped up enough for a comfortable existence. They needed two good seasons on the vineyard to get back in front of the bank loans.

As he slowly strolled past the vines, he became lost in his thoughts, smiling at the beauty of the landscape.

"Hey," a voice called behind him, and he turned.

Casey was walking toward him.

"Hey, yourself," he said, pausing for her to catch up. When she did, he embraced her and kissed the top of her head. "Tell me, what have you learned lately?"

"Oh, I know how to roll a joint."

Hennessy stopped in shock. "Pardon?"

"Yeah," Casey smiled. "Usually, it's my ankle playing volleyball."

Joe laughed enthusiastically at the superb delivery of her joke before he told one of his own. "You know, I heard the world champion tongue twister got arrested in New York last week." Joe smiled. "Yeah, I heard they'll give him a tough sentence."

"Oh, Dad, that's a terrible joke," Casey laughed. "But I like it. Got any more?"

"I have the memory of an elephant."

"Is that right?"

"Absolutely. I remember one time I went to the zoo and saw an elephant."

Casey laughed again, patting him on the shoulder. "They're getting worse and worse as you grow older."

The pair slowly continued, walking amongst the vines as the occasional bee shot past in search of nectar. Joe put his arm around her shoulders, and together, they rounded the end of the vines and continued down the next aisle.

In the far distance, he spotted a red sedan parked on the side of the road. Hennessy tried to get a better look at it.

"Think someone broke down?" Casey asked.

"I don't know," he said.

Joe walked forward and saw something moving amongst the vines further down, a few hundred yards away in the valley. Something rustled in the bushes.

"Hey," Joe called out.

A man in a blue baseball cap walked out. He didn't look back. A few yards out of the bushes and the man began to run. He ran past the vines, jumped the waist-high fence, and ran further down the gravel road.

"Hey!" Joe called out again, jogging forward.

The man didn't stop. He ran to the red sedan. He jumped in and sped off, leaving a cloud of dust. Joe stood on the crest of the hill for a while, staring out at the distance, watching as the cloud of dust disappeared into the air. He was wary. These were dangerous times.

He didn't know who was sneaking around the

vineyard, but he knew it wasn't a good sign.

CHAPTER 32

Joe Hennessy awoke to his cell ringing, buzzing beside his bed at 5am.

Hennessy looked at the number—it was his neighbor, Jack Allen. Jack's property bordered them to the west. He'd lived there his whole life and was as much a part of the landscape as the surrounding vines. Hennessy answered the call.

"You got a fire!" Jack yelled into the phone. "It's near the west edge. I'm heading there now. You got irrigation down there?"

"Irrigation? Running along the fence." Joe leaped out of bed and raced to the window. A plume of smoke rose from the bottom of the valley.

"I've called the fire department," Jack continued. "They're on their way."

"I'm coming," Joe responded.

Wendy stirred and looked up at her husband.

"There's a fire," Joe said as he grabbed his shirt

and ran to the kitchen. Wendy followed a few steps behind. He grabbed the keys to the truck before he turned to Wendy. "Get Casey up. I don't know how bad it is. If it's bad, you've got to get out. Follow the fire plan."

"Oh my," Wendy covered her hand over her mouth and ran upstairs to Casey's room.

Joe ran to his truck, desperate to get to the fire before it spread.

He roared the truck out of the driveway, spinning the tires over the gravel as he tore toward the smoke. The plume grew bigger. In the distance, he saw the flashing lights of a fire engine.

Joe roared the truck to the bottom of the valley. He found Jack Allen spraying the hose over the edge of the flames, trying to stop the fire from spreading.

"You go to that side!" Jack yelled. "It's spreading east!"

Joe covered his mouth with the top of his shirt. He ran to the edge of the flames, reaching down to grab one of the irrigation hoses. He found the tap nearby, twisted it, and attacked the ten-foot flames with the water.

The heat from the tall flames was intense, but the

smoke was worse.

The smoke had become so thick that he could barely see the fire department arrive.

Joe fought hard. The smoke filled his eyes and his throat and covered his clothes. He fought the heat, spraying the hose on the edges of the fire. The flames attacked, swaying in the wind, trying to spread devastation. The heat pushed him back, but Joe wasn't going to stop.

Within minutes of the fire engines' arrival, the flood of water had tamed the flames.

The smoke remained. It was heavy, and the smell of gasoline was strong in the air.

When the flames were reduced to a smolder, Joe looked over the crop. Three rows of vines in the bottom of the valley were burned, and two more were damaged. Devastated, he walked around the edge and found Jack Allen. He thanked him.

"Don't mention it," Jack said. "I got up and saw the smoke. Don't know what could've caused it."

Joe looked across at a firefighter as he approached through a plume of smoke. "This your property?" the firefighter called out.

"Yeah," Joe tried to wave some of the smoke from

his face. "Thanks for coming so fast."

"No problem. It's our job," the man responded. "Looks like we got it under control before it did too much damage." He eyed Joe for a moment. "But I don't like that smell."

"Nor do I."

"I'd hate to guess what the fire investigation finds, but that smells like gasoline to me," the firefighter continued. "You smell it a lot with arson attacks. I'm going to call the cops and get them to come out as well."

"Thanks," Joe managed, the shock starting to set in.

"But if I were you," the firefighter continued. "I'd start thinking if anybody has a grudge against you. That might help the investigation."

Joe didn't have to think for long. He didn't care how much money, power, or influence Longhouse had.

Nothing was going to stop his pursuit of justice.

CHAPTER 33

For the next five days, Hennessy remained at the vineyard.

He attempted to lodge a claim with their insurance, but from what he could work out, it looked like the money would fall short of the costs. Deciding that there would be plenty of time for checking the numbers, he turned his attention to the damage and, together with Wendy, began to clear the spoiled crop.

The smoke damage over the vineyard would have the worst effect. They wouldn't know how bad the smoke damage was for months. When grapes were exposed to smoke, it could result in a burnt taste, which wine judges usually describe as 'smoke tainted.' If that were the case, the entire crop would be ruined.

He returned to Charleston on Thursday afternoon. Jacinta had run the office during his absence, and she looked concerned when he stepped through the door. She wanted to know everything and sat with him in his office as Hennessy repeated the events from that Sunday. He told her about the man he'd seen the previous afternoon, as well as the potential that gasoline was used as an accelerant.

"Speaking of cars." Jacinta got up and as she walked to the window. She gestured for him to follow. Hennessy did, and Jacinta stared out to the street below. She scanned first one side, then the other, and she stopped when she reached the far side. "There," she pointed to the street.

Hennessy looked, and while half a dozen vehicles were dotted along the side of the street, he could immediately see the one she meant.

"The Malibu?"

Jacinta nodded.

"What about it?"

"It's been parked there since early Monday morning. It's here when I get here and leaves after I leave. When I left on Wednesday, I returned to the office after fifteen minutes, and it was gone."

"Did you see who was in it?"

"Two men. I even walked past it on the other side of the road yesterday afternoon, and I could feel them watching me."

Before she could say anymore, Hennessy turned and headed for his desk.

"Joe, where are you going?"

He didn't stop. "I'm going to show them I don't react well to intimidation."

Hennessy took his Glock 19 out of the bottom drawer, and slid it into his pocket. He raced down the stairs as the beating in his chest reached fever pitch. His rage fed off the kick of adrenalin, using it to drive him forward as he walked out the doors. He walked up the sidewalk, never taking his eyes off the target.

He managed to get to within half a block before the lights of the car turned on. To make his presence further known, Hennessy stepped off the sidewalk and continued toward the car as it rolled forward.

He felt his arms tense as he considered taking the gun out.

If the car hinted at trying to run him down, he would pull it out and unload on the stalkers. For a man pushed to the brink, he felt all sense of repercussions fade away.

The car never appeared to aim for him. The dark tint on the side windows hid the identity of the occupants, but that didn't stop Hennessy from shouting at them as they passed. He turned as the car passed him. His eyes were fixed on the driver. Once the vehicle passed, Hennessy stepped into the middle of the road and held his arms wide. He watched as the Malibu disappeared around the next corner.

Once he was sure the car was gone, Hennessy went back inside.

He sat in his office alone for the rest of the day. The pressure he continued feeling didn't appear to give him an inch of forgiveness, continuing to rise with each new event. It should've given him more resolve, more strength, but something felt missing.

Broken wasn't a word he ever used, nor could he contemplate feeling, but the longer he sat in his office staring out the window, the more Hennessy believed it was where he was headed.

For the first time, he wasn't sure how long he could keep fighting.

CHAPTER 34

Hennessy had to swing wild, and he had to swing hard.

He'd been pressured, pushed, and taunted, and it was time to attack with his big gun. He called the local news channels and advised he had photos of Longhouse's affair, expecting them to fight for exclusive rights, but all the news networks steered clear of the pictures. They didn't even want to see them. The editors said the images weren't in the public interest, which Hennessy found absurd.

After a morning of rejections, Hennessy and Jacinta discussed their options. He talked about how Longhouse had contacts everywhere, and any media outlet that published those photos would feel his wrath. Hennessy talked about posting the video online himself, pressuring the media to report on it, but Jacinta had a better idea. She made several calls and had soon set up a meeting across the state border with the Charlotte Observer.

The following Monday morning, Hennessy and Jacinta made the three-hour trip north to Charlotte to meet with Felicity Farrow.

Farrow's offices were slick. In the middle of Downtown Charlotte, she had a corner office on the fifteenth floor, complete with a view of the beautiful city. Spacious and modern, the office felt like an escape from the frantic hustle of the newsroom occurring just outside her door. Her views stretched over Charlotte, and the bookshelf to the left of the room was mostly filled with indoor plants.

A political reporter, Felicity Farrow, had a known distrust for Richard Longhouse, dating back to an event ten years earlier where she accused him of groping her buttocks and breasts at a party. No charges were ever laid, and Longhouse counter-sued for defamation, which was settled out-of-court.

Farrow presented herself well. She was a well-educated woman in her late fifties who had spent her life chasing political stories. She had a reputation for chasing stories that others wouldn't touch. Her reports were delivered with fire and passion, encouraging more than a million viewers to subscribe to her social media channels.

"And you want to release these photos to the public before they've been presented in evidence in court?" Farrow asked. "From what I know about the law, it could damage any hope of winning future court cases, especially related to the jury's deliberations. Are you sure you want me to talk about the photos? Is this really what you want to do?"

"It's a warning shot to Richard Longhouse," Hennessy said.

"And what if it's a doctored photo?" Farrow raised her eyebrows. "Taking a false shot at the man who groped me would end my career."

"You can check the photos, but they're legitimate," Hennessy said. "This is it—your chance to ruin the man who assaulted you."

"And why didn't you take it to the South Carolina media outlets?"

Hennessy raised his eyebrows.

"Right," Farrow replied. "Because he has his fingers in a lot of pies."

"He has a funding amount of two-point-five million, and the media knows it," Jacinta added. "If they publish something bad about him now, they can kiss those advertising dollars goodbye. It's not corrupted—it's just good business sense. But in North Carolina, you're outside his scope for the advertising budget. You can make the report without losing a cent."

Farrow nodded her agreement. "I'll confirm the source, and then I'll have the photos scanned by the technical team. If they find that these photos are legitimate, then I'll publish them. This is quite the scandalous story you've got here. He takes the mother to prom and then has an affair with the daughter decades later. This will attract a lot of focus."

Hennessy agreed, but the nerves were building. Now, the real danger was about to start.

CHAPTER 35

Hennessy had missed twenty-five calls from the office of Richard Longhouse.

He wasn't going to return the calls. If they wanted to play hard, he'd play harder. If they wanted to flex their muscles, he'd flex his muscles. If they wanted to make it personal, he'd do the same. The battle was on, and Hennessy would fight until the end.

The Charlotte Observer ran the story of the Longhouse affair for a week, finding different angles to splash the photos in the papers. The images circled on social media until the South Carolina news outlets had no choice but to report on the pictures. Kathryn had gone into hiding, taking time off her work and avoiding the media. Longhouse's wife was nowhere to be seen.

When chased by the media, Longhouse refused to answer questions about the affair, and there were articles published about deep fakes in the South

Carolina papers next to any article about the scandal. The ploy to create doubt in the photos was some of Al Berry's finest work.

The North Carolina cousins weren't so nice. They went after him with everything they had. Hennessy read every one of the news articles and smiled when he saw an article in the New York Times talking about the scandalous Southern political drama.

Hennessy was at his desk on Saturday morning when Wendy rang.

"Hello, beautiful." When she didn't respond, he continued. "What is it? Tell me what's wrong?"

"The Starks canceled their wedding."

"The Starks? Why?"

Paul and Loretta Stark had booked the vineyard with the most expensive package on offer. The cost of the two-day affair was the equivalent of five regular weddings and would've helped with any shortfall in the finances.

"Paul has been in a motor vehicle accident. It's bad, and they're unsure if he'll make it."

"Oh no," Joe replied. "That's terrible news. Send them my love. I hope he pulls through."

"It's terrible," Wendy agreed. "He's such a nice

man, and they're such a lovely couple. The wedding's postponed, maybe even off."

"Of course. It's terrible for them. Tell them I hope he pulls through, and if they need to cancel, that's ok. I know how much this wedding meant to our bottom line, but it's terrible news."

"Because it's only two weeks out, it's outside their deposit time limit."

"No," Joe said. "Give it back to them. They'll need it more than us."

"Good," Wendy breathed a sigh of relief. "I agree, but I wanted to run it past you first. By the sounds of it, they're going to need every cent over the coming months."

Hennessy felt like he'd received a blow to the gut.

"But if things don't turn around soon, Joe," Wendy's tone lowered. "We may have to consider selling the vineyard."

He stopped, frozen as he considered the prospect. "The insurance," were the only words to come out of his mouth, but he already knew what Wendy would say. "It won't cover the fire damage, not even by half."

In all their years of marriage, Wendy had always

been the realist, and she now knew the truth neither of them wanted to face.

"I can't see us walking away from it," Hennessy whispered, the words feeling like acid on his tongue. "We can't walk away, Wendy. Do you know what that would do to us? It'll be like losing Luca all over again."

Wendy knew how much it hurt her husband and changed the topic. She talked about how they could help the Starks. She would send flowers and offer to help in any way possible. They chatted for a while longer, then said their goodbyes. The distance between them seemed enormous.

Overwhelmed by the prospect of losing the vineyard, Joe got in his truck and drove.

He loved his truck. The beaten-up old girl had been a reliable teammate on the vineyard for the past twenty years. It didn't mind the potholes around the land, it always started first go, and the old girl thrived on the open road. It had its problems, but it was always something Hennessy was happy to fix. He could spend hours under the truck's hood, letting the day disappear in the routine activities.

On his drive to nowhere, Hennessy pulled over at

Uncle Chuck's boiled peanuts roadside stop on US 17.

The streetcar delivered some of the best boiled peanuts in the South. Stirring four pots, Uncle Chuck was always happy to talk about his Virginia peanuts. Hennessy chatted to the owners of the stop, Chuck and Debbie, for a while. They chatted about the weather, about the traffic, and about the tourist numbers. It was a pleasant distraction from his thoughts. As he stood in the shade of the tree off the edge of the road, spitting peanut shells to the ground, Hennessy's cell rang. He looked at the number. It was Barry Lockett.

"Barry."

"Mate, I hope you're ok. I hear you're doing it tougher than an over-cooked steak," Lockett said, his Australian accent stronger than normal.

"That's one way of putting it," Hennessy agreed.

"Well, I have some good news. This might make your day, or week, for that matter."

"Go on."

"Remember the items we received from the insurance company? There was the chainsaw, some water bottles, his gloves, his jeans, all those things?"

"I remember," Hennessy responded as he picked something out of his teeth. "What do you have?"

"We've got a lead."

"How big?"

"Big. They found traces of ketamine on George's chainsaw."

"Ketamine?"

"It's a horse tranquilizer. It's a dissociative drug, and when used by humans, it detaches a person from reality. I was planning on heading over to the lab and—"

"No, wait for me. I'm an hour away. I'll get there as quick as I can."

CHAPTER 36

Hennessy raced the twenty-five-minute drive in under ten.

He sped into the parking lot of the Precision Applied Technical building on Calhoun Street and found his investigator standing in front of his truck. The rest of the parking lot was empty on Saturday afternoon. As Hennessy climbed out of his truck, Lockett walked toward him. They shook hands solidly before Lockett gestured toward the door. "Nicki's waiting for us inside, and I'll let her fill you in."

Hennessy followed Lockett through the glass doors, where they were greeted by Nicki Chang, waiting in the otherwise empty foyer.

"Nicki, this is Joe Hennessy," Lockett said and stepped aside.

Hennessy shook with the young lab technician, and she smiled. She was a pretty young lady of Chinese descent, with nice clothes and a friendly smile. Her black hair was pulled back tightly into a ponytail, and she had two dangling gold earrings.

She led them one floor up to her offices and through the first floor of a recently renovated building. The carpet was soft, and the artwork hanging on the walls was modern. The rest of the floor was empty, as expected on a Saturday. Nicki unlocked her separate office, a small space with a window to the street, and offered the men a seat in front of her white Formica table. Four monitors took up most of the space on the table.

"It's your lucky day," she smiled and walked over to bench on the far side of the room. She picked up a file and waved it in the air. "Not only did we find traces of ketamine on the chainsaw, but we also found it somewhere else."

"Not just on the chainsaw?" Lockett questioned.

"No," Nicki said, directing their attention to her desk, "not just the chainsaw. We also ran tests on everything that the insurance company kept. There are the ladder rungs, his boots, his jeans, and his gloves. Those tests all came back negative. But then we tested his water bottle."

Hennessy raised his eyebrows. "It also contained

ketamine?"

"I wondered how ketamine could've landed on the chainsaw, and I thought there must've been two options. Either the chainsaw was stored near some ketamine, or he expelled the substance from his mouth before he died," Nicki nodded. "Following the second theory, I tested his water bottle and found trace amounts of it mixed in with the remaining water."

"Ketamine." Hennessy shook his head, still coming to terms with the revelation. "How does it affect the system?"

"In small amounts, ketamine produces a dissociative state, characterized by a sense of detachment from the world. It's known as depersonalization and derealization. At higher amounts, users may experience what's called the 'K-hole,' which is a state of dissociation with visual and auditory hallucinations."

"Would a coroner test for ketamine?"

"Not unless there was a reason to test for it."

"He was drugged," Hennessy whispered, the revelation sinking in before he repeated himself. "He was drugged. They knocked him out, held him down, and then hit him with the sharp edge of the chainsaw. The carotid artery at the top of the neck doesn't need a deep cut."

"This is it." Lockett clapped his hands together. "This is a home run. This proves Longhouse was responsible."

"Not even close." Hennessy stood and started pacing the floor. He placed one hand on his head while thinking and then turned back to Lockett and Nicole. "We have two major problems. One—the chain of evidence is a big problem."

"Agreed," Nicki said as she handed Hennessy the report. "I can only testify about what I've found in the water bottle since it came into our possession, which is only five weeks ago. Before that, I can't verify anything. We don't know if the ketamine contamination happened after his death or a long time before it. We can't even be sure that the ketamine was present on the day of his death."

"Any good lawyer will focus on that," Hennessy groaned. "The life insurance investigators originally stored the chainsaw in their storage facility for five weeks before returning it to Maria, where she stored it in the garden shed of her home, next to all of

George's old tools. It becomes a question about what happened between the time of death and the testing. Was it stored in a shed near ketamine? Were the traces of ketamine deliberately planted before this testing round? It's not a clean line of evidence because the items could be tampered with."

"Not a home run, then?"

"Not even first base. If the Circuit Solicitor's Office opens a criminal investigation, they won't be able to prove anything. Any decent lawyer will have the evidence suppressed because of the chain of evidence. And even if it got through, they'll suggest the ketamine was placed in the drink before George arrived at the property, which would clear Longhouse's name." Hennessy paused for a few moments as the thoughts rolled through his head. "This evidence doesn't prove who put the ketamine in the water bottle. You said it was also used as a party drug?"

"That's right," Nicki confirmed. "It's known in the rave scene as the 'K-bomb.'"

"If we present this evidence in the civil trial, Longhouse's lawyers will suggest that he took the amount voluntarily. They'll say that George Santos was an addict and was voluntarily under the influence of drugs when he fell off the ladder. We can't present this at the civil trial. It'd be a disaster for us."

"You've got the report in your hand," Lockett said. "You'll have to enter it into discovery the second you leave here."

"Not quite." Hennessy placed the folder back on the table. "Nicki, can I ask you to retest the items to make sure this is factual? I have doubts about the result, and I'd like it retested to be sure."

"I can do that."

"And could it take at least another five weeks for that to happen?"

She smiled. "I have a lot of things on, so yes, it would take me more than five weeks."

"Thank you," Hennessy said and turned to Lockett. "I can't enter anything into discovery if it's not completed."

CHAPTER 37

Hennessy was the first to reach the office the next morning.

He unlocked the doors, pulled the curtains aside, and turned on the air conditioner. He set up the coffee machine and headed to the boardroom. Fifteen minutes later, Lockett and Jacinta turned up, with the latter carrying a tray filled with cups.

"You grabbed coffee," Hennessy said, a grin forming.

"And donuts," Jacinta replied, waving a bag in her other hand. "These are from Glazed on King Street. I've got plain, raspberry, maple bacon, key lime pie, and berry almond crumble."

"She's worth more," Lockett said as he sat down. "I keep telling you."

"If I won the lotto, I'd pay her more." Hennessy took one cup and grabbed a seat.

"What's the latest in the media reports?" Lockett

asked Jacinta.

"Outside of South Carolina, people love it. There are articles all across the country about the scandal. They love Southern political dramas. But inside the state is a very different story. There have been reports on the case, but they're all very small. And it's interesting how the media have framed it." She opened her cell. "Like this report—it says a South Carolina Senator is the subject of 'rumors' of an affair, and it doesn't even name Longhouse."

"That's what we thought would happen," Hennessy said.

"Will you call Longhouse as a witness?" Lockett asked. "It'd be a great chance to expose his deviant behavior."

"In a civil trial, you should always choose to do what the opposition wants the least," Hennessy said. "However, questioning an adverse witness during your case-in-chief can be a costly mistake, especially one as charming as Longhouse. Using an adverse witness as a spokesperson is not a convincing way to offer evidence at trial. If we called him as a witness, he'd charm the jury with his lies. So no, we won't call him, but if the defense wants to do it, I'd be happy to cross-examine him."

"And what's the big issue you've found?" Jacinta asked as she bit into one of the donuts.

"Traces of ketamine were found on the water bottle that was stored in George's truck. The insurance company tested it for alcohol, but we had it retested and found traces of ketamine."

"And what exactly is ketamine?"

"A horse tranquilizer," Hennessy said as he reached forward for a donut.

"It's also a party drug." Lockett grabbed the glazed donut. "Ketamine is a medicine used by doctors and vets as a painkiller and a sedative, but ravers also use it for its hallucinogenic effects. It can be bought as a white powder that dissolves into a clear liquid. Perfect to put in a water bottle."

"So, they knock him out, pin him to the ground, and cut his neck with a chainsaw?" Jacinta raised her eyebrows as she thought about the situation.

"That looks likely. And they would've got away with it except for this case."

"It makes you wonder what else they've done." A shiver ran through Jacinta. "But if Longhouse drugged Santos, he'd know about the water bottle."

"That's true." Hennessy tapped his finger on the edge of the table. "But it's been in Maria's possession since it left the insurance company."

Hennessy walked to the whiteboard at the rear of the room and rolled it forward. He wrote 'Richard Longhouse' in the middle, and proceeded to fill the whiteboard with names, adding lines connecting them all with what he knew. Soon, the board was filled with scribbles down the side representing Hennessy's thoughts, but Jacinta could barely read his scribbles.

"We could name Workers Compensation in the suit with Longhouse." Hennessy tapped the marker against his chin. "If George was an employee, the Santos estate would also be eligible for workers compensation."

"This isn't about money for Maria," Jacinta said. "We can focus on Longhouse, and if we lose it, we can move onto workers compensation at a later date."

"Agreed." Hennessy walked back over to the board and circled one name. "Jacob Aster, the OSHA specialist, is still the key to winning this case. Although we have all this other information, his testimony is still the key. He's the way we win the wrongful death suit. Everything else is for the police and a criminal case." Hennessy stepped back from the board, staring at the connections. "If I looked at the civil case subjectively, then I would say someone found a dead gardener in the morning, and the local police had little evidence of foul play. But when you add all the surrounding issues, it becomes too much to be a coincidence." He stood back and looked at the board. "Maria's instincts were right all along—this isn't a civil case."

His words hung suspended in the air for almost a full minute, Jacinta and Lockett staring up at him from their seats.

"The hard part is proving it," Jacinta said, and Hennessy returned to his seat, took a sip of coffee, and nodded to her.

"The next hearing for pretrial motions is tomorrow," he said, opened his laptop, and began to type. "Then we'll have the chance to expose him in court."

CHAPTER 38

When Hennessy entered courtroom five of the Charleston Judicial Center, two reporters were already in the courtroom seats. Hennessy smiled. Finally, the local media were paying attention to the case. He was breaking down the barriers, getting the word out, and he was sure that once the dam wall broke, the flood of coverage would be massive.

Jacinta led Maria Santos into the courtroom, and she was joined by two of her daughters-in-law. Hennessy had told her she didn't need to appear in the courtroom for the pretrial hearing, but she wanted to be there. She wanted to be there every step of the way, waiting for justice for her husband.

At 10.05am, five minutes late, Christian Brockman, Leonard Milton, and Al Berry entered the courtroom. They laughed as they entered, jovial in their attitudes. Brockman and Milton stepped through the gate and sat at the defense table while Berry sat behind them.

Richard Longhouse was nowhere to be seen.

Fifteen minutes later, the clerk at the front of the room read the case number and then asked the room to rise for Judge Justine Griffin. The judge walked in, followed by one assistant, and took her time before sitting down. In her sixties, Judge Griffin looked like someone who hadn't smiled in decades. Her jaw was clenched shut, her black hair was cropped short, and her glasses were square and thick. Although she had a small stature, she intimidated most people with her icy stare. After a minute, and only once she was settled, Judge Griffin looked out to the waiting courtroom.

"Welcome to all parties. We have several motions to get through in case number: 2023-AE-07-155. Santos vs. Longhouse, a wrongful death suit under Section 15-51-10 of the South Carolina Code of Laws." Judge Griffin's tone was flat. She moved a piece of paper, rustled it loudly, and then stared at the defense table. "We'll start with the motion to redact all identifying information for the defendant. Counselor, please explain."

"Your Honor." Brockman stood. "This is a preposterous claim aimed at destroying the reputation of a Senator of the state of South Carolina. Under the South Carolina Code of Laws, section 30-2-330, supported by Rule 41.2, we have a motion to redact any identifying information of the defendant until such time as the case is completed."

"Your Honor." Hennessy's voice was firm. "This case is in the public interest. It involves case law and Occupational Safety and Health Administration regulations, which are clearly in the public interest. It would be a disservice to the public if these records are not available in full."

"Hmm," Judge Griffin replied. "I agree, Mr. Hennessy. This is in the public interest."

"Your Honor," Brockman argued. "This is sensitive information and a sensitive situation. We ask that the court redacts the identifying information in this frivolous claim. We—"

"You can stop there, Mr. Brockman," she interrupted him. "It's highly unusual for courts in this state to grant that motion, and while there have been recent precedents, they don't apply here. I already have a decision. After considering the affidavits, memorandums, and the arguments, under the South Carolina Code of Laws, section 30-2-330, the motion to redact identifying information is denied."

"Your Honor," Brockman stood, shocked at the denial. "Can we please ask you to reconsider that decision based on—"

"No," Judge Griffin stated. She glared at him and pursed her lips. "You may not ask me to reconsider my decision on the motion. In this courtroom, my decision is final. Do you have a problem with that, Mr. Brockman?"

"No, Your Honor," Brockman stated meekly and sat down.

Judge Griffin moved another piece of paper. Again, she rustled it loudly. "Next, we have a motion to suppress. Please present your argument, Mr. Brockman."

"The defense applies to suppress evidence regarding the death of Miss Sofia Ortez. Mr. Longhouse employed Miss Ortez as a housekeeper, and she died of natural causes five years ago. The police report, along with the coroner's report, definitively state that Miss Ortez died of natural causes. We believe that referencing the unfortunate accident that happened on the same property would be very prejudicial against the defendant."

"Mr. Hennessy?"

"We object to the suppression of this evidence. We believe that the death of Miss Ortez speaks to a pattern of behavior on the defendant's property and shows that he's negligent when caring for his staff."

"Hmm." Judge Griffin reviewed the reports in front of her before looking at the lawyers. "At this point, the motion to suppress is denied. However, I will state that during the case, we're not to stray into hearsay, and we're not to stray into unfounded accusations. These reports state that Miss Ortez died of natural causes, and there will be no suggestion otherwise."

"Yes, Your Honor," Hennessy responded.

"Next, we have another motion to suppress. Mr. Brockman?"

"Your Honor, we have filed this motion to suppress these photos, as they're highly prejudicial against the defendant. These photos picture the defendant and a young woman together. They have nothing to do with this case and presenting them to the jury will only prejudice them against the defendant."

"These photos were taken by Mr. Santos only days

before his death. They're very relevant to the case, Your Honor."

"Mr. Hennessy, are you suggesting foul play in the death of Mr. Santos?"

Hennessy drew a breath, trying to find the right words to respond.

When he didn't respond immediately, Judge Griffin continued. "Because everything I've seen in these case files points toward an argument of the defendant's negligence. If you're arguing about foul play, this dramatically changes the case. And I will warn you that you need direct evidence for an argument of foul play, and if you have none of that, then a summary judgment may go against you. So, I'll ask you again, Mr. Hennessy, will you argue for foul play during this court case?"

Hennessy swallowed his pride. "No, we will not, Your Honor."

"Then I see no reason to submit these photos as evidence. Considering the affidavits and memorandums presented, the motion to suppress is granted." She moved another piece of paper. "Now, I see we have a motion for a summary judgment. Mr. Brockman, I've reviewed your arguments and memorandums, and you may speak to that motion now."

"Thank you, Your Honor." Brockman stood again. "Given the extraordinary lack of evidence in this case, the defense submits a motion for a summary judgment. What we have is an accident that occurred with an independent contractor on the defendant's property. As the person was an independent contractor, as stated in the police report and the life insurance claim, there are no legal grounds for this claim. Legally, we must not proceed."

"Mr. Hennessy?"

"The independent contractor was in name only. He was an—"

"Your Honor, this is ridiculous. The police report clearly states he was paid as an independent contractor. This case has no legal grounds."

"Your Honor," Hennessy's voice was firm. "I would like to present my argument without being interrupted."

"Agreed," Judge Griffin stated. "Please hold off on your argument until directed, Mr. Brockman."

"Thank you, Your Honor," Hennessy said. "Mr.

Santos was an independent contractor in name only. He was an employee of the property owner and was entitled to the safety requirements of the Occupational Safety and Health Administration regulations. The OSHA has recognized the wrong classification of an employee is a problem nationwide. The OSHA has several ways to determine whether a person is an independent contractor. One, they consider the work process, and two, they consider workflow control. The employment of Mr. Santos at the property fails both those tests. He was an employee being paid as an independent contractor. As per the OSHA regulations, the responsibility for his safety rests with the employer."

"He was paid as an independent contractor," Brockman growled.

"In name only."

"He submitted a 1099 form every year!" Brockman tapped his fist on the desk. "He was not an employee!"

"Quiet!" Judge Griffin yelled. "Gentlemen, you will not behave like children in my courtroom. I expect that all the lawyers in this courtroom will behave with the utmost respect for this court and each other. Understood?"

"Yes, Your Honor," Hennessy and Brockman replied together.

She raised her eyebrows and stared at them for a long moment before she looked back at the files in front of her. "Considering the nature of the claim and what's in dispute here, and having reviewed all the documentation, including the affidavits and memorandums you have both presented, I have a decision on the summary judgment. Upon consideration of the South Carolina Rules of Civil Procedure, applicable case law, briefs, and oral arguments, the defendant's motion for a summary judgment is denied." She stared at Brockman, almost daring him to speak. When he didn't, she continued. "And I see the parties have yet to enter into mediation?"

"That's correct, Your Honor," Hennessy said.

"Then I recommend, strongly, that a mediation session is held before trial." Judge Griffin closed the file. "And if there is no further progress, then we will have the court date on the docket on September 15th."

CHAPTER 39

After the success of the first hearing, Hennessy worked through the weekend.

He was alone on Sunday. He saw the time at 1.55pm and took a lunch break. He walked outside, needing to get some blood back into his legs. He knew sitting down for hours wasn't doing him any favors. He walked two blocks to one of the local cafes, ordered a meatball sandwich, and took it outside.

The August heat continued to rise. The humidity was drenching Charleston in heavy moisture and draining the energy out of all its residents. People moved slower when the humidity reached its peak. They had to. Trying to move quickly through the humidity was a recipe for heatstroke.

He returned to Waterfront Park and sat in the shade of the densely populated oak trees, watching the children splash in the nearby Pineapple Fountain.

Charleston was an easy city to fall for—the historic architecture, the beautiful rivers, the gorgeous marshes. The Palmetto trees, the secret gardens, the stately mansions. The outdoor lifestyle was alluring, the easy access to the rivers was enticing, and the friendly people were filled with Southern hospitality. The city had a major place in America's past, filling the streets with stories of war and struggles. He loved his home city. He loved finding new snippets of history that he'd never learned before. He only recently discovered the city's layout was nearly identical to the Barbados city of Bridgetown. When the British arrived in 1670 and found sugar cane, they tried to recreate the place they'd just traveled from. Cobblestone streets, colorful colonial buildings, and crepe myrtle trees were mirrored in each city.

Hennessy smiled. The sun, the people idly chatting all around him, and even the passing traffic on the street added to the weekend's serene atmosphere.

His cell buzzed in his pocket, and he pulled it out and looked at the number.

"Joe Hennessy," he answered the call.

"Mr. Hennessy, this is Officer Hamish Manson from the Greenville Police Department."

Hennessy's first thought was something had happened to Wendy or the girls. He found himself unable to answer, almost paralyzed by the fear which continued to tighten around him. In the split second when the name hit his brain, a massive hit of adrenalin flushed through his system, sending his body into a near shock. Fear gripped him like a vice, his heart instantly slamming awake inside his chest.

"Sir, are you there?"

"Yes." His voice shook. "How can I help you?"

"You reported seeing a vehicle parked on the side of the road the day before the fire at your vineyard. Is that correct?"

"Ah," Hennessy said as relief flooded over him. His shoulders relaxed from their height of tension. "That's right. It was a red sedan, possibly a Ford. Several of the staff on the vineyard saw it at different times of the day as well."

"One of our officers found a vehicle that matches the description. It was abandoned outside a strip mall without any plates. We were able to match it to a car that was stolen two days before the fire. We've had some forensic tests run on the vehicle, and what we've found is quite interesting."

"Go on," Hennessy said, feeling his curiosity stir awake.

"We found evidence of an accelerant in the back seat of the car. Two empty cans of gasoline, which also matches the fire report on your property. We also lifted a couple of prints from the steering wheel, and after running them through our system, we got a hit. Does the name Frank Diaz mean anything to you?"

"No, but he has a record?"

"He does, and quite an extensive one. He's currently on parole but hasn't reported for weeks. The arson attack appears to be something he's known for. He's had a few arrests over other minor arson activity."

"And you're trying to find him?"

"Yes, sir, we are, but he hasn't reported to his parole officer for weeks, and we don't have another address for him. I'll be sure to keep you up to date the second we find anything."

"Thank you, Officer Manson. I appreciate you and everything your office has done," Hennessy said and ended the call.

For a moment, he found himself unable to move. The anger of losing his crop returned. Rage inundated his system, and without thinking, he looked at his cell again, thumbed through his contacts, and made a call. A few seconds later, Barry Lockett answered.

"Barry, do you know a man named Frank Diaz?"

"I've heard the name. Why?"

"I've had a call from Greenville PD, and Frank Diaz is the prime suspect in the vineyard fire."

"Seriously?" The line went silent for a few seconds. "I'm down the coast with the family at the moment, but give me a few hours. I don't think he'll be too hard to find."

Lockett didn't wait for a reply. He hung up, leaving Hennessy to listen to nothing but silence. His brain went into overdrive, taking on multiple trains of thought at once. Longhouse, Wendy, his daughters, the fire, all of them intertwining into a mass of concern, anger, and fear.

He thought back to the man he'd seen at the vineyard. He'd been wearing a baseball cap and was too far away to identify.

Hennessy shut out the rest of the world and concentrated on his breathing, feeling the sweat build on his brow. He went back to the office, but couldn't focus. One hour and fifty-five minutes later, Lockett called back.

"Tell me you found him," Hennessy answered, his tone hopeful.

"I have."

"Is he close by?"

"He's in North Charleston. He doesn't have a place, but his girlfriend lives on Marilyn Drive. He's known to be staying there."

"North Charleston?" Hennessy looked at his watch. "I can be there in fifteen."

"No, Joe. I've already called the Greenville PD, and they've assured me they'll get the North Charleston Police Department to arrest him."

"I'll go past to make sure he doesn't run. An extra pair of eyes wouldn't hurt."

"Joe, don't. Diaz is known to be unstable," Lockett said. "Listen to me. Let the cops do their thing. They'll grab him, and we can question him once he's in custody. Maybe, with enough pressure, he'll roll over on Longhouse."

"That's good." Hennessy paced the room. "But I'll go to the address on Marilyn Drive now and just look out for him. I'll stay back. The more help, the better."

Hennessy heard a muffled groan from his

investigator, but he ignored it. This was personal, and he couldn't let the suspect get away.

CHAPTER 40

It took Hennessy less than fifteen minutes to reach the address Lockett had provided.

He parked his pickup behind a sprawling oak tree and watched the house from a distance. The oak tree was at the edge of an empty, overgrown block, and if he stayed in the shadows, he wouldn't draw attention to himself. Five cars were around the address—three in the driveway and two on the front lawn. A young man walked out to one of the cars, fired it up, and then roared down the street, leaving behind tire marks on the grass.

Five minutes later, another car pulled up, and another young man emerged. He walked inside, and not five minutes after that, he drove away again. Hennessy figured it was a drug den, a place where deals were happening, and that meant the people inside would be armed.

While waiting, he flicked on the radio in his truck.

He listened to a few tunes, tapping his finger on the steering wheel before breaking news came in. There was a shooting in North Charleston, and residents were warned to stay away from the Liberty Mall Shopping Center. The shooter was still active, the news stated.

Hennessy groaned and hit his palm on the steering wheel. He knew what it meant. All the police resources would be diverted to the shooting, and rightly so. But it also meant no police resources would attend the Marilyn Road address anytime soon.

Within five minutes of hearing the news of the shooting, Hennessy saw a figure leave the address. The description matched Frank Diaz. The man entered a late-nineties Ford Escort, revved the engine heavily, and drove out of the driveway.

Careful not to be seen, Hennessy followed at a safe distance.

The drive didn't last long. Five minutes later, the blue Ford Escort pulled into the 555 Bar and Steakhouse parking lot, located at the end of a small strip mall. Diaz parked across two parking spaces next to the front door, and then stepped out of the car and went inside.

Hennessy parked five cars from the front entrance and listened to the radio reports. They warned the shooter was on the run. All police resources would be diverted to the location and would most likely be there for the rest of the day.

He gripped the steering wheel tightly. He knew, logically, that he shouldn't go inside. He knew, logically, that he shouldn't confront Diaz. And he knew, logically, that he should remain in the pickup.

But after months of being pushed to the edge, he couldn't control his rage.

He reached across to the glove box and removed his Glock 19.

With a last look in the rearview, he opened the truck's door and slid out. As he closed it, he stuffed the gun down the back of his pants, but rather than letting it sit there, he kept one hand on it for good measure.

Hennessy walked with a sense of purpose, caution coming a distant second. He'd been pushed to his limits and then past it. His rage and anger had reached its breaking point. He didn't think. He couldn't. The red mist filled every part of his body. He was ready to unleash a rampage, and if Diaz so much as twitched in the wrong direction, the resulting damage would be final.

The hip-hop music from inside the bar reached his ears long before he reached the steps leading up to the front door. His fingers tightened on the handle of the gun. Aware of the adrenalin, Hennessy paused long enough to take a deep breath. His body was shaking with anger.

He pushed through the front doors. He spotted Diaz at the bar. The arsonist was ordering a drink.

"Hey," Hennessy called out. "Frank Diaz. We need to talk."

Diaz looked up. He saw a man in a suit and reacted. Diaz pulled a pistol from his jeans. He didn't hesitate.

The sound of the shot echoed through the bar. Hennessy dived to his right, drawing his gun from his belt. Someone screamed. The sound of another shot echoed. Hennessy looked up. The emergency exit door was swinging open. An alarm was going off somewhere.

Diaz was gone.

Hennessy ran to the door, gun out, ready to fire. He stopped at the exit. Peered around the corner into the parking lot. He saw nothing. He stepped out. He couldn't see Diaz. He spotted a man hiding behind a Dodge Challenger.

"Did you see where he went?"

"Drove off in a Ford. Not sure which direction. Kept my head down during the shooting."

Hennessy groaned and leaned against the Challenger. He gently punched his fist against his forehead, more than aware of his error of judgment. "I lost him."

CHAPTER 41

Hennessy waited for news of Diaz's capture for two days.

Each morning, he checked his cell the second he woke up, then rechecked it every few minutes during his morning routine. By the time he reached the office, he'd already checked for any kind of news no less than two dozen times. Hennessy beat himself up over his mistake to confront Diaz. He lost an opportunity because the anger became too much. He felt helpless.

Lockett said nothing. There was no 'I told you so,' or any negativity. When he spoke with him, Lockett remained positive they would get their man.

The news came at 10am that morning. Hennessy sat at his desk reading the files in the Santos case when Jacinta came into his office. When he looked up from his laptop, she was leaning against the doorframe, with a distinct look of dread.

"I'm not going to like this, am I?" he asked, his tone barely audible in the silence of the room. Rather than answer immediately, Jacinta shook her head before casting her eyes down.

"Go on then," he said. "Let me down gently."

"Frank Diaz has left the country."

"Are you positive? How can you be so sure?"

She tried to smile for him, but Hennessy felt his insides drop. "A contact phoned me earlier. She said Diaz had fled the country. I messaged Lockett, and he called one of his contacts at immigration. They confirmed he was on a plane from Atlanta the same day you saw him."

"Does anybody know where he's gone?"

"Flight left for Honduras, but after that, nobody knows."

Hennessy felt like screaming, his hands tightening into balled-up fists as he considered the news. "I did this," he whispered to himself. "It's all my fault."

"You can't think like that," Jacinta said. "Even though he's gone, you still have a case to work on. Maria Santos is still here, and her husband deserves justice, remember?"

Hennessy looked up and tried to grin. "Can't I

even have a few minutes to wallow in my self-pity?" He thought he could use a bit of humor to break the tension, but Jacinta wasn't biting.

"No, you cannot," she said, dropping into the chair opposite him. "This is too important, and you, of all people, should know that."

"I know," he said, leaning back in his seat. "I'm sorry. It's things with the vineyard could already be out of our hands, and catching Diaz would've helped me deal with the emotional carnage."

"That bad, huh?"

"That bad." He closed his eyes and rubbed his temples.

"Is there anything I can do to help?"

He opened his eyes and smiled at her. "Unfortunately, not," he said. "This is our problem."

"Well, look at the bright side."

"What's that?"

"If nothing else, you get to see Longhouse tomorrow."

It took him a moment to understand. "The first mediation session."

"It is," she said. "This time tomorrow, you and I will be sitting opposite Richard Longhouse, trying to come to a settlement."

CHAPTER 42

Hennessy met Maria Santos at the entrance to the O.T. Wallace County Office Building at 101 Meeting Street. They greeted each other before Hennessy led them inside.

The receptionist led them to one of the smaller boardrooms, where they were asked to sit on one side of the table. The room was small and tight, with the wooden table taking up much of the space. The walls were bare, with not a patch of color, and there were no windows. It smelled like the table had just been cleaned with a lemon-scented cleaning product.

"Now that depositions have been taken, the next step in the lawsuit is the court-ordered mediation sessions," Hennessy explained. "This is where you and I meet with Richard Longhouse and his lawyers to determine whether a fair settlement can be reached. The mediator will be a retired attorney who'll listen to both sides to determine what we need for a settlement. We'll then be split into two rooms, and these are referred to as separate 'caucuses.' The mediator will go from one to the other and relay offers, messages, demands, questions, and counteroffers. The mediator's job is to resolve the dispute by showing both sides how much there is to lose at trial. Usually, given the unpredictable nature of jury decisions, a settlement would be best because both sides have so much to lose. The court has suggested we go through five sessions. However, if the mediator suggests that no settlement will be reached, we can end it after one."

"And after that?"

"If no settlement can be reached, we prepare for trial."

"Good," Maria stated. "My husband deserves justice, Mr. Hennessy and that's what I'll be sticking to." Her tone was intense, and her conviction almost final. "That man has already tried to scare me once, and I can promise you, he will not succeed."

"So that we're on the same page, I need to know what amount you would consider settling at."

"Nothing."

"There must be a price, Maria," Hennessy said.

"Ten million?"

"He could offer me a hundred million, and I wouldn't take it," she replied. "I want justice for my George. Not money—justice. If the police won't investigate it, then I'll take it to court myself. If Mr. Longhouse admitted that he had a hand in my husband's death, then I would settle. Without a confession, I won't take a deal. Tell him that—a signed confession and this is over."

"And the monetary amount?"

"It could be anything. Without a confession, I won't settle." Maria thought for a moment. "But you can tell him fifty-million-dollars for damages."

Hennessy nodded. Her line in the sand was clear— a confession from Longhouse. If nothing else, he knew her moral compass couldn't be questioned.

Jacinta entered the room and said hello. Five minutes later, the mediator entered. Stephen Johns was a skinny man in a loose suit, a former lawyer who had retired when he turned fifty but found he had too much time on his hands. Golf wasn't his thing, nor was sailing. He enjoyed returning to the office to mediate settlement discussions, his one day a week in the middle of the action. Johns apologized for the small boardroom before explaining that the larger boardroom had been double-booked.

Johns confirmed the purpose of the mediation and then left to bring in Longhouse and his lawyers.

"Joseph," Longhouse cheered as he entered the room, greeting Hennessy like an old friend. "It's so good to see you again."

Hennessy ignored him but could already feel the adrenalin kick in as Longhouse sat down. Brockman and Minton followed him in, and they sat on either side of their boss. Johns sat at the head of the table and explained the process for each party. When no questions were raised, he invited the parties to begin.

"Joseph, my dear old friend, why do we insist on being so formal?" Longhouse grinned, sarcasm dripping off his words. He looked directly at Maria. "He hasn't changed in thirty years, still as professional as ever. I keep telling him to loosen up a bit, but he never listens to me."

"We're not old friends, and as Mrs. Santos has already told you and your lawyers, she isn't interested in your money alone. To settle this case today, we need a signed admission of guilt for the death of Mr. Santos. And in addition to the signed statement, we can negotiate on the amount of damages, but we'll start negotiations with a fifty-million-dollar payout."

Longhouse laughed, and when he turned, Brockman and Minton did the same.

"That's outrageous," Brockman chuckled. "Our counteroffer is $500,000, and Mrs. Santos will sign an NDA to never discuss it. It's a substantial offer, and I suggest you take it."

Maria turned and looked at Hennessy, leaned in closer, and whispered into his ear. He listened, never taking his eyes off Longhouse. When she was done, he stated. "Money alone will not settle this case. We need a signed statement that has admission of guilt."

"Listen to me," Longhouse hissed and leaned forward, pointing his finger at Maria. "You need to take the deal. What's the matter with you?"

"Now, that's not how we behave in these meetings," Johns interrupted. "I'll ask you to refrain from any such attempts at intimidation, Richard."

Minton reached over to try and calm his boss, but Longhouse shrugged his arm away.

"We believe half a million is more than fair in this matter," Minton continued, doing his best to turn the attention of the meeting on him. "Our client was not responsible for this accidental death, and this offer is very generous."

"The monetary amount can be discussed, but we're not budging on the admission of guilt," Hennessy responded. "That's non-negotiable."

"Good," Johns said, trying to calm the tension in the room. "We have a starting point for the negotiation. You might not believe it now, but it's a very important step in the process." Johns looked over to Longhouse. "Richard, I would like you and your lawyers to come and sit in the room further down the hall, and then I will go between the parties and try to get us onto one page."

Longhouse stood and walked out of the room without another word. His lawyers followed a few steps behind.

For the next fifty minutes, Johns went between the rooms, bringing new offers to each party. He explained the importance of not putting undue pressure on the legal system and the costs that could be involved in taking the case to court. He tried his best to convince Maria to take the money, but she wouldn't budge without an admission of guilt. And it was clear to Johns that Longhouse would never give her that.

Looking exhausted, Johns entered the boardroom for a fifth time. He drew a breath and sat down across from Maria. "At this point, it's clear to me that neither you nor Mr. Longhouse will get what you want from further mediation sessions. I don't see the need for further sessions, and I recommend we finish the mediation today."

Hennessy thanked Johns for his hard work and shook his hand. When Johns had left the room, Hennessy looked at Maria. She nodded. It was time to take the case to court.

CHAPTER 43

Richard Longhouse sat down in the leather armchair and grinned.

He liked this place. Entry into the Quest, a speakeasy bar, was by invitation only. The bar didn't advertise anywhere, there was no website, and the only door didn't have any signage. It was a favorite of the rich and powerful of the city, a place to do deals without the judging eyes of the public. Dripping in nostalgia and bourbon, and with room for only twenty-five patrons, the dimly lit bar showcased locally distilled, small-batch spirits produced in the heart of the South Carolina Lowcountry. Gold trimmings laced the furniture. The service was quiet and impeccable. The scent of cigar smoke hung in the air.

"A distant cousin?" Longhouse asked as he sipped his neat bourbon.

"He's a second or third cousin on the father's

side," Al Berry stated, seated on the armchair opposite, one leg crossed over the other. "I'm not sure if they've even met."

"That doesn't matter. How long has he been in prison?"

"Two years ago, Javier Santos was sentenced to twenty-five years for murder and other drug offenses. He's in prison in Mexico City, and a lot of people don't leave that place. I'm sure he's a member of a gang by now."

"Do you think we can pull it off?"

"Of course," Berry laughed as he sipped the whiskey. "George might never have met his cousin Javier Santos, but they're still family. The Santos family are murderous drug dealers. The papers will love it. I can see it now, 'Mexican Family of drug dealers try to sue local Senator.' If anything, this sort of story might get more people to vote for you. It shows you can stand up against Mexican drug gangs."

"And that's the angle we run?"

"As soon as anyone hears their family are Mexican drug dealers, the Santos clan will lose all credibility. The general public will dismiss them as a money-hungry, drug-dealing family." Berry chortled. "And

I'm sure we can spin it a hundred ways. It would be gold if we could find out which gang Javier is in."

"And when will the first stories run?"

"The day before the court case is due to start."

Longhouse grinned as another man approached. Mark Taylor was an advertising man known in many circles as the powerful wizard of the television commercial. His persuasive ads could change the course of entire elections. The two men shook solidly, each with something to gain from the other. Taylor wanted a piece of Longhouse's massive campaign money, and Longhouse needed Taylor's touch to swing the voters. They chatted briefly, laughed more than was required, and wished each other a good night.

When Taylor had moved on, Longhouse moved his attention back to Berry. He sat back down and leaned forward in his chair.

"It's starting to bite," Longhouse said. "I could see it in Taylor's eyes. There's doubt in people now. They think this might destroy me."

"Then we need to be strong," Berry said. "If this trial is going to land in the media, then we need to discredit George Santos. We'll start with discrediting the family and then move on to discrediting George as the court case progresses."

"I know how." Longhouse looked around and lowered his voice. "Let's say George Santos was under the influence of drugs at the time of his death. How would that affect public opinion?"

"That would work. We paint him as the bad, money-hungry drug addict, and you're the vulnerable local landowner who was taken advantage of. Yes, that would work very well."

"And if we could prove he took drugs on the day of his death?" Longhouse asked.

"It would be magic if you could present it during the trial. The media will have a field day with that."

"Then we have a solution." Longhouse smiled and sat back in his chair. "I know exactly how to play this."

CHAPTER 44

"Did you see the news?" Jacinta opened an article on her cell and showed it to her boss.

On the morning of their return to court for further pre-trial motions, Hennessy met with Jacinta and Lockett in his office boardroom to discuss the final details. Hennessy leaned across and read the headline of the small article. "'A drug-dealing family accuses local Senator of Negligence.' Who's the drug dealer?"

"George's cousin in Mexico. I asked Maria, and she said they've never even met."

"It's a media play by Longhouse and his team. It has Al Berry's dirty fingerprints all over it. He's dug deep to find that link, no doubt." He turned his focus back to the case. "In the case, we'll open with the coroner, then call the forensic experts before we move on to the character witnesses. How are we with the character witnesses for George?"

"Five have confirmed," Jacinta said. "We're still

waiting for one more to come through, but they've all responded to the emails, which is a good sign."

"What about Stephen Harrison?"

"Our bloodstain pattern analysis expert is ready," Jacinta said. "Any further thoughts on calling Richard Longhouse to testify?"

"It's too much of a risk in our case. As evil as he is, Longhouse can be very charming. We don't need the jury to fall for that charm." Hennessy clicked his pen. "And the defense won't call him to the stand. It's too much of a risk for them to call him. Under cross-examination, I could ask him anything. No, he'll be too exposed."

"And you're comfortable with only one OSHA specialist?"

"Jacob Aster is just about the perfect witness. He's experienced, respected, and charming. Our case hinges on him stating that George was an employee," Hennessy said. "But we have a backup OSHA expert, if needed. Mary Powell is a good witness, although not as experienced as Aster. Let's hope Aster does his job and seals the deal for us."

Hennessy and his team had spent weeks interviewing the potential witnesses. He interviewed the Deputy Coroner, the insurance researcher, and the insurance assessor. He drafted testimonies with chainsaw specialists, accident investigators, and crime scene experts. He spoke with forensic specialists and five OSHA professionals. He spent hours reviewing documents, preparing witnesses, and researching precedents. After months of hard work, the day of reckoning had almost arrived.

"Time for the next step," he said as he packed up his notes and placed them in his briefcase.

Twenty-five minutes later, they met Maria Santos in the foyer of the Charleston Judicial Center. She talked to Hennessy about the news article. She was angry about it. She stated their family had no connection to Javier Santos. He was a second cousin of George, and they'd never met. She couldn't believe the media would discredit her name without even a phone call.

Hennessy led his team into the courtroom. He sat next to Maria, set his briefcase down on the floor beside him, and patiently waited. He checked his watch a couple of minutes later and was about to ask Jacinta to check hers when the doors to the courtroom finally opened.

Brockman and Minton entered, but there was still no sign of the defendant.

The bailiff called the room to rise, and Judge Griffin entered the courtroom, looking sterner than she had before. Her face was devoid of emotion as she sat down and read over the files on her desk. She opened her laptop and typed several lines before turning to the lawyers.

"Now, I see that both parties have engaged in a mediation session." She looked down at the two groups over her thin gold-wired glasses. "How did y'all go?"

"Your Honor," Hennessy said, rising to his feet, "we have met with Mr. Longhouse's team and haven't reached an acceptable solution. It's clear we won't be able to find a resolution."

Brockman stood as well. "Unfortunately, Mr. Hennessy is correct, Your Honor. Despite our best efforts to make Mrs. Santos an acceptable offer, her continued refusals have left us with very little choice but to take this to trial."

The judge looked down at her paperwork, disappointed by the news.

"Well, that's a shame," she said. "Given that there

has been no acceptable agreement reached between the two parties, this court finds no other alternative but for the matter to proceed to trial." She looked down at her calendar, appeared to calculate something, then peered back at the parties over the top of her glasses again. "I'll see both parties back here two days from today for voir dire. That's Thursday at 10am."

The time for justice had arrived.

CHAPTER 45

The Charleston Judicial Center was in the beating heart of the historic city.

It sat behind the famed Four Corners of the Law at the historic intersection of Broad and Meetings Streets. On each of the four corners, the buildings represented a level of the law—state law with the Charleston County Courthouse, God's law with the beautiful St. Michael's Episcopal Church, city law with Charleston City Hall, and federal law in the Federal Courthouse.

Joe Hennessy stopped at the intersection and took a breath. He loved the history of the great city and often stopped to gaze upon the architecture. On the northwest corner of the Four Corners sat the Charleston County Courthouse, representing state law. First constructed in 1753 and reconstructed in 1792, the neoclassical building had a long and colorful history, including the first reading of the Declaration of Independence in South Carolina from the balcony on the second floor.

After he took a moment to calm himself, he continued into the Judicial Center, and his heart rate increased with each step. By the time he walked through security, his heart was pounding like he'd just run five miles.

After twenty-two years of heartache and after two months of turmoil, Richard Longhouse had to face his day in court. The defense had put forward several deals in a last-ditch attempt to settle, all including a million dollars plus. Maria Santos refused each offer. Hennessy suggested she should consider the deals, but without an admission of guilt, she wasn't moving.

Hennessy was surprised at the speed of the trial, but he shouldn't have been. Longhouse could make backroom deals, pull strings, and move mountains. He needed the case resolved before he started his electoral campaign, and his contacts in the system had helped him.

The media had sided with Longhouse. After the initial scandal of his affair died down, Longhouse spoke to the press, giving very calm and measured responses to any questions. Elise was smiling by his side, but she wasn't a very good actor. It was clear she was forcing the smile through hatred for the man.

When asked about the court case, Longhouse dismissed it as if it had no legs to stand on. The media ran with that opinion. Under guidance from Al Berry, they painted the civil case as a frivolous lawsuit from a money-hungry family.

The lawyers spent two days in voir dire, the jury selection process. Finding suitable people who hadn't heard of Richard Longhouse or the affair with his much younger neighbor was difficult.

The defense needed locals on the jury. Longhouse looked Southern, spoke Southern, and charmed everyone with a broad Southern grin, so they needed people who would warm to him. They needed people who had South Carolina running through their veins. They needed people whose family history was tied to the state. And they needed jurors who were biased toward locals. The defense dismissed anyone with Latino heritage and anyone who didn't profess their love for South Carolina.

Hennessy needed the opposite. He needed people from off. People who had chosen to live in the beautiful state but weren't blinded by their love of all things local. He needed people with open minds and open ideas. He needed people with experience and a subjective eye.

After two days of questioning and arguing and dismissing, the lawyers had their twelve.

Six jurors were middle-aged, two were younger, and four were older. Most had children, one was a foster parent, and another was retired and childless. One was a bartender. Another was a tour guide. There was a finance worker, an administration assistant, and a janitor. Five were White, four were Black, and three were Asian. Seven men, five women. The alternative jurors were also selected.

After the jury was finalized, Judge Griffin called an end to the week. The following Monday morning, at fifteen minutes past ten, the court had resettled. Longhouse sat with a straight back, nodding to himself, keeping his eyes forward. His lawyers, Brockman and Minton, whispered to each other, confident they had the upper hand.

The seats behind the lawyers were almost full. The Santos family sat behind the plaintiff. They filled two rows. Her sons were there, as were their wives. Her sisters and their husbands were also there. Friends had gathered. Her support was strong.

The casual observers sat on the other side of the gallery. None appeared to be friends of Richard Longhouse. Elise Longhouse, Richard's long-suffering wife, looked reluctant to be there. Their thirty-year-old son, whom Richard hadn't spoken to in years, would never attend. Longhouse didn't have friends that he hadn't bought, and no backer wanted to risk sitting behind him.

Hennessy's legs were weak as he waited in his seat. Nerves filled his stomach. His hands were cramping. After sitting down, he looked up at the vacant jury box. It was there his chance for justice would come.

"All rise," the bailiff called out, alerting everyone that Judge Griffin would soon enter the courtroom and the trial was about to begin. "The court is now in session, the Honorable Judge Griffin presiding."

Judge Griffin walked into the courtroom, in no rush to begin the case. Once she sat down, she looked over the names on the file, coughed, and moved the microphone closer. She clicked her pen five times, coughed again, and then raised her eyes to look at the courtroom before her. She clicked her pen again, wrote a note on a piece of paper, and then looked back to the lawyers.

She didn't bother to welcome the parties to the court. She began by detailing the rules for conduct in her courtroom. When she was satisfied everyone understood the rules, she instructed the bailiff to open the jury door. They walked in, and all looked at Maria first and Longhouse second.

The jurors took their oath under instruction from Judge Griffin, "Ladies and Gentlemen of the Jury, please stand and raise your right hand to be sworn: You shall well and truly try the issues joined in this case and a true verdict give according to the law and evidence. So help you God."

After they confirmed their oaths, Judge Griffin moved her laptop, adjusted her glasses and further explained to the jury their roles and responsibilities. She spoke at length about their responsibility to the court. She detailed the procedures and talked about what was likely to occur over the coming weeks. She made sure the jurors were clear on her expectations. No one dared to talk back to her. She talked to the jurors like they were school children, and she was the principal, ready to admonish them at a moment's notice. When she was satisfied that everyone was clear on the process, she took a piece of paper from her folder and read from it, just like she had done hundreds of times before.

"Under the constitution and laws of South Carolina, you, the jurors, are the finders of the facts in this trial. During this trial, you will hear testimony and receive evidence from the plaintiff and the defendants. While I will guide you on the definition of the law, it's your duty to determine the effect, value, weight, and truth of the evidence presented. As the trial judge, it's my responsibility to preside over the trial and to rule upon the admissibility of the evidence. You're to consider only the testimony which has been presented from this witness stand, together with any exhibits which have been made a part of the record. You are not to bring any outside bias into this courtroom. You are not to use any outside information to make a decision in this court. As the presiding judge, I'm the sole judge of the law in this case. It's your duty as jurors to accept my decisions as correct and apply the law as I state it to you. However, I do not have the right to express any opinion on the facts or evidence of this case, because this is a matter solely for you, the jury, to determine."

When she was sure the jurors understood her statements, she stated, "This trial, like most trials in this state, will begin with the opening statements. The opening statement is not a testimony of evidence. It's an outline of what the lawyers will present during the case. The lawyers are not here to entertain you, nor are they here to testify. They are here to provide an overview of what the actual evidence will be."

The jurors nodded obediently, and then Judge Griffin invited Joe Hennessy to begin his case-in-chief.

*****

"Your Honor, ladies and gentlemen of the jury, my name is Joe Hennessy, and I represent the claims of the plaintiff, Mrs. Maria Santos. In this opening statement, I'll provide an overview of the evidence which will be presented in this trial for you to consider.

In this case, the facts are simple.

On January 15th, Maria's husband, Mr. George

Santos, went to work on the property of Senator Richard Longhouse. Over the past five years, Mr. Santos had worked on the property's sprawling grounds for two days every week.

On that day, one of the coldest days in recent memory, Mr. Santos was asked to cut the branches off one of the oak trees. His employer, Senator Longhouse, provided Mr. Santos with a ladder. That ladder was stored outside overnight. It was cold that night, and there was frost on the ground.

Senator Longhouse asked Mr. Santos to cut the branches. He told Mr. Santos to use the ladder that leaned against the shed. Under the direction of his employer, Mr. Santos used that ladder.

Mr. Santos was not provided with fall protection from his employer.

While using that ladder, he cut one branch off the oak tree before moving on to the next. While attempting to cut the second branch, he slipped and fell.

When he landed, the chainsaw fell on top of him. While the chain had stopped spinning, the sharp edges of the chainsaw fell onto his neck. This impact cut his carotid artery, and he bled to death.

Those are the facts. They are not in dispute in this case. They were stated in the police report and confirmed in the report by the life insurance company, Mutual Life.

This court case is not about those facts. This court case is about what protections Mr. Santos should've been afforded under the Occupational Safety and Health Administration, also referred to as OSHA, regulations.

Under the OSHA regulations, Senator Longhouse, the property owner, had an obligation to ensure the safety of Mr. Santos. He did not do this. Senator Longhouse took no steps to remove the ice. Senator Longhouse, according to his own words in the police report, did not warn Mr. Santos of the danger. Senator Longhouse took no steps to ensure the property was safe.

Mr. Santos was paid as an independent contractor. However, per the OSHA and the Internal Revenue Service definitions, Mr. Santos was an employee. As South Carolina law does not provide a definition for who qualifies as an independent contractor, we must rely on the definition of the OSHA, IRS, and the United States Department of Labor.

Throughout this trial, we will call witnesses who will show this information in more detail.

You'll hear from the coroner and the lead detective in the investigation into the death of Mr. Santos, and they will discuss the circumstances around the incident. You'll hear from a bloodstain pattern analysis expert and a forensic expert. You'll hear from crime scene experts and workplace safety experts. We will call character witnesses, and they will testify that Mr. Santos was meticulous in his safety preparation. You will hear from former work colleagues who will testify the same thing. Over and over again, you will hear from people who will declare that Mr. Santos always put safety first.

You will also hear from witnesses who will state that Mr. Santos should have been paid as an employee of Senator Longhouse.

For example, you will hear from Mr. Antonio Smith, a gardener who used to work for Senator Longhouse. He will testify that Senator Longhouse treated him as an employee, despite paying him as an independent contractor. He will testify that Senator Longhouse directed him to work outside his contract, including helping the cleaning staff inside the house.

Most importantly in this case, you will hear from OSHA specialist Mr. Jacob Aster.

Mr. Aster will testify that, according to OSHA regulations, Mr. Santos was not employed as an independent contractor. Mr. Aster will explain that there are important distinctions that mean someone is an employee, regardless of how they're paid. Mr. Aster will testify that Mr. Santos' employment met all the regulations to be defined as an employee.

According to the law, Mr. Santos was an employee.

This is the most crucial distinction in this case. Although he was paid as an independent contractor, according to the law, Mr. Santos was an employee.

As an employee, he should've been provided with safety equipment. He was not.

As an employee, he should've been provided with undamaged and unfaulty equipment. He was not.

As an employer, Senator Longhouse had a duty of care to provide a safe working environment. He did not.

As an employer, Senator Longhouse provided faulty equipment that caused Mr. Santos' death.

Now, during this case, you'll hear tricks from the defense about what defines an employee. Do not be fooled by stories that have no basis in fact. Remember, you're here to assess the facts and make a judgment on the law.

On the law.

Once we arrive at the end of this case, once you've heard all the evidence, there will be no doubt that Mr. Longhouse is liable for the wrongful death of Mr. Santos.

As Judge Griffin explained earlier, a civil claim differs from a criminal charge.

In a civil claim, the burden of proof is based on a preponderance of the evidence. This is a more lenient burden of proof than a criminal case and requires establishing only that there is a greater than fifty percent chance the claim is valid. Therefore, if you believe the claim is more likely than not, you must find in favor of the plaintiff.

When we arrive at the end of this case, and you make your decision, you'll then be asked to make a judgment on the amount that the defendant is responsible for. We are asking for damages at $50 million for the wrongful death of Mr. Santos. There are rules you need to consider when determining a monetary amount, and the court will explain those to you at a later time.

As jurors, you've been tasked with an important responsibility. You're tasked with evaluating the evidence presented to you and making a decision based on the rule of law.

Remember that you must look at the evidence, not the stories. You must apply the law.

At the end of this case, I'll address you again and ask you to consider all the evidence we have presented and conclude that Senator Longhouse is liable for the wrongful death of Mr. Santos.

Thank you for your service to the court."

*****

During Hennessy's opening statement, juror number one stared at Maria, looking at her with judging eyes. Juror one was a lifelong South Carolina man who distrusted anyone not from his home state. His face was stern, his expression cold, and his jaw was clenched tight. He didn't trust Maria.

When Hennessy finished his opening statement,

he looked at juror five and nodded. Juror five nodded back. She was already convinced. An older woman who had relocated to Charleston from Chicago, she was drawn in by Hennessy's strong tone and charming looks.

After Hennessy was seated, Judge Griffin invited Christian Brockman to open. Brockman took a moment, read over his notes, and then stood. He moved to the lectern, offered the jury a fake smile, and then began.

*****

"Ladies and gentlemen of the jury, Your Honor, my name is Mr. Christian Brockman, and along with Mr. Leonard Minton, we represent the defendant, Senator Richard Longhouse.

Mr. Hennessy was right—this case is plain and simple. Mr. George Santos had a workplace accident and fell from a ladder. As he fell, the chainsaw he was using also fell, and it hit his neck. Unfortunately, and tragically, the chainsaw cut his carotid artery, and he bled to death.

I'll be clear right here and right now—the property owner was not responsible for the safety of the independent contractor.

Under South Carolina law, a plaintiff cannot receive damages if they're determined to be 51% or more responsible for the accident. Remember that. If you determine that 51% of the responsibility for safety rested with Mr. Santos, you cannot find in favor of the plaintiff.

Mr. Hennessy wishes you to believe that the property owner was negligent in his duty of care. To prove negligence, we must look at the legal terms that define it. In law, negligence means someone behaves in a way that a reasonable person would not, and that unreasonable behavior causes an injury to another. There are four distinct factors that define negligence.

First, the plaintiff must prove a duty of care. As Mr. Santos was an independent contractor, Mr. Longhouse had no obligation to provide a duty of care.

Secondly, they must prove the negligence breached the established legal duty. The plaintiff needs to prove that not only did the defendant owe a duty of care but also breached that duty in some way. Senator Longhouse did not breach any legal requirements for duty of care.

Thirdly, they must prove damages. For wrongful death, damages are measured by the losses the victim's family members have suffered as a result of the death. Simply put, the defendant's breach of their duty must be the cause of the plaintiff's grievances. It was not.

And lastly, they must prove causation. This is as simple as it sounds: did the person cause the wrongful death?

The answer is clearly no.

Over the coming weeks, we will present witnesses who will prove that Senator Longhouse did not breach any duty of care, and legally, had no responsibility for the death.

You will hear from expert witnesses who will state that Mr. Santos was paid as an independent contractor and that the Occupational Safety and Health Administration regulations did not apply to his working conditions. You will hear from crime scene experts who will testify that this was nothing more than a tragic accident. And you will hear from workplace safety specialists who will state that Mr. Santos' safety was solely his own responsibility.

At the end of this trial, I will stand before you again and show you how the plaintiff has failed to show Senator Longhouse was responsible for this accident.

When you're asked to make a decision in this case, you can only conclude in favor of Senator Longhouse. At that point, you will have already determined that Mr. Santos was more than 51% responsible for the incident. Remember, if you determine that Mr. Santos had 50% or more of the responsibility for his safety, you cannot find in favor of the plaintiff.

Thank you for your time."

CHAPTER 46

The public interest was growing.

Members of the public had filed in, filling the first two rows in the courtroom. The bailiffs stood at the front of the room, scanning the crowd. Media filled the space to the side of the room, each reporter with their notepads ready. The smell was stuffy, the crowd was unsettled, and the atmosphere was tense. Hennessy moved to the lectern, looked at the stern faces of the jurors, and then called his first witness.

"We call Deputy Coroner Dr. Benjamin Sutton to the stand."

Dr. Benjamin Sutton entered the courtroom through the tall wooden doors at the rear. Dr. Sutton looked like a car salesman's dream—an innocent smile, tubby waist, and an almost boy-like wonder in his eyes. His shirt was tucked in, his jeans were ironed, and any remaining hair was brushed over the top of his balding scalp. He took his oath, bowed his head to the judge, and sat in the witness stand.

"Dr. Sutton, thank you for coming to the court today," Hennessy began. "Can you please confirm your name for the court and give the court a brief overview of your occupation?"

"My name is Dr. Benjamin Sutton, and I'm employed as a Deputy Coroner with the Charleston County Coroner's Office. I was previously an ER doctor before becoming a member of the South Carolina Coroner's Association. I've worked for the Charleston County Coroner's Office for the last five years, where I've conducted hundreds of independent investigations into certain types of deaths. I've conducted these investigations to establish the cause and manner of death and to understand the circumstances surrounding the events that have led to the deaths."

Hennessy submitted the doctor's report into evidence and continued. "Dr. Sutton, did you conduct the medical examination of Mr. Santos after his death?"

"That's correct."

"And can you please tell the court how he died?"

"Mr. Santos died on January 15th as the result of

exsanguination."

"Can you please define exsanguination to the court?"

"Exsanguination is death caused by blood loss. Depending upon the individual's health, the average human usually dies after losing half to two-thirds of the blood from their body. However, any more than one-third of the blood volume can be deadly. It occurs most often after a major artery is severed and the bleeding is not stopped."

"What caused the loss of blood for Mr. Santos?"

"Mr. Santos had a laceration of the carotid artery near the top of his neck, on the left side. Upon further investigation, it was confirmed that this laceration was the cause of his blood loss."

"In your report, do you define what caused this laceration?"

"Yes. The cut is consistent with the chainsaw found at the scene. We've seen many cuts with chainsaws, and all the lacerations have the same pattern. Assessing the scene, it was reasonable to assume that he fell from a height of around ten feet. He slipped off the ladder, and the chainsaw fell on top of him." He made the action with his hand, karate chopping the left side of his neck with his right hand. "He wasn't wearing any safety equipment, and one of the sharp points of the chainsaw hit the top of his neck."

"The time of death?"

"Based on several factors, we can place his death between 8.05am and 8.15am."

Hennessy began his case-in-chief by asking factual questions. He was attempting to consolidate the truths, drilling into the jury the small facts that would become a mountain of evidence. "Did you also conduct a toxicology report on the deceased?"

"That's correct."

"And what was found in the toxicology report?"

"Nothing of note."

"Was there any alcohol found in his system?"

"No."

"Was there any other foreign substance found in his blood?"

"I tested for a range of drugs, including amphetamines and depressants. Nothing was found in his blood."

"It says in your report that Mr. Santos most likely fell off a ladder while holding onto the chainsaw. Why do you believe that?"

"Mr. Santos had bruising on the back of his head consistent with a fall. Given the scene where he was found, the injury is consistent with a fall from height."

"Do you believe, in your medical opinion, that Mr. Santos would've died from the fall alone?"

"No. The fall off the ladder was unlikely to have killed him. It was most likely that he fell while holding onto the chainsaw. During the fall, he didn't let go of the chainsaw and then the chainsaw cut his neck. This was the most likely action that caused the death."

For the next hour and twenty-five minutes, Hennessy continued to build the facts around the scene, from the weather to the state of the ladder. He took the jury on a journey, asking Dr. Sutton to describe every small detail that was stated in the report. Dr. Sutton talked about the position of the body when it was found, the state of the chainsaw found next to the body, and the lack of safety equipment at the scene. He talked further about the examination of the body, he talked about Mr. Santos' bloodied clothes, and he talked about how deep the laceration was.

Throughout it all, Hennessy kept looking at the jury, nodding and smiling, building a rapport with them. The jury warmed to Dr. Sutton, trusting every statement he made, as if he was an authority on all that was right.

"No further questions," Hennessy stated as the afternoon drew long.

Judge Griffin considered calling a recess, but when Brockman stated he only had a few questions for the witness, she allowed him to cross-examine.

"Dr. Sutton," Brockman began, seated behind his desk, "was there any evidence that anyone else was involved in this accident?"

"No."

"So, it was an unfortunate accident?"

"I don't think that's in dispute."

"A yes or no to that question would be nice," Brockman stated in a condescending tone. From their reactions, it was obvious the jury disliked him. "I'll repeat myself—was it an unfortunate accident?"

"Considering the circumstances, yes."

"And what you're saying is that Mr. Santos was involved in an accident and died as a result of that accident?"

"Objection," Hennessy called. "Asked and answered."

"Sustained," Judge Griffin stated. "Move on, Mr. Brockman."

Brockman nodded and clicked several keys on the laptop beside his desk. "Let me ask you this, Dr. Sutton—was there any indication that Mr. Santos was pushed off the ladder?"

"Objection," Hennessy stated. "Again, this question has been asked and answered."

"Sustained." Judge Griffin agreed. "It's been established that Mr. Santos fell off the ladder of his own accord."

Brockman turned to the jury. Several jury members squinted, trying to gauge the moral decency of the man at the defense table. When Brockman saw their faces, he arrogantly waved the witness away. "We have no further questions for this witness."

Judge Griffin called a recess, marking the end of the first day of the trial. Hennessy left the room buoyed by the start of their case, but he knew there was still a long way to go.

CHAPTER 47

"The plaintiff calls Detective Joshua Brooks."

The crowd turned to watch as the detective entered the room to begin day two.

From the moment Detective Brooks walked in, he eyed Hennessy with hostility. Brooks was a heavy man with the skin of a heavy drinker, with a red nose and red cheeks laced with broken capillaries. He had dressed in a cheap, ill-fitting suit for the occasion. He huffed as he walked and grunted as he sat down. It was a risk to bring the investigating detective to the stand so early, but Hennessy's plan was to establish the facts of the scene before launching into the legality of who was responsible.

"Thank you for taking the time to come to court today, Detective Brooks. Can you please begin by telling the court your name and profession?"

"My full name is Joshua Andrew Brooks, and I'm employed as a detective with the North Charleston

Police Department. I've served in this role for the past ten years. Before that, I was in the Navy for many years. Being a cop can be confronting sometimes, certainly when dealing with deceased persons, but it's part of the job."

"Were you the detective that investigated the scene where Mr. Santos had died?"

"That's right." Detective Brooks shifted in his seat, leaning to his left. "We got a 911 call at 8.25am on January 15th from a person on Ashley River Road. The caller said they'd found their gardener injured on the property. They said there was a lot of blood and didn't think he was alive. Along with my partner, I received the call over dispatch at 8.30am, and we arrived at the property at 8.40am. The EMTs arrived five minutes before us and informed us that the man was deceased. Due to the blood loss, it was obvious to everyone that he wasn't alive."

"What did you do at that point?"

"Like any death we're called to attend, we established an investigation. We sealed off the surrounding area and looked at the possible causes of death. We took photos of the area and interviewed anyone who was around at the time."

"And who did you interview?"

"Firstly, we interviewed Senator Richard Longhouse. He was the person who found the body. He said he'd arrived back at the property and saw the body on the ground as he drove into his driveway. He said he ran to the body, and his instincts kicked in. He tried to place pressure on the man's neck to stop the bleeding, but it became obvious the man was dead. That's when Senator Longhouse called 911. When we arrived at the scene, Senator Longhouse had a lot of blood on his hands and clothes, which we found consistent with his story. The poor guy was covered in blood and quite upset."

"Was it icy at the time you arrived?"

"You can see from the body-cam footage and the photos that there's ice on the ground."

Hennessy introduced photos of the scene into evidence. Copies of the photos were handed to the jurors. "And are these the photos you took of the event?"

"That's correct." Brooks shifted in his seat again. "As you can see, the EMTs had covered the body by the time we were taking photos, but you can still see the blood on the nearby grass. It was quite a mess. It appeared that he fell, then the chainsaw fell on top of him, and he struggled for a few moments, trying to crawl toward the house. It was quite a confronting scene."

"And in the fifth photo," Hennessy typed into his laptop, and the photo appeared on the monitor screen at the side of the room. "Is this the ladder that Mr. Santos slipped off?"

"That's correct."

"And is there ice on the rungs of the ladder?"

"That's what we noticed as well. There was ice on the rungs of the ladder, and we concluded that this is what most likely caused him to slip off. You can see that he started to cut a branch on the tree to the left of the ladder. From our initial investigation, we thought he hit a knot in the tree, slipped, lost control, and fell to the ground. He would've still had the chainsaw in his hand when he hit the ground."

"Was it obvious to you that the grounds were icy?"

"That's right."

Hennessy nodded and took the photo off the screen. He didn't show any photos of George Santos after his death, as the images were extremely confronting. The cut from the chainsaw was wide, and the jury didn't need to see that.

For twenty-five minutes, Hennessy took Brooks through the photos he'd taken of the scene. They reviewed the location of the ladder and where Longhouse had stored the ladder outside overnight. They reviewed the photos that showed frost on the ground and ice on the windows. And they reviewed photos showing the location of the body. When the facts were established, Hennessy flipped over a page on his desk and continued. "And did you ask surrounding properties if they had surveillance footage that pointed toward the defendant's property?"

"We did. It appeared that one of the neighboring homes might've had a camera angle on the area where the incident occurred, but they informed us the cameras hadn't worked for a while and were more of a deterrent than a security measure."

Hennessy squinted. "That isn't in the police report on Mr. Santos' death. Why was that not included?"

Brooks shifted his weight to the other side of the chair. "The report mentions that we asked the neighbors if they saw anything. There was no need to go into any more detail than that."

"And which neighbor was that?"

"The Moore household."

Hennessy froze for a moment, before grabbing his notepad and writing several lines. When he was finished, he turned his attention back to the defendant. "And had you met Mr. Longhouse before that day?"

"Objection," Brockman called out. "Relevance."

"Your Honor, I'm establishing if there was any personal link between the detective and the defendant."

"The objection is overruled for the moment, however, don't stray too far into the personal relationship without due cause." Judge Griffin was cautious. "You may answer the question, Detective Brooks."

"I'd met him before, yes."

"And have you investigated previous deaths on the Longhouse property?"

"Objection," Brockman jumped to his feet. "There's no relevance to this case with any past events."

"Your Honor," Hennessy argued. "We're merely trying to establish the facts in this case, and the detective can provide those facts."

"The objection is overruled for the moment. However, don't stray into hearsay, Mr. Hennessy," Judge Griffin stated. "Please answer the question, Mr. Brooks."

"Five years ago, we investigated the death of a housekeeper on the property. In that instance, we determined she'd died from natural causes. The coroner later confirmed this."

Hennessy nodded, and for the next fifty-five minutes, he asked question after question about the day of George Santos' death and the subsequent investigation. Every question had a direct answer, but Brockman objected where he could. As the lead investigator into the crime, Brooks introduced most of the hard evidence to the court. After the facts of the scene were established, Hennessy finished his questioning.

"Your witness, Mr. Brockman," Judge Griffin said.

Brockman took his time reviewing his notes before he stood and walked to the lectern. "Detective Brooks, can you please tell the court if you investigated if the ladder had been tampered with?"

"We did."

"And was there any sign the ladder was tampered with?"

"No, there was not."

"Was there any sign that the scene was tampered with?"

"No."

"And was there any sign that the chainsaw had been tampered with?"

"No."

"Was there any sign that the tree had been tampered with to increase his chances of falling?"

"No."

"Was there any sign that Mr. Santos' body had been interfered with after his death?"

"No."

"And in your professional opinion, with years of investigations into these sorts of occurrences, was there any chance that this was something other than a tragic accident?"

"No."

"No chance at all?"

"None."

"Thank you for your time." Brockman returned to his desk, having done damage with only a few questions. "Nothing further."

CHAPTER 48

Over the coming days, Hennessy called witness after witness, and they all delivered as expected.

The testimony of the bloodstain pattern analysis expert, Mr. Michael Turro, went as predicted. Yes, the blood stains were consistent with a chainsaw injury. No, there was no evidence of foul play. Yes, the blood would've sprayed quite far. All very precise and comprehensive. Forensic expert, Miss Julia Sha, spoke about the scene. Yes, Mr. Santos moved after the chainsaw cut his neck. Yes, his movements were consistent with someone who had sustained this type of injury. No, there was no evidence of anyone else at the scene. Construction workplace safety expert, Mr. Michael Starr, was next. Yes, the ladder had ice on it. Yes, it was enough ice to cause a person to slip. No, there was no evidence of foul play.

After days of experts and specialists building his case full of facts, Hennessy turned his attention to the character witnesses.

The first character witness, former colleague Mr. Raymond Sullivan, spoke well. Yes, Mr. Santos was meticulous in his preparation. No, he never took risks. Yes, he would trust his life in the hands of Mr. Santos. Next-door neighbor Mr. Harrison McVeigh was equally as well-spoken. Yes, Mr. Santos had worked in his garden. No, he'd never seen Mr. Santos take any risks. Yes, Mr. Santos was always very well-prepared for the job.

By day five of the civil trial, Hennessy's case was building nicely.

Longhouse barely moved or said a word during the days of testimony. He whispered occasionally to his lawyers, but mostly, he was on his best behavior. He knew the reporters were watching him, waiting for him to break and give them something interesting to write about. He deliberately gave them nothing. His tactic had worked. By Friday morning, only one reporter returned to the courtroom. The story had faded from the papers, and Longhouse wanted to keep it that way.

Hennessy called Antonio Smith to start the fifth day. Even under the pressure of the courtroom,

Antonio Smith appeared relaxed as he swore his oath. There was an innocence to his smile. He looked unfazed by the world, unfazed by life, and unfazed by the court. He wore a checkered shirt with blue jeans and a large belt buckle.

"Mr. Smith, thank you for coming to court to testify. I understand that this must be hard for you. Can you please tell the court how long you had worked alongside Mr. Santos?"

The man needed no time to think. "Five years."

"And did you enjoy working with Mr. Santos?"

"That's an understatement," Smith said. "I enjoyed each and every day working with George. He was the kind of colleague you could call a friend for life."

"And during those years, how would you describe Mr. Santos as a worker?"

Again, no pause to think. "If I had to choose just a single word, I'd say meticulous. George maintained a level of safety that I'd never seen before or since." Smith looked across the courtroom. "Many might assume our job is relatively safe, given we spend our days in people's gardens, but it can be very dangerous. With the types of tools we work with, as well as some unpredictable situations."

"Could you name one of those situations?"

"Excess wind blowing trees over. Sometimes, the trees don't fall all the way to the ground, and we have to go in with chainsaws to try and clear things up."

"Have you ever injured yourself during such a situation?"

"I did, about a decade ago," Smith said. "A tree fell on my leg and broke my ankle in five places."

"When you say meticulous about Mr. Santos, could you elaborate?"

"The man spent more time ensuring the safety of himself and others than he did on an actual job."

"And Mr. Smith, can you please tell the court if you have ever worked for Mr. Longhouse?"

"I worked for Mr. Longhouse on the same property before George. I was employed there as a gardener around five years ago, but I left after one year."

"And why did you leave?"

"Because of the way Mr. Longhouse treated me. I'm an independent contractor, so I go around doing jobs on people's gardens. I'm my own boss, and I like it that way. I don't have to answer to anyone, and I get to make my own decisions. But working for Mr.

Longhouse was different. He wanted me there at 8am, not a second later, and even if I finished the work, I wasn't to leave before 4pm. I was just another employee for him."

"Were you an employee or an independent contractor?"

"I was paid as an independent contractor, but it was clear I was an employee. I had no choice over how things were done on the property. If grass needed cutting, Mr. Longhouse would tell me how. I would start using the riding lawnmower, but he would stop me and tell me to do it with the push lawnmower. If trees needed cutting, he would tell me how to cut them and what to use. It was very frustrating. By every definition, I was treated as an employee, but without the benefits. He paid me as an independent contractor, but it wasn't right. We had a dispute about it, and then he told me not to return."

"Can you give us another example of those work directives?"

"There was one time when I finished the job at about three o'clock. I'd done everything I needed to, and I was packing up to leave. Mr. Longhouse saw me, came out of the home, and said I had to stay until

4pm. He said if I wanted to get paid, I had to go inside and help the housekeeper. I thought he was joking, but he wasn't. So, I went inside and helped her."

Over the next hour, Hennessy drilled into the workflow of Mr. Smith's employment at the Longhouse property. He found five different ways to ask the same question over and over again. When he was sure the jury understood that Mr. Smith was paid as an independent contractor but treated like an employee, he turned the witness over.

Brockman stood but remained behind his table. "Mr. Smith, how long would you say it's been since you last directly worked alongside Mr. Santos?"

Smith looked up as he thought about the time. "Two years."

"And given what you know of the man, would you say it's possible his safety standards could have slipped in any way?"

"Objection," Hennessy interrupted. "Speculation."

"Sustained," Judge Griffin said almost immediately.

"Ok," Brockman whispered under his breath before raising his voice again. "Let me try this. How do you think Mr. Santos felt when Mr. Longhouse treated him like an employee?"

"Objection to the word 'felt,'" Hennessy said. "It asks the witness to speculate."

"Sustained," Judge Griffin said. "Please choose your words more carefully, Mr. Brockman."

"Yes, yes, Your Honor," Brockman tapped his hand on the table in front of him. "Mr. Smith, what do you consider he was—"

"Objection to the word 'consider.' Again, it calls for speculation."

"Again, the objection is sustained."

"Ok, ok," Brockman whispered under his breath. He composed himself and looked at the witness. "How did it seem—"

"Objection to the word 'seem.' It calls for the witness to characterize the events."

"Sustained," Judge Griffin agreed. "Mr. Brockman, the witness is allowed to talk about what they know but is not to make assumptions or characterizations. Please choose your words more carefully."

Frustrated, Brockman offered a fake smile to the judge and then waved his hand at the witness. "No further questions."

CHAPTER 49

After lunch on Friday, Hennessy called his last witness of the first week. "We call Brittany Howell to the stand, Your Honor."

As Brittany Howell walked through the doors, nobody looked at her. They seemed disinterested. She was a small brunette woman in her thirties with an average build and an average appearance. She wore regular clothes, jeans and a shirt, and her make-up was pleasantly done but not noticeable.

The bailiff went through the routine of swearing her in, and once done, Miss Howell turned her attention to Hennessy. He looked down at his paperwork for a last time, then stood and walked closer to the witness stand as he thanked her for making the effort to come to court.

"Miss Howell, could you tell the court if you recognize the man sitting next to his team of lawyers over there?"

"Yes, that's Senator Richard Longhouse."

"And how do you know the Senator?"

"I worked for him as a housekeeper at his property on Ashley River Road."

"Could you tell us how long you worked for Senator Longhouse?"

"Around five years," she replied. "But I haven't worked there over the past twelve months."

"And how would you describe working for Mr. Longhouse?"

"The best word to describe the experience would be unprofessional."

"Unprofessional? Can you please expand on that?"

"He was mean to us and often swore and shouted at all his staff. Everyone was required to be on call at a moment's notice. You could never relax at that job. If he saw you take a moment, even if you were eating lunch, he'd tell you off for being lazy. He'd yell at us, throw things on the ground just so we had to clean it up, and be very rude."

"Did you ever find yourself in an uncomfortable situation with Mr. Longhouse?"

"Yes, once, when he tried to kiss me."

"Objection. Relevance."

"She's allowed to testify about the truth of her working conditions," Hennessy responded. "This speaks to the conditions of employment."

"Agreed. The objection is overruled," Judge Griffin responded. "You may continue."

"Mr. Longhouse tried to kiss you. What did you say?"

"I told him I was married and didn't want him to kiss me."

"How did he react to that response?"

"He tipped his glass of red wine on the carpet and told me to clean it up."

One member of the jury gasped.

"Is that the worst thing that happened while you worked there?" Hennessy continued.

Another pause. "No... no, there was another incident."

"What sort of incident?"

"One of the junior housekeepers, Sofia Ortez, was found dead in Mr. Longhouse's bedroom. She was only twenty-five."

Another gasp rose from the gallery and seemed to strengthen into a rumble of voices washing across the crowd. Judge Griffin struck her gavel several times to bring the crowd back under control.

"Could you elaborate for us?"

"It happened about five years ago. At the time, rumors swirled about Richard and her—"

"Objection." Brockman leaped to his feet. "Rumors are speculation and don't have a place in this courtroom."

"Sustained," Judge Griffin agreed. "Miss Howell, please only talk about the facts as you know them, and don't reference any rumors."

Brittany Howell nodded.

"Miss Howell," Hennessy continued. "Where in the bedroom was the body found?"

"Objection," Brockman interjected again. "Relevance. The police report into that death clearly stated that the person died of natural causes, and the location of the body has no relevance to this case."

"Again, I agree with the defense," Judge Griffin stated. "The objection is sustained."

Hennessy spent the next twenty-five minutes asking more questions about the working conditions on the Longhouse property. All the women on the jury shook their heads when Howell stated that Longhouse had patted her bottom many times. When it was clear that working for Longhouse was unprofessional, Hennessy finished his questioning.

"Thank you, Miss Howell," Hennessy said. "At this time, we have no further questions."

When instructed to begin by Judge Griffin, Brockman took more than a minute before he turned his attention to the witness.

"Miss Howell, isn't it true that the investigating officers interviewed the entire staff at the time of the death of Miss Ortez?"

"Yes, that's true."

"And two staff multiple times, you included, I believe?"

"Yes, I spoke twice with them."

"And according to subsequent reports, the officers uncovered that the deceased had a criminal record, did she not?"

"I wouldn't know."

"Well, we can pull the report, if you like, but from what I've been told, two counts of possession, a fact she withheld from her employer."

"Again, I wouldn't know," Howell repeated.

"Did you know she died of a heart attack?"

"That's what we were told."

"Do you know what effect drugs have on the heart?"

"Objection," Hennessy stated. "The witness is not qualified to answer that question."

"Sustained. Move on, Mr. Brockman."

For fifty-five minutes, Brockman drilled Brittany Howell about her time working for Longhouse. Brockman was attempting to make Miss Howell look like an unstable witness, a person who couldn't be trusted, but his intense questioning had the opposite effect. He looked like a bully. A courtroom thug. A man in power picking on a timid woman. Miss Howell shed some tears, but Brockman didn't care. He pushed forward, oblivious that he was destroying his own case.

Hennessy tried to help her where he could, objecting at every opportunity, but he could do little. When Brockman finished, Howell wiped her cheeks with a tissue.

"Redirect, Mr. Hennessy?"

"Two questions," Hennessy responded. "Miss Howell, were you surprised by the death of Miss Ortez?"

"Yes. She was a perfectly healthy woman."

"And do you believe Miss Ortez would've died if she didn't work for Mr. Longhouse?"

"Objection!" Brockman shouted. "That's speculation."

"Withdrawn," Hennessy said, but by the look of shock on some of the jurors' faces, the question had the required impact. "No further questions."

CHAPTER 50

The following week, Hennessy kept piling on the indisputable facts of the case, leaving little doubt that George Santos had died as the result of the fall from the icy ladder.

Crime scene experts testified about the details of the property. Chainsaw experts testified about every aspect of the equipment. And more workplace safety experts talked about the lack of safety equipment provided to Mr. Santos. By the time they arrived at the court on the second Friday morning, the jury was clear about how the scene looked, what type of person George Santos had been, and what had happened in that tragic moment.

There was only one thing left to dispute—who was responsible for ensuring George Santos' safety.

After two weeks of presenting witnesses and arguing, Hennessy only had one more witness to call. One more chance to seal the deal. His star witness to consolidate everything.

On the second Friday morning, Hennessy stood. "Your Honor, we call Mr. Jacob Aster."

Jacob Aster walked to the stand with his chin held high and his chest out. In his fifties, his shoulders reached for his ears, tense under the focus of the court. He wore clean black pants, a white shirt, and an expensive gold watch. He entered the courtroom, watched by almost every set of eyes, the silence almost unnerving as the only sound came from the man's boots on the tiles. He took his seat on the witness stand and was subsequently sworn in by the bailiff.

One reporter in the crowd was taking notes on his notepad, and another was flicking through her cell. Five more people entered the courtroom, sliding into the back row, trying to make as little sound as possible. The gallery was full, and the tension was high.

"Thank you for testifying, Mr. Aster." Hennessy began seated behind his desk. "Can you please begin by confirming your name and your occupation?"

"My name is Jacob Aster, and I'm employed in the Federal   Occupational   Safety   and   Health

Administration as an OSHA specialist. I've had this role for the past five years, and prior to that, I was employed by the South Carolina Occupational Safety and Health Administration. In total, I've spent twenty years working with the OSHA."

"And what does an OSHA specialist do?"

"This means I go to work sites to analyze whether a site is adhering to safety regulations. Part of my role in the South Carolina Occupational Safety and Health Administration was as an investigator. Unfortunately, part of that job was to analyze workplace accidents and sometimes deaths."

"Did you analyze the scene of Mr. Santos' death?"

"No, however, I have reviewed the reports of the scene."

"What was the first thing that stood out from the report?"

"The lack of fall protection at the scene."

"And what is fall protection?"

"In OSHA literature, there's a definition of the 'Big Four' working hazards. One of those 'Big Four' hazards are falls."

"Can you please define further?"

"The OSHA states that regardless of the fall

distance, fall protection must also be provided when working with dangerous equipment, such as chainsaws. Similarly, the employer must ensure that contractors have the correct tools for the job, such as ladders, and the employer must maintain this equipment properly. The OSHA regulations state that portable ladders should be checked routinely to ensure they're free of faults." Aster shifted in his seat as he caught Maria's eyes. "There must be adequate fall protection, whether by railings or a personal fall protection system, such as a harness. Any ladder must be positioned so that it's steady on even ground, and the ladder should be checked before use to ensure it's free of defects or damage."

"Interesting." Hennessy rose to his feet and moved to the lectern. "And from reviewing the report on Mr. Santos' death, could you see if this fall protection was provided to Mr. Santos?"

"It was not."

"And," Hennessy paused for impact. He looked to the jury, who were all paying attention. "Can you please tell the court who was responsible for providing the safety requirements?"

"I've reviewed the work situation for Mr. Santos.

Given that he attended the same property two days every week for several years, it's clear that while Mr. Santos was being paid as an independent contractor, he was performing his duties in line with someone who should've been classed as an employee."

"And how does the OSHA regulations come to that conclusion?"

"It's clear in the regulations what makes an independent contractor, and while there are several things to look at, the most critical is the work process. When you hire a true independent contractor, you request a specific outcome. You can specify what result is acceptable and what's not. The contractor then applies their expertise to arrive at the end result. If you employ an independent contractor, you don't get to dictate their process. If you dictate someone's work process, you control their safety. It's that simple. If you dictate someone's work process, the OSHA regulations have to be followed. If safety violations occur, the OSHA will use the Economic Reality Test, which considers the crucial nature of workflow control. The less control the independent contractor has over their work, the more responsible an employer becomes."

"Are you aware of the IRS definition of an independent contractor?"

"Yes, we often refer to the IRS definition in our reports. The IRS states an individual is an independent contractor if the payer has the right to control or direct only the result of the work. Given this definition, it's clear Mr. Santos was not an independent contractor and should've been classed as an employee."

"And given Mr. Santos had no control to dictate his work process, how would he be classed under the IRS definition?"

"Although he was paid as an independent contractor, it's clear he was an employee."

"Given that he should've been defined as an employee, who was responsible for providing the safety equipment?"

"According to the OSHA regulations, the fall protection should've been provided by the employer, who in this instance was the owner of the property."

"The owner of the property," Hennessy repeated. "And in your report, did you state that Mr. Longhouse had provided this fall protection anywhere?"

"There was no evidence that Mr. Longhouse provided the required fall protection."

"And who was responsible for the ladder?"

"By OSHA standards, it's the employer's responsibility to ensure proper safety gear and training of the employee."

For the next three hours and forty-five minutes, Hennessy fired out question after question, drilling into the jury that although George Santos was paid as an independent contractor, his workflow indicated he should've been an employee.

"Thank you, Mr. Aster." Hennessy looked at the jury. The front row of the jury were all nodding. "No further questions."

Brockman stood. "Mr. Aster, did you see Mr. Santos fall from the ladder?"

"What a ridiculous question. No, I didn't."

"There's no need for commentary, Mr. Aster," Brockman noted. "Are you aware if Mr. Santos lodged a 1099-Non-Employee Compensation form with the IRS?"

"Yes, but receiving a 1099-NEC doesn't make you an independent contractor. The Department of Labor has stated that misclassifying employees as independent contractors is a major issue nationwide. The OSHA regulations and the IRS clearly define the standards for defining an employer-employee relationship."

Irritated, Brockman exhaled loudly and turned back to the defense table and waved the witness away. "No further questions."

"Redirect?"

"Thank you, Your Honor." Hennessy stood again. "Mr. Aster, despite his wealth and social status, is Mr. Longhouse above the law?"

"Nobody is above the OSHA regulations."

"No further questions." Hennessy looked to the jury, and when he saw several heads nod, he turned to the judge. "We rest our case, Your Honor."

Hennessy smiled. He was winning. Justice was coming.

CHAPTER 51

Hennessy walked deep in thought, hands tucked into his pockets, smile on his face, taking in the Saturday morning sunshine as it spread across Colonial Lake.

Tucked into a residential section of the Charleston peninsula, Colonial Lake was a locals' retreat—away from the tourist destinations, where local residents enjoyed jogging, walking, or strolling around its half-mile distance. Created in 1881, Colonial Lake Park was a place where people could daydream, relax, and generally feel happy. The calm landscape was beautiful and well-tended, with the scents of jasmine and pink wisteria floating all around.

Hennessy felt better than he had in a long time. Not only was his mood reminiscent of the morning sun hanging in the sky, but his confidence had returned. He was winning. If they finished strong, the media couldn't ignore the story anymore. It would be over for Longhouse.

He spoke to Maria and her family for a long time after court on Friday afternoon. They were happy that George was about to get justice.

And for the first time in months, the tension had eased from his shoulders.

"I thought you'd come back," a voice called out from a bench as he passed. "Second lap?"

Hennessy looked up and saw Brenda Moore sitting on one of the park benches. She was dressed casually in sports clothes, like she was ready to run a lap of the lake.

"Good morning, Brenda." Hennessy was cautious as he approached.

"I need some lawyerly advice, Mr. Hennessy." She stood and walked beside the tall lawyer. "And you're a lawyer."

Hennessy kept walking, waiting for her to continue.

"You said an NDA can be broken, but you never finished the sentence. When can it be broken?"

Hennessy looked over his shoulder, and when he saw no one was following, he answered. "It can be broken for several reasons, including criminal activity.

Any criminal activity voids an NDA."

"Well." She looked around as well. "I need to break an NDA."

"Go on."

"This is an interesting meeting," a voice stated ahead of them.

Hennessy looked up. "Detective David Farina."

"I hope this is just a coincidence that you two know each other." Farina hitched his pants up as he walked closer. He eyed Brenda Moore. "I hope you just accidentally bumped into each other."

Brenda avoided eye contact with Farina, looking at the ground instead. "Just a coincidence," she mumbled, not looking at him. "I was going for a jog and ran into Mr. Hennessy here. We've met before, and I thought I'd say hello. I'm a single woman and he's a very handsome man. There's nothing wrong with that."

Farina grunted and looked at Hennessy. "Is that right?"

Brenda looked at Hennessy. "I've got to go." She stepped forward and began to jog, pretending to start her watch.

Hennessy watched her jog away before he turned

back to Farina. "What's going on here?"

"I've got nothing to say to you." Farina turned away and started walking back to the street.

"You're following her, aren't you?" Hennessy called out. "Why?"

Farina didn't look back.

Confusion set in for Hennessy. He looked at Brenda, who was a hundred yards away and then back to Farina, who was walking toward his dark sedan.

Hennessy completed the remaining part of the walk and then returned to his apartment in confusion. He didn't see Brenda Moore or David Farina on the walk again.

When he arrived back at his apartment, he poured a coffee and sat on the front porch, looking out to the view of the park nearby.

He tried to call Brenda, but there was no answer. He left a message, but he doubted she would return the call. She was scared of Farina. There was fear in her eyes when he arrived.

At midday, he began the journey to his office. He stopped at Sabatino's for lunch, picked up a large pepperoni pizza, and a bottle of Coke. For Joe, it was the best pizza in the state. Together with his laptop, he didn't need anything else for the afternoon. With a slice of pizza in one hand, he reviewed the depositions given by the potential upcoming defense witnesses.

Late in the afternoon with half the pizza gone, Hennessy was leaning against the back of his chair, Coke can in hand, when his cell rang. He pulled it out of his pocket and answered it.

The moment he heard the voice on the other end, his heart sank.

"I'm sorry, Joe," Nicki Chang said. "They came in here with a subpoena. Two lawyers and a cop. I tried to stop them, but there was nothing I could do. I'm so sorry."

"What did they take?"

"They took the water bottle and the reports. I told them that the reports weren't finalized, but they took it all anyway."

"Thank you for letting me know." Hennessy hung up the phone and dropped his head.

In the space of one phone call, his chances of winning the civil trial had dived to almost zero.

CHAPTER 52

Hennessy couldn't sleep again.

He woke with a start, sitting bolt upright as drops of sweat shot from his brow. He rubbed his eyes, a thumping headache already in the works as he felt the familiar pain behind his right eye. Knowing time was of the essence if he wanted a chance at suppressing the headache before it took hold, he went to the bathroom and prioritized painkillers. He poured three caplets from the bottle, looked at them questioningly, then added a fourth, popped them in his mouth, and swallowed with the help of a glass of water.

The drive through the Sunday morning traffic didn't provide any reprieve from the storm churning up his head, with bumper-to-bumper traffic courtesy of Charleston churchgoers. On a Sunday in Charleston, it was nearly impossible to go for more than fifteen minutes without hearing a church bell ring. The bells chimed all Sunday long. As he approached his office, he passed people in the street dressed in their Sunday best—suits and bowties for the men, dresses and hats for the women. Proud families gathered on the steps outside the many churches of the Holy City, greeting each other with smiles and hugs.

Hennessy didn't have time for them. He raced past the churches and around the streets toward his office. He parked on the street and was met by Lockett.

"Geez, Joe, you look terrible," Lockett said as he greeted him on the street outside his building. "Did you sleep at all?"

"Didn't sleep a wink," he said as he unlocked the building. "And I can always trust an Aussie to be charming."

Jacinta's car pulled up to the sidewalk, and she jumped out without hesitating. "What's so urgent this morning?" she asked as she approached.

"We'll talk inside." Hennessy led them through the building and into the boardroom. "We have a major problem," he said as he slumped into one of the chairs. "Nicki Chang phoned me late yesterday. Longhouse's lawyers subpoenaed the water bottle."

"And they've taken it?" Jacinta asked.

"They have."

"What does this mean for the case?"

"It means their case is going to target George as a drug user. With the evidence that there was ketamine in the water bottle, they'll say he was addicted to the drug and was under the drug's influence when he fell off the ladder, which legally lifts all responsibility from Longhouse. If he was using drugs while using a chainsaw, no amount of safety regulations will save us." Hennessy groaned. "Their media strategy makes a lot more sense now. They were always building to this."

"Can't you dispute the chain of evidence?"

"I will, but we'd had it tested and found the same results. The judge will take that into consideration."

"How do we fight it, then?"

"We could say that George had the ketamine in his shed," Lockett suggested. "That it fell into the water bottle after his death."

"That just plays into their hands." Hennessy shook his head. "Ketamine is a controlled schedule three drug. Why would a gardener have it in his shed unless he was using it for personal reasons? It's a good idea, but the jury will see straight through it."

Lockett stood and rubbed his hand over his head. "I thought we'd won it."

"So did I."

For the next five hours, they planned a new defense strategy. With the introduction of new evidence not mentioned in the defense's opening statement, they would have the chance to present rebuttal witnesses. That would be their chance to present a new strategy.

They considered calling Longhouse to the stand as a rebuttal witness. After discussing the strategy for an hour, Hennessy concluded, "We can do it, but it's a last resort. If it looks like we're going to lose, we'll call him as a rebuttal witness. We can say that Longhouse's statement to the police contradicted that George was a drug user. That's our way to get him on the stand."

"In his statement," Jacinta flicked open a file and read over the first page, "he said that 'George Santos was the best worker. The man was a model citizen.'"

"That's perfect." Hennessy looked at Lockett. "And there's something else."

"What is it?" Lockett asked.

"Brenda Moore tried to talk to me yesterday, but we were interrupted by David Farina. He was following her, and she was scared of him."

"Why?"

"I don't know." Hennessy tapped his finger on the table. "But I need you to find out why she signed an NDA. She could be the answer to all this."

CHAPTER 53

Hennessy broke the news to Maria in the morning.

She was shocked, angry, and upset. She'd never even heard of ketamine. She didn't even know what it was. George was no drug addict, she insisted. He barely drank alcohol. Never smoked. She demanded that she have the chance to take the stand and denounce such information, but Hennessy advised against it.

Longhouse drugged George because he tried to blackmail him, she stated. Hennessy explained that, although likely, they had no evidence of that and couldn't say it in court.

The anger radiated from her as they entered the courtroom on Monday morning.

Judge Griffin came to her seat, looking as angry about her job as she always did. "Before we bring the jury in, I see we have a motion to add a new witness. Care to explain, Mr. Brockman?"

"Yes, Your Honor." Brockman stood and held a report in his hand. "New information has come to us yesterday. As you can see by the date on this report, it was filed and completed only this morning after our team worked frantically all weekend."

Judge Griffin waved him forward. Brockman handed the report to the bailiff, who then gave it to the judge.

"Your Honor," Hennessy began. "We strongly oppose any new witnesses or evidence at this late point in the case. It severely disadvantages the plaintiff."

"That's ridiculous," Brockman argued. "The plaintiff has had access to this information for five months. Five months! They've known about this evidence all along, and in fact, we found this evidence in a private lab, undergoing testing requested by the plaintiff."

"Which wasn't completed," Hennessy retorted.

"Wasn't completed?" Brockman laughed. "Are you serious? You were trying to bury this information. You were trying to keep it out of the court case because it categorically disproves your case."

"That's outrageous," Hennessy raised his voice.

"We did no such thing."

"Gentleman," Judge Griffin called out, calming the situation. "Please keep it civil."

"We also have an objection based on the chain of evidence. There's simply no way to prove any substance entered any water bottle either before or after Mr. Santos' death."

"Your Honor, that's ludicrous. The chain of evidence is stated in the report you have in your hands. The evidence went from the police to the insurance company and then into the hands of the estate of Mr. Santos. If there's any change to the evidence, it must've been intentionally caused by the plaintiff."

"Agreed," Judge Griffin kept reading the report. "Regarding this new evidence, is it legitimate?"

"It is, Your Honor," Brockman responded. "The plaintiff paid a different forensic lab to assess the result and had the same preliminary results."

"Then, given the plaintiff already had access to this information, I will allow this new evidence." She closed the report and looked at the lawyers. "We'll recess for the morning while the plaintiff and her team reviews the new evidence, and then we'll reconvene after lunch."

After Judge Griffin left the room, Hennessy slumped down into his chair. He could feel his chance for justice slipping away.

Three hours later, the courtroom was already filling up with people. There was a buzz back in the air. The reporters had filled the side gallery again. Hennessy searched the crowd and saw Al Berry. Berry waved to him, smiling. Hennessy realized this was their plan all along, and he was sure the next day's headlines would exonerate Longhouse, long before the jury returned their decision.

When the buzz in the courtroom settled, Judge Griffin invited Brockman to call his first witness.

"The defense calls Ms. Fiona Finch."

Fiona Finch's dark hair was cropped short. The thirty-five-year-old had a nose ring and an earring in the left ear. She had enough tattoos on one arm to be considered a sleeve, and on the other, a long snake tattoo jutted out from beneath her short-sleeve white business shirt. As the crowd in the room watched the woman walk down the aisle, a low rumble of hushed voices seemed to follow her.

It took the bailiff just a few moments to swear the

witness in, and once finished, Brockman walked closer to her.

"Thank you for coming, Ms. Finch," Brockman began, and the woman gave him an acknowledging smile. "Would you mind stating your experience for the record?"

"Absolutely," Finch said. "My name is Fiona Finch, and I work as a lab technician in forensics. I began my career a little over ten years ago as a chemical engineer for Malcom Industries but moved into forensic science five years later. For the past five years, I've been employed as a forensic researcher, mostly focused on the medical industry."

"That's quite a resume for a young woman."

"Thank you. I've worked hard to get to where I am," Finch said as she looked at the jury.

"Ms. Finch, did you run any tests on the water bottle that was found in Mr. Santos' truck after his death?"

"I did."

Brockman used the opportunity to introduce the water bottle into evidence. "And what did you find in the water bottle?"

"We found a small amount of water, which we

tested. Firstly, we tested for alcohol, and the result came back negative. Next, we tested for amphetamines and depressants, and the result also came back negative. Thirdly, we tested for dissociative drugs and found a hit."

"Can you please tell the court what a dissociative drug is?"

"Dissociative drugs act on different chemicals in the brain to produce visual and auditory distortion and a detachment from reality. They're a subclass of hallucinogens, which include ketamine, phencyclidine, which is more commonly known as PCP, and nitrous oxide, which has a street name of nangs."

"And which of those dissociative drugs did you find a hit on?"

"We tested further and found a hit on the drug ketamine."

"To clarify, your testing showed traces of ketamine in the water bottle owned by Mr. Santos?"

"That's correct."

"Ms. Finch, can you please tell the court what ketamine is?"

"Ketamine is a dissociative anesthetic that has hallucinogenic effects. Used properly, it's a short-acting anesthetic used on humans and animals, and can induce a state of sedation, immobility, and ultimately, relief from pain. Unfortunately, it has also been used as a party drug. It's popular with the rave culture because it can distort a user's perception of sight and sound, making them feel disconnected from their body. It has many names, but the most popular terms are a 'Special K trip' or a 'K-hole.' It's popular because it makes users feel detached from their pain and environment."

"And what are the effects on the body when used recreationally?"

"Hallucinatory effects. For partygoers, it's considered better than LSD or PCP because its hallucinatory effects are relatively short in duration, lasting approximately 30 to 60 minutes, as opposed to several hours. Users report that they can see, hear, smell or taste things that don't exist, or can perceive them differently to how they really are."

"Sounds like quite a powerful drug," Brockman quipped. "Ms. Finch, can you please tell the court if you read the coroner's report on Mr. Santos' death?"

"I did."

"And can you please tell the court why there

would've been no traces of ketamine found in his system?"

"Ketamine has a short half-life within the bloodstream of around forty-five minutes. Mr. Santos could've still been under the influence of the effects at the time of his death, but it wouldn't have shown up on the testing."

"Interesting," Brockman noted. "And since your employment in the forensic field, how often would you come into contact with ketamine?"

"In South Carolina, we've seen a recent increase in the use of the drug by partygoers over the past five years."

Brockman continued for another fifty minutes, asking question after question about the drug and how it affected the human body. He repeated the word 'ketamine' as much as he could, drumming the word into the jurors' brains. When he was sure the jury was convinced, he ended the questioning with a sly grin.

Not wishing to make the situation any worse, Hennessy declined to cross-examine.

Next to him, he could feel Maria's heart break.

CHAPTER 54

The week went well for Longhouse and his team.

Since the presentation of the drug evidence, their case grew stronger. They framed their entire argument around the evidence of the ketamine found in the water bottle.

The testimony of another drug expert went even better. He talked about the impact that ketamine would have on climbing ladders. He stated that George Santos could've been thinking about anything when climbing the ladder. The witness said George could've thought he was a bird and the chainsaw was his lover. The jury laughed but stopped when they heard Maria sobbing.

Brockman lined up a procession of witnesses to consolidate the drug evidence, almost making it indisputable that George Santos was high on ketamine when he attempted to cut the tree branch. Chainsaw specialists talked about how nobody should ever use dangerous machinery under the influence of drugs.

During the week, Brockman used every opportunity to repeat the word 'ketamine,' having said it at least five hundred times.

Studying the jury, Hennessy saw several confused faces. Here was a man who was a good citizen, a good family man, a reputable member of society, taking a restricted substance such as ketamine. Something about the story didn't fit, and there were missing pieces to the puzzle.

Where was he getting it from? How did he afford it? How did an older man who barely drank alcohol get hooked on a raver drug?

Hennessy would target those questions when he had the chance to call rebuttal witnesses.

Hennessy continued to try and contact Brenda Moore. She didn't return his calls. He drove to her address and attempted to talk to her, but the gates were locked. As he looked for a way into the property, Detective Farina arrived. Hennessy questioned Farina, but the detective told him to get out of there. Hennessy went to push Farina, but Farina drew his gun. He yelled at Hennessy to go and not return. Reluctantly, he left.

Over the week, Hennessy drove past the property several times, but there was always a car parked opposite her driveway. She had a twenty-four-seven tail, sheltering her from any potential questions. Farina was protecting her, and he needed to know why.

The media ran with the drug-user story. They reported the case as a money-hungry drug-using family chasing a good Senator. They said a gardener who was high on drugs had fallen and cut himself with a chainsaw. With all the twists and turns of the Longhouse drama, people were hooked. There was talk of a documentary, perhaps even a television series. Public opinion sided with the lack of responsibility that Richard Longhouse had to take. So did the law. Even if he was an employee, the OSHA regulations were void if the worker was willingly under the influence of drugs.

The story of Longhouse's affair with Kathryn Moore morphed into something else. Some younger men called talkback radio and laughed that Longhouse was living the dream. Others called him a hero for all sugar daddies. His wife, Elise, was forgotten in the discussion.

Brockman ended the week with five character witnesses for Richard Longhouse. They spoke about his fundraising efforts and his eagerness to help better the community and aid those in need. They talked about his dedication to the state of South Carolina and how much his family had given over generations. They were proud to call him a friend, they all said.

Hennessy couldn't believe it, but somehow, someway, Richard Longhouse's reputation grew better with the court case.

After a week of evidence, Brockman rested the defense at 4:05pm on the third Friday of the trial. Judge Griffin called for a weekend recess and asked Hennessy to prepare any rebuttal witnesses.

The chance of justice was slipping away.

CHAPTER 55

Hennessy had had enough.

Late on Friday night, he stormed into the Vintage Lounge. The bar was full of patrons, mingling and laughing. He had no time for that. He looked for Kathryn Moore and spotted her behind the bar. He charged forward, leaning across the bar as she made a cocktail.

"Kathryn, I need to know why your mother signed the NDA."

"You again?" she raised one eyebrow. "Get lost, mister. I'm working."

"Kathryn, this is important. That sleaze deserves to go down. Why did your mother sign the NDA with Richard Longhouse?"

"I have no idea what you're talking about." She moved away, walking further down behind the bar.

Hennessy followed her. "Your mother signed an NDA with Richard Longhouse and then came into some money. That's not a coincidence."

"Ask her yourself," she scoffed as she grabbed a bottle behind the bar.

"I can't. People are stopping her from talking to me."

"And what am I supposed to do?"

"Talk to her for me. Convince her to come to my office. Tell her to talk to me and give me the truth."

The security guard, a burly six-foot-five thug dressed in a suit, approached and stood beside Hennessy. "Everything alright?"

Hennessy ignored him. "Kathryn," he stared at her. "This is your chance to stop that creep. Talk to your mother. Tell her to call me."

"Hey pal, Kathryn's busy." The security guard rested a hand on Hennessy's shoulder.

"Kathryn, please. Talk to your mother. Help her end this."

"Alright, pal. It's time to go."

Hennessy turned to the security guard. The guard removed his hand from Hennessy's shoulder and nodded toward the exit. Hennessy turned back to Kathryn, but she'd already moved on, focused on making the next drink. Feeling the chance had gone, he walked to the exit.

At the exit, he looked back and caught her eye. For a moment, he saw a vulnerable girl who had to do things she never wanted to. Then she turned away.

Hennessy walked out of the bar and back to his truck. Inside, he hit his steering wheel with the open palm of his hand. He hit it again. And again.

Longhouse had covered every base and every angle. He had money, power, and influence. He had connections on both sides of the law. He was the bully, laughing at the little people. He was the rich man patronizing the poor.

And Hennessy couldn't touch him.

CHAPTER 56

At 5:05am Saturday morning, Hennessy's cell rang.

"Joe Hennessy," the voice was shaky. "This is Brenda Moore. I'd like to meet you at your office. Farina isn't here right now, but I'm sure he'll return later today. I'm going to drive to your office now. If you're not there in twenty-five minutes, I'm leaving."

She ended the call without a response from Hennessy.

Hennessy jumped out of bed, put on his clothes, and grabbed his keys. He jumped in the truck, roared the engine, and raced to his office. Early on Saturday morning, with a city still bathed in darkness, the traffic was quiet. He parked on the street, and when he stepped out of his car, he saw Brenda and Kathryn standing in the shadows near the front door.

Hennessy greeted them and opened the office door. They followed him inside without a word between them. He could feel the nerves coming off them.

"Thank you for doing this," Hennessy said as he led them inside.

"No, thank you," Brenda said. "It's about time someone put that man in his place." She turned and looked at Kathryn. "I'm so sorry for not doing this sooner. I know I should have, but I was scared, and for that, I'm sure God will judge me in time."

Hennessy guided them to the boardroom and offered them a seat on one side while he sat two chairs down. "It's been quite hard to talk to you, Brenda."

"It's Farina, that detective from Beaufort. He won't let me out of his sight. He's going to be furious when he realizes we're not home this morning."

"Why doesn't he want you to talk?"

Brenda swallowed hard and looked at Kathryn. "I'll tell you everything, but you need to protect us until they're behind bars. Promise me you'll protect Kathryn and I."

"My investigator has a lot of contacts that can keep you hidden for a while." Hennessy nodded. "You said, 'behind bars.' Why do you think they'll end up there?"

"Because they killed him."

"Who?"

"The gardener."

"Who killed him?"

"Longhouse and Farina. They killed him."

Hennessy sat up straighter. "You witnessed them kill George Santos?"

"Better than that, I've got it on footage." She looked down. "That's what I signed the NDA for. $250,000 to delete the surveillance footage from the side of my house that overlooks the fence. I was asked to delete the footage and never speak of it."

"I didn't know." Kathryn stood and moved to the end of the room. She crossed her arms. "I thought we'd just come into money."

"I hated that he was paying Kathryn to sleep with him." Brenda's face scrunched up. "I hated it, but we'd lose the house otherwise."

"You knew?" Kathryn whispered.

"Of course, I knew. Where else would you be getting thousands from every week?" Brenda looked at her hands. "I appreciated that you wanted to save the house."

Kathryn didn't say anything, a blank look on her

face.

"I love you, Kathryn." She looked up at her daughter. "And it's time I stopped that evil man."

"You're an accessory to murder," Kathryn whispered, keeping her distance from her mother. "Why didn't you go to the police?"

"How could I go to the police?" Brenda pleaded with her arms out wide. "There's a cop in the footage. He's bought them all. They would've had me killed like him. I couldn't go to the police. I didn't want to die."

"What are we going to do now?" Fear washed over Kathryn's face. "You said this was bad, but I didn't know it would be this bad."

Brenda swallowed and turned her attention back to Hennessy. "Can you present this in court? That's the only way I can see us bypassing the police. I can put it in a public forum where it can't be taken back." She eyed Hennessy. "I can't trust the police, but I trust you."

"Do you still have the footage?" Hennessy asked.

She pulled out her cell, scrolled through her videos, and then showed Hennessy the footage.

It was a five-minute clip. No one said anything

while it played. After it was completed, Hennessy stood, shocked by what he'd just seen.

THE SOUTHERN TRIAL

CHAPTER 57

Lockett worked all weekend to hide the Moore family.

He drove them to Myrtle Beach in the back of an SUV rental, where he had a contact that would keep them safe. He stayed with them to ensure nothing went wrong.

Hennessy spotted Farina outside his office twice on Sunday, no doubt searching for Brenda Moore. When Farina realized they weren't home, his blood pressure would've just about exploded. When Hennessy drove to his apartment on Sunday night, he spotted Farina following him. Hennessy pulled up to his parking spot and exited the truck to confront Farina, but he drove past without stopping.

Brenda and Kathryn Moore returned to Charleston on Monday morning in the back of a different black SUV rental, complete with dark-tinted windows. Lockett drove them into the parking lot across from the courthouse, but they remained in the car's back seat, hidden from Longhouse and Farina, waiting for a call from Hennessy.

Hennessy's nerves were running high when Judge Griffin entered the courtroom. Longhouse looked agitated, and nervous. No doubt he'd spoken to Farina.

Judge Griffin came to her seat and read the note before her. "Before we bring the jury in, I see we have a motion for an additional witness. Care to explain, Mr. Hennessy?"

"Yes, Your Honor." Hennessy stood and looked at Longhouse. Longhouse didn't look back. "Due to the new information about the drug use presented in the defense case, we wish to add a rebuttal witness to dispute their claims." He picked up a file and passed it to the bailiff. The bailiff then passed it to the judge. He picked up a second copy and handed it to Brockman. "This new information came to us yesterday."

Brockman opened the first page, and shock swept across his face. Longhouse noticed and leaped to his feet. He looked over Brockman's shoulder, and his face went white. "No, no, no," Longhouse repeated.

"No, no, no."

"Your Honor," Brockman began. "We strongly oppose any new witnesses at this late point in the case. It severely disadvantages the defense. These claims are outrageous. They're…" he stumbled over his words. "They're…"

Judge Griffin squinted and looked at Hennessy. "There's evidence from the surveillance footage from the house next door?"

"That's correct, Your Honor. In the folder, there are copies of the still photos taken from the footage. The footage clearly identifies Mr. Longhouse at the scene of the crime at the time of death."

"No, no, no," Longhouse stated. "No!" He slammed his fist on the table. "These claims are the subject of a non-disclosure agreement."

"Which is null and void because it involves criminal activity," Hennessy responded. "As you see in the folder, Your Honor, the NDA also forms part of the evidence against the defendant."

"Your Honor," Brockman argued, the panic setting in. "These claims are offensive. We cannot possibly air them in court. This… this… this… is outside the scope of the civil suit."

"I argue it's not, Your Honor. This civil suit is for the wrongful death of George Santos, and now we have evidence that Mr. Longhouse was more than involved in his death."

Judge Griffin put the file down and leaned back in her chair. She rocked on her chair for a moment. "Have you contacted the police over these claims, Mr. Hennessy?"

"We sent the evidence to them this morning."

Longhouse's head snapped toward Hennessy. His mouth was hanging open, shocked at the developments.

"Well, given the gravity of this evidence, we're going to recess for two hours so that the defense can review the new information. After that time, we'll have another hearing to discuss whether this new evidence can be submitted in this case. If the defense needs more time to prepare, given the gravity of the evidence, I'm willing to allow that to happen. I expect you both to have arguments prepared for that."

Judge Griffin tapped her gavel and exited the room.

Hennessy looked across to Longhouse.

"You're dead." Longhouse's teeth grit together.

He pointed his finger at Hennessy. "You hear me? You're dead!"

A bailiff stepped forward while Brockman tried to hold his client back.

"Where is she?!" Longhouse yelled. "Tell me where she is!"

The bailiff stepped between Longhouse and the plaintiff's table. Hennessy remained standing, unfazed by Longhouse's aggression.

Al Berry leaned across the bar and told Brockman they needed to prepare a response. Quickly, Brockman and Minton shuffled out of the room, followed closely by Longhouse and Berry.

Hennessy looked at Maria. "We got him."

CHAPTER 58

For the next two hours, Maria Santos sat on one side of the table in the courthouse conference room, while her burly sons stood next to the wall. The air conditioner above their heads pumped in cold air, providing a calm background noise to the tension. The long wooden table that occupied most of the space was spotless and recently cleaned. The walls were white, the chairs were leather, and framed photos of Charleston hung on the walls. The smell of coffee filled the air.

"Why does this take so long?" Maria asked. Her coffee was untouched. "Minutes feel like hours in here."

"Longhouse is falling apart right now." Hennessy was calm. "We should allow them to take all the time they need. The surveillance footage from the roof of the two-story house next door looks over the fence and into the yard of the Longhouse property. In the top of the footage, it clearly shows Detective Farina goes to George's truck and takes out a water bottle at 8am. At 8.05, Farina gives George the water bottle and Longhouse is also there. George takes a drink and then they walk off. What happens next is outside the frame, but there's no doubt both were present at the time of death."

"Did he even climb the ladder?" Maria's voice was shaky.

"Given the bruise on the back of his head, we think so. I would suggest that he had the drink, and once Farina and Longhouse saw the effects of ketamine start to take hold, they told him to climb the ladder and cut a branch."

"Longhouse pushed the ladder over, didn't he?"

"Only Farina and Longhouse know what happened there." Hennessy paused. "But I would assume they pushed the ladder over."

"The chainsaw didn't fall on him, did it? He fell, and they cut him with it, right?"

"We can't prove that, but that appears to be the case."

"What happens now?"

Hennessy looked at his watch. "We've given the

surveillance footage, the NDA, and the witness statements to the police, and they'll assess it before they make an arrest. I contacted Chief Myers this morning, but he warned me that given the people involved in the accusations, it won't be a quick process. They will want to get this right."

"He killed our father?" one son asked.

"It appears so."

The second son clenched both his fists and punched the wall lightly. "I'll kill him myself."

"No," Maria scolded him. "You have your children to think about. This is what we wanted. Justice. We've got it now. Just be patient."

Hennessy agreed before he excused himself and walked through the hallway until he came to the meeting room five doors down. He knocked. Barry Lockett opened the door slowly, and when he saw Hennessy, he stepped aside. Jacinta sat on one side of the table. Brenda and Kathryn Moore sat on the other.

They looked worried.

"What's he doing now?" Brenda asked.

"Hopefully, falling apart," Hennessy responded. "But you're safe in here. And now that the footage has been submitted to the court and the police, there's no wiping it from existence. It's on the public record. There's no way Longhouse can buy himself out of this one."

"And the other cop?" Kathryn asked. She looked pale and washed out. "Where's he?"

"Hopefully, about to be arrested," Jacinta said.

Kathryn looked at Lockett. "Can you please stay with us until he is?"

"Of course," Lockett said. "Don't worry. You're safe here."

Hennessy checked his watch. It was two hours after the recess. He drew a breath, thanked Brenda and Kathryn, and exited, walking toward the courtroom. Jacinta followed.

Maria was already seated at the table in the courtroom, awaiting her moment of justice. The sons stood at the side of the room, unable to control their rage enough to sit down. Hennessy stepped through the gate and checked his watch again. It was five minutes past the scheduled court time, but the defense table remained empty.

They sat and waited for another ten minutes, but there was no sign of the defense team.

Fifteen minutes late, Brockman arrived first with a worried look. Minton came next, also pale. Al Berry entered the courtroom next.

They waited for Longhouse to arrive. He didn't.

Hennessy asked Brockman where Longhouse was, but Brockman blanked him. He didn't say a word.

The bailiff checked the lawyers had arrived and then called the room to order. Judge Griffin entered and squinted when she didn't see Longhouse at the defense table. She sat down and turned her attention to Brockman.

"Where's your client, Mr. Brockman?"

"Your Honor," Brockman stood and drew a deep breath. "At this time, we're not sure where he is."

"What do you mean?"

"He left to grab a bite to eat, and we've been trying to reach him since." Brockman looked at Minton. "We're concerned for his welfare."

"Have you notified the police for a welfare check?"

"We were waiting to see if he showed up to court in time, but we will do that right away, Your Honor."

"Considering the circumstances, we're going to recess until you locate your client, Mr. Brockman."

Judge Griffin was firm. "I want regular updates, understood?"

"Yes, Your Honor," Brockman responded, standing as Judge Griffin exited. Once she had left, he raced back out the doors, followed closely by Minton and Berry.

"Where is he?" Maria asked.

"I don't know, Maria."

Hennessy turned and looked at Jacinta. He nodded toward the exit, and Jacinta agreed. Once out the doors, Jacinta whispered to Hennessy. "Think he's going to end it all himself?"

"No, he won't do that. He's too arrogant for that," Hennessy said as they hurried toward the room with Brenda, Kathryn, and Lockett. "He knows he's beaten. He's going to run."

"I'll stay with Brenda and Kathryn if you want to go," Jacinta said.

Hennessy nodded and knocked on the door. Lockett pried it open a little. He saw Hennessy and raised his eyebrows. "It's over already?"

"Longhouse has done a runner," Hennessy said.

"Where?"

"My guess is the nearest airport." Hennessy took

his keys out of his pocket. "We need to stop him."

CHAPTER 59

Once in the parking lot, Lockett pointed to Hennessy's truck.

Hennessy tossed Lockett the keys and focused on his cell. He scrolled through his contacts and, once seated in the truck's cabin, hit the call button. Lockett squealed the tires into traffic, cutting someone off. Hennessy listened to the ringtone and asked for Chief Myers once the cop answered.

"Have to patch you through, Mr. Hennessy," the voice told him, and before he could answer, a second ringtone lit up in his ear.

Lockett raced through the streets of Downtown Charleston. In under five minutes, they reached Rutledge Avenue, and Hennessy pointed for Lockett to turn left instead of right.

"You sure?"

Hennessy gave him a thumbs up. "Quicker to take the left, then up the express—" he began but stopped when a new voice cut in.

"Joe?" Chief Myers answered the call.

"Roger. It's Joe Hennessy. Longhouse is doing a runner."

"A runner? To where?"

"Anywhere but here is my guess. I'm on our way to the airport to hopefully—" but Myers didn't listen to the rest, cutting in.

"Why are you chasing him?"

"You've got the evidence we've sent you. You know he's guilty of murdering George Santos."

"I told you, Joe, we need to tread carefully here. I talked to the Circuit Solicitor this morning, and they advised us to validate the video before we even bring him in for questioning. We need to investigate the evidence before we can reopen the case. We're pushing it through, but we won't be able to make a move on this until tomorrow at the earliest. Right now, I'm waiting on the information on the video to make sure it's legitimate."

"Roger," Hennessy groaned. "He's getting away."

"I wish I could help you, but my hands are tied. We can't stop him yet. I'm not going to arrest a South Carolina Senator without the backing of the Circuit

Solicitor's Office."

Hennessy ended the call. "No help from the cops," he told Lockett, but Lockett didn't flinch.

"So, we'll do it alone," he said, gripping the steering wheel tighter and picking up speed.

While Lockett sped through the streets, Hennessy watched on, gripping his cell tightly.

"Wait," he said, peering down at his cell. Lockett looked over at him.

"Here," he said. "Take this exit instead."

"What? Why?"

"Just take it."

Lockett did, veering the truck toward the exit, squealing the tires again, then following Hennessy's instructions for the next five turns. They crossed the Wappoo Creek Bridge, turned right onto 700, then continued over the Stono River Bridge a couple of miles further down.

"Here, take the next left," Hennessy said, pointing to the sign which confirmed Lockett's suspicions.

"Really think he's going to Charleston Executive?"

Hennessy looked at him, meeting Lockett's brief gaze. "We only get one shot at this."

While Charleston had one major airport further

north, it also sported several smaller airfields. Hennessy didn't think Longhouse would risk trying the major airport, in case someone was watching him.

Hennessy slipped his cell back into his pocket, reached forward, and opened the glove compartment. He pulled out a locked metal box. He reached under the seat and grabbed a key. He unlocked the box and took out the Glock 19.

"You got yours?"

Lockett patted a hand on his jacket. "Always do," he said. "Let's hope we don't have to use them."

"Let's hope he's there," Hennessy said, correcting him, and as they reached the crest of the hill, they felt the tension rise as the airport came into view.

CHAPTER 60

"If anything happens to me," Hennessy began, catching Lockett off guard.

"Don't even start that stuff, mate," the Australian said. Hennessy didn't want to hear it.

"Listen to me," he said. "If anything happens to me, tell Wendy I did this for me and no one else. It was for my own selfishness that I pursued him."

"You did it because of what he did to your son, Joe," Lockett said. "No one will ever judge you for that."

"You tell Wendy. Tell her this wasn't about her. If anything happens to me, I don't want her to think I died because of something she wanted me to do. This has nothing to do with her." When Lockett didn't respond, Hennessy looked at him and raised his volume. "Promise me."

"I promise," Lockett said.

Lockett brought the truck back down to a normal

speed as they passed by the Coast Guard facility, and Hennessy felt his fingers cramping around his gun. He relaxed, switched hands, and began flexing and releasing his fingers until they loosened up.

Nerves gripped him. A mix of fear and dread was surging through his veins.

"There," he said as he spotted the familiar black Mercedes sedan near the front of the parking lot. "It's him."

The sedan was parked near the main building, with the rear door swung open and someone leaning into it. Lockett pulled into a parking spot two lanes across, with parked cars between them.

"There's someone with him," Lockett said. He pulled out his Smith & Wesson M&P. "I want you to stay down. Once we're out, we stick to this row of cars, duck if you have to. The closer we get to them, the more chance we have of ending this with no shots fired."

"He won't go down quietly."

"Which is why I want you to stay behind me."

"You might be big," Hennessy said, "but you ain't bulletproof."

Lockett grinned as he scouted the parking lot,

neither wanted to risk the lives of innocent bystanders who might unwittingly walk into the firing line. Once he was sure the place was clear, Lockett gave the signal.

"Let's go," he said. He gently opened the truck door and climbed out.

Hennessy did the same. They didn't run.

With Longhouse still in the backseat of the sedan, the two men tried to stealth their way as close as possible before making their presence known. If they could reach him within a few yards, just holding their weapons on him might have been enough.

Farina emerged from the front of the sedan. He spotted the lawyer and pulled his gun. "Hennessy's here!"

Farina fired two shots.

The noise echoed across the parking lot, bullets tinkering into nearby cars. Hennessy ducked.

Farina called for Longhouse to take cover. Two more gunshots rang out, firing in Hennessy's direction. Then another two. The pop of bullets peppering into the vehicle continued in short bursts.

"Stay down!" Lockett yelled behind another car, holding his weapon ready. "We need to fall back!"

Hennessy looked around and pointed to the fence. Lockett nodded. Together, they retreated, pushing back behind another car.

"You're not getting away!" Farina yelled. "I'm coming for you!"

Two more shots fired. Farina and Longhouse moved to the right of the parking lot, blocking the only exit.

They fired more shots.

Lockett retreated, moving back behind another row of cars. Hennessy followed, keeping his head down.

"The fence is too high to jump," Lockett called out from one car across. "We can't retreat any further. We're cornered."

Hennessy tried to peer forward through one of the car windows. He saw a shadow scamper between the cars.

"They're going down fighting," Lockett called out. "What do you want to do? I don't know if we can hold them off until backup arrives."

"We fight," Hennessy called out, feeling sweat dripping down his face as the reality of the situation hit home.

Lockett nodded. "Wait until they reload."

When a pause in gunfire appeared, Lockett swung himself up and across the hood of the car, firing his weapon in rapid succession. He landed behind another sedan. Hennessy sneaked to the car's rear, looked around the corner, and spotted the two men.

"It's Farina," Hennessy called to his investigator. "He's on your right."

They settled behind the car, but five more bullets shot in their direction.

It was time to fight back.

CHAPTER 61

Hennessy looked across at Lockett.

Lockett didn't appear nervous, his calm demeanor amplified by the way his index finger kept tapping on the side of the pistol, waiting for the mental signal to pop off a few shots of his own. He saw the look on Hennessy's face and snuck between the cars, moving one car across from Hennessy.

"When I say so, you run to the Chevy parked three spots down. Stay low, and don't look up. Just keep running." Lockett tightened his grip on the handgun. "Ready?"

Hennessy nodded, ensured he had a decent grip on his gun, and prepped himself.

"Go." Lockett snapped and spun sideways. Bullets shot out of the end of his barrel as he unloaded in slow, almost rhythmic bursts.

Sprinting fast as he could, Hennessy remained hunched over and ran for the vehicle Lockett had guided him to. Unable to slow himself quick enough, Hennessy dropped as he reached the car and slammed into the door hard enough to set off the alarm.

The blaring siren punctuated the air.

Longhouse and Farina returned fire toward Lockett.

Hennessy dropped onto his gut, rolled closer to the edge of the car, and prepared to draw their fire.

He spotted the advantage they needed.

As Hennessy lay low, he peered under an SUV and, from his vantage point, could see where Longhouse and Farina were holed up. He could see their feet. Without thinking, he aimed for the ankles and opened fire.

Sparks exploded underneath the SUV as his bullets struck the undercarriage.

The far tire nearest to Longhouse's shoes erupted, shrapnel and debris filling the air. Longhouse dropped to the ground. The other set of feet began to run.

"I've got him covered," Lockett screamed, but Hennessy remained focused on the fallen man. Hennessy was up in a heartbeat, sprinting across the lot to where Longhouse lay bleeding.

Lockett peeled off to give chase to Farina. Two more shots echoed through the yard before Lockett yelled, "Got him!"

As Hennessy neared the SUV, he kept his distance and began circling toward the back, his weapon raised and locked on to where he could hear Longhouse struggling to move. By the time he rounded the edge of the vehicle and saw him, the fallen Senator was crawling away. Blood was pouring from one of his legs.

"You won't get far." Hennessy aimed his weapon at Longhouse's torso. "Your time is over."

Hennessy felt his trigger finger tightening.

Longhouse rolled over onto his back, looking up at Hennessy. Hennessy felt sweat run down the side of his face.

Longhouse began to laugh. He looked up into the sky and laughed even louder.

"You should see your face right now," Longhouse said, pointing at Hennessy with a shaking finger. "Twenty-two years, and you're still carrying your burden of grief like some sort of little child."

"Don't speak," Hennessy said, readjusting the gun's aim.

"Or what? You'll shoot me? That's my best option right now. That video has me and Farina cooked." He shook his head and looked up again. "Who would have thought this is how we'd end up, huh? Twenty-two years and here we are." He wiped his brow with the back of his hand, tried to adjust his leg, and winced at the pain. "That hurts," he whispered to himself.

"Good," Hennessy said, and Longhouse scoffed at him.

"Really? Well, how does it feel knowing your son died for nothing more than a distraction?" Longhouse groaned. "Nothing more. If it hadn't been for you lodging that complaint against me, things might have never gone as far as they did." He paused and looked around the ground. "But could you leave things alone? No, of course not. Not good boy Joe Hennessy with his halo and godly conscience. Couldn't look the other way, could you?"

"You took bribes," Hennessy said.

"I did, and if you'd been smart, you could've made a lot of money yourself, instead of living your pauper existence." He chuckled again, edged a little further away, and paused. "Just a distraction, Joe, that's all it was supposed to be. It was unfortunate Luca died because of that junkie I used, but it wasn't supposed to go down that way."

Hennessy spotted what Longhouse had been trying to get close to. He was edging closer to where his gun had fallen.

"Don't do it," Hennessy said as he stepped forward and raised his pistol a little higher. "Don't."

"Joe," Longhouse sighed in frustration. "Why couldn't you just turn a blind eye?"

"Don't, Richard. This isn't the justice I want," Hennessy said, feeling his trigger finger tighten again as he saw Longhouse move closer to the pistol. "Not this way."

"And what are my options, Joe? Give up?" Longhouse laughed. "If I go back with you now, it's over. That footage shows everything. I'll be sentenced to life in prison. That's no way to live. That's no way to spend your golden years."

"Don't do it."

"Or I can take a risk. Take a chance and see if I can get a shot off."

"Don't, Richard."

Longhouse smiled. With the pistol just five inches

from his fingers, Longhouse pounced for the weapon.

A single shot fired, echoing through the parking lot.

CHAPTER 62

Joe Hennessy spent twenty-four hours in lockup.

He called criminal defense attorney, Jill Harper, and she walked him through the interviews. The surveillance footage in the parking lot of the Charleston Executive Airport clearly showed Farina fired first, followed by Longhouse. Both Hennessy and Lockett acted in self-defense, their lawyers argued. The police weren't as convinced and opened a case.

Hennessy was patient, calm, and responsive during the talks. Detective Chris Reeds led the investigation into the incident. The detectives treated him well, but they needed to get everything right. Hennessy had shot a sitting South Carolina Senator, and they couldn't mess up the investigation.

Richard Longhouse was declared deceased at the scene. That didn't surprise Hennessy. The vision of the hole in Longhouse's chest was burned into his brain.

David Farina had survived. One bullet in his leg, another in his shoulder. Hennessy was told that as Farina recovered in hospital, he was arrested for his involvement in the murder of George Santos.

When Hennessy walked out the doors of the Charleston Police Department, a large media pack had gathered. He refused to answer any questions. Wendy was waiting in a car as he was released, with Casey and Ellie in the back seat. They drove back to his apartment, where Jacinta was waiting. He called Lockett, who had been released an hour earlier. The next day, they met for a quiet beer at Lockett's house. Lockett said he was fine. The police were good to him as well.

Two days after the shooting, Maria Santos arrived at his apartment. They shared some sweet tea and said little.

After she'd finished her drink, she stood and rested her hand on Joe's. "Thank you," she said through tear-filled eyes. Joe nodded and walked her to the exit.

On the third day after the shooting, Hennessy returned to his office. Chief Myers and Detective

Chris Reeds had requested a meeting. Lockett arrived with his lawyer, and Jacinta arrived with Jill Harper.

Reeds was calm as he spoke to them. "We've interviewed Farina, and he said you fired first. We've looked at the footage from many different angles, and it's clear that many shots are fired before you return fire. The vision shows that you try to retreat, but they cut you off. You were cornered and had no choice. If you didn't try to retreat, you'd be facing manslaughter charges, possibly even murder, but the vision is clear. They were attacking you, you retreated, and in that instance, you had the right to defend yourself. Farina is sticking with his story, but it's not washing with us." Reeds drew a deep breath. "The estate of Richard Longhouse may be able to argue for a wrongful death suit and claim he was acting in self-defense as both of you had your weapons drawn, but in terms of a criminal case, you're cleared. We're not laying charges."

Hennessy leaned back in his chair and sighed. He nodded his response.

"What will you tell the media?" Jill Harper asked.

"We've drafted a media release and will have a press conference tomorrow," Reeds said. "We'll tell the media that Richard Longhouse was under investigation for the murder of George Santos and was attempting to flee the country. At the airport, he chose to shoot at a lawyer and an investigator. The lawyer and investigator tried to retreat but were cornered and had no choice but to return fire in self-defense."

"I would like to see a copy of the press release before it goes out, but I like the tone of it," Harper said.

Chief Myers spoke next. "Richard Longhouse's funeral will be next week. The family is holding a small affair at a local church, but I ask that you both stay well away from it."

Hennessy nodded. He hadn't spoken much since the shooting.

"And we found Frank Diaz," Myers continued.

"Where?" Jacinta asked.

"He tried to reenter the country yesterday. I guess he saw that Longhouse was gone, and he thought it was over. He's been arrested for the fire at the vineyard, along with a long string of parole violations."

Hennessy nodded his thanks.

"What happens to Maria Santos' case?" Jacinta asked Chief Myers.

"For the wrongful death suit?" Myers responded. "Well, Joe will know more than me, but the defendant is dead. Unless Mrs. Santos wishes to sue the estate of Richard Longhouse, then it's finished. But that's up to Mrs. Santos to decide her next steps."

A silence hung over the room before Reeds and Myers rose to their feet. Joe stood and offered his hand to Myers.

"Thank you, Roger," Joe spoke for the first time in the meeting.

Myers shook his hand, nodded, and then exited.

It was over.

CHAPTER 63

Joe wandered around the vineyard, checking on the grapes.

Ten days after the shooting, the colors seemed brighter. The air smelled cleaner. The breeze felt fresher. He went to the sheds and talked to the workers for a while. They told some old jokes, laughed at each other, and talked about the grapes. One said the smoke damage didn't seem as bad as first thought. Another joked that smoky should be a new flavor of wine. They were good workers—a tight-knit group.

Joe spent time on the irrigation lines, ensuring they worked well after the fire. With the help of two workers, they laid down a new line. They tested it, and it worked well. Joe smiled most of the afternoon. He loved rolling up his sleeves and working hard. He loved the land. He loved the outdoors.

He spoke to Maria Santos on the phone. She

declined to sue the estate of Richard Longhouse and offered to pay Joe his fees out of the funds from the life insurance claim. Joe thanked her but declined her offer.

Ellie arrived home from New York for a week. Wendy picked her up from the airport, and Joe greeted her with a tight hug. He didn't want to let go. Ellie had to push him away with a smile on her face. Over the week, he spent the afternoons with his daughters, playing cards on the kitchen bench with Casey, and completing crosswords with Ellie's help. They didn't talk about the shooting. The girls didn't mention it once.

On the last night of Ellie's stay, the family shared dinner. For Joe, it felt nostalgic, sitting at the head of the table watching his family enjoy a home-cooked meal. He laughed when they laughed, listened to the great tales of the city from Ellie, and chuckled when Casey talked about the dramas of high school.

"Mom, this is amazing," Casey said as she took another piece of pork crackle. Watching her daughter crunch through it brought a smile to her face. "You could charge top dollar for this."

"Hey, leave some for the rest of us," Ellie slapped

her sister's hand as she reached for her own. As she bit off one end, Ellie looked over at her father. "So, with everything wrapped up now, does that mean you're here for good, Dad?"

"I wish," he said, "but not yet. We still need to get in front of the bank loans, and with the damaged crop, we're not going to have a big year."

"Back to Charleston?" Ellie questioned.

"For now, yes. I still need to earn money down there. Once we've fed the bank enough coins, I'll be back for good." He looked at Ellie. "And you?"

"Law school," Ellie said. "That's the plan, anyway. Maybe Charleston School of Law?"

Joe nodded with a grin. "You could intern for me."

"Intern?" she laughed. "No way. I'd need to be paid a lot to work for you."

They laughed together, and Joe couldn't have been happier. His soul was full. When dinner was finished, he cleaned up the pots and pans, placed the plates in the dishwasher, and returned to the living room. The girls had put on a romantic movie, something Joe was keen to avoid.

"Should we take our drinks out onto the porch for

a bit?" Joe whispered to Wendy.

She picked up her glass and followed him out.

A clear night sky greeted them, the moon sitting halfway up toward its eventual peak. Joe dragged one of the chairs over while Wendy dropped into the other. He set his glass down and held his wife's hand.

They sat in the still air for a few minutes, with the only sound coming from the girls inside the house. Their constant chatting drowned out the movie. Their voices floated out through an open window, and each time he heard them laugh, Joe gently squeezed Wendy's hand.

"Isn't that the most amazing sound in the world?" Wendy whispered.

"It really is," Joe said and turned his head to hear it a little better.

A gentle rain started to fall. It was soft and calm.

"Luca would've loved this rain." Wendy squeezed his hand. "He always loved the rain."

Joe smiled.

It was not a smile laced with sadness or regret. Not a smile used to hide his pain or cover his feelings. It was a smile he felt deep inside, something that grew from love.

And it was there, under the gentle rain of South Carolina, that Joe Hennessy found peace.

THE END

ALSO BY PETER O'MAHONEY

In the Joe Hennessy Legal Thriller series:

THE SOUTHERN LAWYER
THE SOUTHERN CRIMINAL
THE SOUTHERN KILLER

In the Tex Hunter Legal Thriller series:

POWER AND JUSTICE
FAITH AND JUSTICE
CORRUPT JUSTICE
DEADLY JUSTICE
SAVING JUSTICE
NATURAL JUSTICE
FREEDOM AND JUSTICE
LOSING JUSTICE
FAILING JUSTICE
FINAL JUSTICE

*****

In the Jack Valentine Series:

GATES OF POWER
THE HOSTAGE
THE SHOOTER
THE THIEF
THE WITNESS